I am Magdar, disciple of the Lord God Sa'yen, and known as the Left Hand of the Lord!

I am the one that was by His side all those long years He fought to bring His faithful southward on the sacred pilgrimage! I am the one that first acknowledged Him as the Lord; Sa'yen, God of War and Healing; Lord of the Wrathful Vengeance and Miraculous Healing! I am the Magdar who stood with Him when the high walls of Imperial Hakad of the Far North came tumbling down from His wrath!

With His permission, I will put to these scrolls all that truly happened to me, to the Inner Few, and to the Lord God, the Sa'yen, while He was with us upon this world.

"And He shall come, like a newborn babe, to stand among His kind young and invincible and not knowing truly His own magnificence."

BANNERS
OF
THE
SA' YEN

B. R. Stateham

Fowler's Books
Buy - Sell - Trade
323 N. Euclid
Fullerton 92632
or
2634 W. Orangethorpe
Fullerton, 92634

DAW Books, Inc.
Donald A. Wollheim, Publisher

1633 Broadway, New York, N.Y. 10019

FIRST PRINTING, JULY 1981

1 2 3 4 5 6 7 8 9

DAW TRADEMARK REGISTERED
U.S. PAT. OFF. MARCA
REGISTRADA. HECHO EN U.S.A.

PRINTED IN U.S.A.

TABLE OF CONTENTS

PROLOGUE

I am Magdar. Once known as Magdar the Ha'valli. And as Magdar the Bull. And most recently, Magdar the Madman. All these names I have been known by in the past. A past that stretches out so many long, tumultuous years. A long life, the prophets would tell me wistfully, looking at my ancient and cracked skin and my white hair so thin upon my head. A long and wondrous life. A life to be proud of. A life songs should be sung of. A life legends are born from.

And aye, there are legends already about me. Many legends that are sung around the campfires of my father's tribe about me and, more importantly, of He whom I followed. And songs sung by the wandering minstrels who wander from city to city by the hundreds. But aye, there are legends and there are songs about me and my deeds while I served the Lord.

But not by what I am known now. Nay, few who know me now or who have known me in the last twenty years have truly known me by the name legends and songs are sung of. No, pilgrim, the last twenty years few people have known me. For if many had, I confess my life would have been swiftly extinguished many long years ago by most unpleasant methods. Aye, the hordes of howling banshees that would take sword and shield and track me down if they knew me by my real name would be numberless!

Aye, you find this hard to believe. An old and dying shell of a man, writing these many scrolls with a shaking, palsied hand and living in a cave high above the desert floor, is it not possible to believe such a claim as that I have just made? Aye, it is. And even I, in my youth and strength and arrogant confidence, would have laughed at such a boast if I had come across these scrolls as you have. But then, would your mind change perhaps if I mentioned my real name?

Well, pilgrim, know you by the title I truly am. I am Magdar, disciple of the Lord God Sa'yen, and known as the Left Hand of the Lord!

Aye! The true Magdar! The sole survivor of the Inner Few that served the Lord while He was among us! I am the one that was by His side all those long years He fought to bring His faithful southward on the sacred pilgrimage, the Wha'ta. I am the one that first acknowledged Him as the Lord; Sa'yen, God of War and Healing; Lord of Wrathful Vengeance and Miraculous Healing! I am the Magdar who stood with Him when the high walls of Imperial Hakad of the Far North came tumbling down from His wrath! And aye, pilgrim, I am the Magdar who pulled the Lord God Sa'yen, the True One, from the depths of the Pictii's most sacred fortress sanctuary deep underneath the mountains, known as Halls of the Ancient Kings!

I am he that the Pictii, those priests of the brown robes, have sought these long years to find and punish. They have, in their merciless ways, tracked down and extinguished the lives of all the few that were part of the Lord's Inner few. All except me. I am the only one left. And it is Lady Death, as the Lord called it, and not the Pictii that soon will lay claim upon my soul. Lay claim upon me soon unless what was promised to me by Him, just before the shimmering fire consumed Him, does not happen first. Aye, it will be a fast and hard race to see which contestant will win. The Lord's promise, or that patient, ever-present vague form the Lord called Lady Death, whom I have known intimately these long, hard years, I must admit. It never has been easy to be a follower of the Sa'yen among a world that looks upon the brown robes of the Pictii as their true emissaries from the divine gods. And one, if he claimed to be of sane rationale, who dared not mention the Lord's name among strangers after He was consumed by the shimmering fire while in the process of tearing down the Hidden Garden Sanctuaries of Pictii. The Pictii, being of minds that defy logic, rose from the ashes the Lord left them from His wrath and in only a few decades began to exterminate that which the Lord God had sought so valiantly to achieve!

Aye, I have known Death intimately these long years! And soon, apparently, shall know her even more intimately unless the Lord's promise is not realized shortly. But I am of the Sa'yen! I believe! I heard the Lord's voice, before the green shimmering fire engulfed Him with a roar. He promised to return! To return and take me with Him to the beyond. And all I had to do was wait for Him. Wait for His return deep within this high desert valley where He last walked among us.

And I have waited, waited these thirty years for His return. I have waited, and watched, and never journeyed for more than a month's hard march from the desert valley my mountain cave overlooks. And I shall continue to wait until either His promise or that dark-robed lady of many charms finally lays claim my soul.

Aye, you laugh and scoff at my words, pilgrim! I know, and I cannot deny, that you have cause to! Why would Magdar, the Left Hand of the Lord, the last survivor of the Inner Few, as we were known, be alone and old and penniless and dying in a mountain cave high above a lonely, desolate desert valley. Aye, you have reason to wonder, pilgrim, why this strange tale I am now putting to ink has come about. And, with His permission, I will, in my short time left, put to these many ancient scrolls that lie about my feet all that truly happened to me, to the Inner Few, and to the Lord God, the Sa'yen, while He was with us upon this world.

I shall write a scroll at a time. And I shall start at the beginning. I shall start on the first that I saw Him among us. That night, so long, long ago, high up in the Tors Mountains in Northern Hungar. And, pilgrim, keep in mind the one promise left to us thousands of years ago by the prophets.

"And He shall come, like a newborn babe, to stand among His kind young and invincible and not knowing truly His own magnificence."

I

$\bullet\!\!-\!\!\circ\!\!-\!\!\bullet$

The Sa'yen Appears

Aye, I remember the Sa'yen. Even now, in my old and
decrepit age, I can still recall with all the startling clarity
every detail of the Sa'yen's sudden appearance among us
mortals! Aye, and I become as thrilled now, nay all these
years long that have passed, as I became on the night He
first came among us. The Sa'yen! How long have we of
the rugged Northern Regions waited for the Sa'yen? Eons;
generations after generations have sat patiently, staring up
into the vaulted darkness, with the millions of lights Our
Lord called other suns, and waited for the Fiery Chariot
that would bring Him among us. And He came! He came
just as the legends foretold He would. He came among us
with sword and shield in hand, with fire and madness in
His eyes and with wrath and destruction in His heart.

And I was there! I was the first officer on the old
Princess Tagia, when the five black-hulled Aggarian ships
attacked. And the night He appeared! Such a wild tempest
I have never lived through before or since. His appearance! The winds were blowing with such a fury the old
Princess Tagia leaned heavily to starboard, even though all
sails were furled except for a few fliers on the for'mast.
And the rain was pelting us, whipped by the shrieking
wind with such a fury that my arms became numbed from
the pain of it all. Five Aggarian black hulls against a lowly,
meager prize such as we! How could I ever forget His
coming? Aye, that was a fight that I was in that night!
With sword and shield all of my crew fought the bearded

11

pirates from the high-mountain pirate's nest in the Aggarian Mountains with every ounce of strength we had. We knew what our fate would be if we failed that night. Still, when the five ships of the Aggarians descended down to us through the broken cloud cover of that night, the bright moonlight illuminating the countryside we flew over and glistening off the hundreds of swords and shields on the Aggarian ships, I knew that this was to be my last fight. Aye, do we not remember the reputation of the Aggarian pirates before His coming? None escaped the raiding pack of the black-hulled ships when they descended from above onto their intended victims. None, that is, until the Sa'yen came to our rescue.

But none of us on that round, slow, old ship knew that our lives, our destinies, would be changed that night with the Sa'yen's appearance. We fought that night in desperation, against forces that only had to bide their time before they wore our thin ranks down to the last man! But I fought! I fought with shield and sword like I never have before! And as fierce as the many tales were of the prowess of the Aggarian swordsmen, I knew that night, for the first time in my life, that few men could stand before me with sword and shield. With stroke after stroke my arm flew and pirates clambered over bodies as they tried to kill me. But my shield was strong and my blade true; I fought with the madness of fighting lust in my veins, roaring in my ears, and so wild was I that I even jeered and taunted these fabled pirates of the high Aggarian Mountains when one would fall and another stepped up to take his place. Yet for all the mad lust that was surging through my body, one quick glance behind me showed that the fight would soon be over. Our ship, the old *Princess Tagia*, had a meager crew of fifty. When the first grappling hooks of the black-hulled ships flew through the night air and dug into our sides, followed by the swarming hordes of the bearded pirates themselves, our crew was rapidly cut down to only a handful in a matter of seconds. But we fought, all of us wounded at least once, and we made the pirates that tried to overwhelm us pay a heavy price for their victory. And then, just as I saw our captain go down from a sweeping blow of a pirate's halberd, the impossible happened!

In the melee, with three of the black-hulled ships lashed to our sides and the other two hovering just above the upper spars of the mainmast, none had watched in what direction we drifted. The howling of the storm, not once letting up from beginning to end of the pirates' attack, had pushed us down the vaulted corridors of a high-walled valley. The valley floor and walls were heavy forests of Yab'lal wood, the broad-leaved, thick, heavy trunks of wood that our ships of the rugged North are made of. Drifting down, descending all the time as we flew, and pushed by the rain-splattering, screeching wind, we eventually were warned of our imminent danger when one of the black-hulled ships lashed to us crashed into the first limbs of a Yab'lal tree. There was a shout of panic and suddenly the pressure of the pirates, already close to overwhelming the handful of us that yet survived, wavered then disintegrated as Aggarian officers shouted orders to their men to save their ships! A few of the pirates still tried to cut us down, yet exhausted as we were, we met these few bearded warriors and dispatched them with some difficulty. I saw through the panic and rain of the storm a chance for us to escape with our lives. The old ship that had been ours was of no value to us, and we were desperately few to try to contest the issue. Since I was the only officer left after the captain died, it was my decision to make. I did not hesitate. I ordered to abandon ship.

Turning, I said nothing as I motioned with my sword for the few of us yet alive to follow me. Through the darkness and the rain we few stepped across the dead bodies that littered the deck of our ship and darted between masts to make for the prow of our ship. We had crashed prow-first into the high walls of the valley, the crash so intense that two of the black-hulled ships had lost masts that had fallen into the upper reaches of the Yab'lal forest, pinning the whole melee to the forest. The wind was from the stern, and as we paused to catch our bearings, it appeared to me that the wind was rising in its fury. In that case, it helped our cause because it continued to push the littered mass of the three black-hulled ships lashed to our sides farther into the tree-lined wall of the narrow valley, making it impossible for the pirates of the Aggarian Mountains to cut free and rise above the valley into safety. I grinned in the rain-whipped winds of the storm, for the first time feeling that we few had a chance to escape with our lives. With sword and shield in hand, I motioned the five remaining men to follow me as we began to climb down through the crushed beams of the prow and into the waiting arms of the Yab'lal trees.

But alas! We were discovered and with a roar a mass of bearded pirates swarmed back onto the deck of the old ship and sped for our position. I turned and yelled for the few men alive, only five of them, to turn and hurry for the trees! And then like the fool that I am at such times, I turned and jumped forward to meet the rush of the bearded pirates alone!

They were upon me in an instant! My shield arm was beyond pain from the incessant pounding of swords being deflected. My sword arm felt like heavy stone as I parried blows and cut and slashed. Yet I was laughing and taunting them with every breath I took. I knew that night I was a dead man, so what did it matter to me? If I died, then I died with sword and shield in hand, fighting like my father, an old Ha'valli warrior of the Ha'valli plains, had taught me to fight. Laughing and talking like a madman, I fought on, hoping that at least a few of my comrades yet had time to escape the clutches of the pirates' grim-humored torture. Bearded pirate after bearded pirate stepped up to face me and died as my sword slipped under their shield and found its target. But the fight was unfair from the beginning, the odds too much for me to handle alone. A vicious blow to the back of my head from a shield staggered me to one side and suddenly the searing pain of a sword thrust into my shoulder was my reward! And then, He came. From out of the night, out of the dark black forests of the Yab'lal woods, He came. The Sa'yen!

There was a tremendous crash of thunder, the sky lighting up with the jagged flash of lightning, and the bearded pirates stepped back in that instant to catch their breath for the final rush. Wounded, blood flowing freely from my shoulder, yet I stood with shield in one hand and sword in

the other, back up against the for'mast, glaring at the forty
or fifty bearded pirates that faced me with a thin grin on
my lips. There was another rolling crash of thunder, and
from above, one of the five black-hulled ships staggered,
struck by lightning. A shout, heard faintly in the wind,
then amazingly the night was filled with the licking, hungry flames of fire rapidly spreading across the smooth deck
of one of the black-hulled ships! Another bold crash of
lightning crashed through the howling, rain-swept night,
followed by the staggering clap of thunder. A bearded pirate before me, already stunned by the sight of his ship
being consumed by fire, cringed from the bolt of lightning
and looked upward to another side of the night. My eyes
were upon him as I saw his face pale suddenly in the glow
of the roaring flames above us, and then he dropped sword
and shield from his hands and screamed in terror as he
pointed upwards into the spars of the for'mast. All eyes
turned to gaze upwards and all were stunned at what they
saw. The Sa'yen! The Sa'yen in His magnificence! He stood
on the for'mast main spar, long-bow in hand with arrow
notched to the string. The long, heavy blond beard was
blowing in the wind, curling over His shoulder, as was His
shoulder-length hair; and dressed in the rags that once had
been strangely cut clothes, to all of us below he looked like
a Forest Ghoul.

How can I describe this man-god? He was an apparition
before our eyes that none of us could believe. Wide shoulders swept down into narrow waist, He stood with His feet
apart, His legs thick and powerful looking. With His long
beard and hair blowing in the wind, we all stood there
looking up, too stunned to utter a sound. But this did not
stop the Sa'yen! With sudden swiftness that took the
breath away from me, the string of His bow twanged in
the night wind, and a bearded pirate screamed his death
scream, an arrow through his throat! In a blinking of an
eye, five more pirates died by the sudden swiftness of the
Sa'yen's bow. The bearded pirates before me sulked back-
wards, bunching closer together from the sudden assault
from above, shields rising to protect themselves.

The Sa'yen's voice bellowed in the night, the first my
ears heard of His commanding deep voice, and He jumped

from the for'main spar to the deck of the ship beside me!
Landing on His feet, three more arrows swiftly left His
bow, and three more bearded pirates fell to the deck lifeless. It was unbelievable! I had never seen such deft, su-
perb bowmanship in my life. The Man, the weapon He
used, was unknown to me and I knew not what to think.
But the bearded pirates before me suddenly surged forward, overcoming their shock at a new assailant, and attacked with vengeance in their hearts! I stepped forward,
raising my shield to protect Him and me as well, but a
strong hand gently pushed me away. Leaning up against
the for'mast, blood still flowing from my wound, I
watched with speechless wonder as He met the rush of
thirty armed Aggarian pirate warriors alone with only a
bow and a quiver of arrows for weapons. And what did
my eyes witness that night? A fight, a show of martial arts
that I have never seen another man equal! And, in the
first few minutes of that night, I knew the Sa'yen was before me. I knew the legends of His Coming were true! For
what I saw then was impossible for a mere human to do
alone. Only a god could accomplish the feats of prowess
He completed before me. Only the Sa'yen could do what
He did that night.

They came in a rush, bunched together with shields
forming a solid wall before them. But two warriors were
over-eager to meet the Sa'yen and rushed ahead of their
comrades to cut the almost weaponless warrior down with
their swords. One warrior, a giant of a man, came forward, sword raised high over his head, shield up, and
screamed in triumph as he slashed downward with his
heavy blade. But the Sa'yen stepped to one side, an arm
coming up to catch the wrist of the man's sword arm, and
suddenly the bearded giant was thrown bodily into the air.
He went screaming to his death to the valley floor a thousand feet below, and stunned, I watched the Sa'yen bend
down to pick up the warrior's heavy curved sword just in
time to meet the rush of the second charging warrior. The
second warrior made a sweeping slash from the left to the
right, but the Sa'yen calmly parried this, and tripped the
warrior with one of His feet and free hand! He cut the
fallen warrior's throat with a calm dispatch, turned and

faced the oncoming mass of Aggarian pirates as casually
as I've ever seen a man do anywhere!

There was the tremendous roar of the aft'mast crashing
to the deck, engulfed in white, searing flames. Flames
from the mast lit the rigging of the main'mast, and before
anyone knew what came next, the entire ship was a roaring inferno. The shield-wall of the attacking pirates
slowed, then halted, then turned and fled in panic. I
grinned at their flight, the loss of blood making my knees
weak and forcing me to kneel to the deck. I remember
dropping my sword and shield to the deck, too weak to
hold them any longer and my eyelids felt like heavy
stones. I started to fall, the flames of the consuming fire
licking close beside me, but I felt strong hands grab me
and lift me from the deck entirely. As if I were a young
child, He carried me from the burning pyre of the four
ships lashed together. I grinned, looked up into His
bearded face and thanked Him. I saw a face with a long,
thin nose, dark blond hair and bright gray-blue eyes. His
face was set into a mask of determination that I've never
seen on another mortal, and as easily as carrying a newborn babe, He carried me through the smashed prow of
our ship and descended down into the depths of the
Yab'lal forest with a swiftness and agility I found amazing
even then. And I closed my eyes and fell into a well of
unconsciousness, too exhausted to care about anything any-
more.

I opened my eyes with the sudden sensation of something cool and wet being placed on my brow. I looked up
and found that I was lying under the green canopy of a
Yab'lal forest, with Him kneeling down beside me, smiling
as He ministered to my wounds. For a moment or two,
panic swept through me as I could not remember why I
was here. But a restraining hand and the look of kindness
in His eyes made me pause and swiftly the memory of the
desperate fight filled my mind. Smiling weakly, I said
thanks and found my mouth dry and parched. He
frowned, then smiled, and held up a finger. From a large
leather bag strapped to his waist He pulled out a strange
object and held it up between us. He nodded, and,

puzzled, I could only stare back at him. He smiled patiently, then motioned to me by pointing to His lips with His finger and then to the machine He held. He did that several times again, over and over, and for a moment or two I was puzzled. Was this apparition a mute? I found this impossible to believe, and hesitantly I spoke a few words.

"What is it You wish me to do, Lord? I, I do not understand."

He nodded in satisfaction suddenly, and then the machine spoke! A strange sound came out of the machine and I almost jumped to my feet in fright. But He put a hand out to restrain me and smiled. His smile had magic for all that He smiled upon. I relaxed hesitantly, hearing the strangeness of the sound coming from the machine He held between us. As I lay on the ground, the cool wrap over my brow, He spoke in the tongue of the Gods, and the machine translated into the tongue of us mortals.

"Do not have any fears, warrior. You are with your friends and I mean you no harm."

I blinked my eyes several times, looking first at the machine He held in His hand, and then into His face, mystified at what I was seeing and hearing. He saw my confusion, smiled, and spoke again.

"This that I hold before you is only a machine, warrior. It is a language translator. It takes in your language and converts it over to a language that I can understand. Do not be afraid; nothing will harm you."

I nodded, still confused, relaxing somewhat from the strangeness before me, but cautious about whom I was speaking to. Yet I knew deep within me who this manthing was. He was the Sa'yen! Our Lord and Deliverer! Gulping, I hesitated before at last asking Him who He might be, telling him, "I am Magdar, called the Bull by my kind."

He nodded after the strange machine translated to the tongue of the Gods and spoke into the machine.

"I am called Alexander; Alexander Synn."

I heard voices behind me, and turning, I gazed upon the faces of the five of my crew that escaped the clutches of the Aggarian pirates. They all had gasped in sudden realization when the machine spoke His name, understanding then as I knew all along what to be the truth. Had not the legends prophesied that He would come back to us in the flesh of a mortal disguised in a new name that yet was His name? Alexander Synn! The Sa'yen! I wanted to shout in triumph! I wanted to sing praises to His ears, but young Hagbash, the younger ship carpenter, suddenly fell to his knees and bowed three times to Our Lord in humble supplication. Quickly the other four old ship members fell to their knees and copied the devotions of young Hagbash. The Sa'yen looked at this sudden desire to fall and worship Him in dismay clearly written across His face, then turned and looked at me as He spoke into the machine.

"What are they doing, warrior? What is the matter? Are they ill?"

"No, my lord," I said, grinning like a happy youth at last included in the ranks of manhood for the first time as I answered His query. "They are only offering you praise of supplication and gratitude. They are a few of your devoted followers, my Lord. And I, too, follow your banners as a humble servant as well."

"Follow my banners? What madness are you speaking of, warrior? Why are these men on their knees and bowing to me as if I were some kind of god?"

Aye, then is when I wanted to laugh like a delighted child! Had not the prophets told us that Our Lord would act as He did when He first arrived among us? Had not the prophets said that even the Sa'yen would not know he was Our Lord when He first reappeared before our eyes again to lead us to the Halls of the Mountain Kings? Aye, I was so happy that day I wanted to shout and dance in delight! Sitting up slowly, wincing from the pain, He reached out to help me up with His hands, and I took a hand of His and kissed it excitedly.

"What!" He bellowed, pulling His hand back quickly and looking at me as if I had gone insane. "Are you mad, warrior? What is the matter with you all?"

"Aye, we are all insane, Lord! Insane with ecstasy! Our Lord, the Sa'yen has returned among us again to lead us. A thousand Ha'las to Your return, Lord!"

Amazement clearly on His handsome, bearded face, He

sat before me as I and the five of my old crew began
dancing and singing in our salvation. It was a madness
that gripped us that day. Under the thick, green canopy of
the Yab'lal forest we danced and praised the prowess of
Our Lord, the Sa'yen. He looked on as if we six had left
our senses. And in fact, we had. We were filled with a
sense of deliverance that cannot be expressed in words.
We were overjoyed! We knew that among us was the
Promised One. The Sa'yen! What else could we do but
sing and dance and praise Our Lord with every fiber of
our being?

I will never forget the look that filled His face as we
sang to Him. At first He was mystified with our antics,
then as time passed on and we continued with our joyous
celebration, a look of deep concern filled His eyes. Here
He sat, a bearded, dirty Forest Ghoul, in rags that hung to
His hard, tanned frame much like rags hang from a
scarecrow in a plowed field, looking at us with eyes of
deep concern. I could see, as time passed on, the mystifica-
tion in His eyes as we celebrated. And I was pleased. Did
not the prophets foretell that He would not understand His
own divinity? Did not the prophets foretell that the Sa'yen
would be wrapped in the body of a mere mortal in order
that He may feel as we feel? Did not the prophets before
us, and down through the ages, prophesy that years would
pass before He finally would see that He was indeed the
Promised One? Years in which only a few of His most
devoted followers would be with Him and share His tribulations? Aye, all that the prophets foretold around the
campfires from our ancestors down to the present was
coming true. I danced with my comrades, forgetting the
pain of my deep wound, convinced that sitting among us
was Our Deliverer. And He would, ultimately, lead His
banners southward to open all the Halls of the Mountain
Kings.

II

---•◦◉◦•---

We Take a Ship

Days passed in the forests of the large Yab'lal trees and we all grew to know Our Lord. And He was a strange man-god. We insisted that we take over the routine chores of the camp, allowing Our Lord to sit and contemplate and think. And Our Lord smiled upon us. Two days after the big fight with the Aggarian pirates, old Fidor the sailmaker discovered the hulks of two burned out black-hulls still entwined in the high tops of the Yab'lal trees. We all raced through the dark paths of the forest to gaze upward through the limbs at the still buoyant hulls of the pirate ships. Our Lord, the Sa'yen, had said little since we told Him who He actually was, but now, standing at the base of a truly huge grandfather Yab'lal tree and looking up through the green canopy at the black hulls of the burnt-out ships, He turned to speak to me at last.

"You and your planet are a strange race, Magdar the Bull. I have never seen such strange craft as these before! They are like blimps, or dirigibles. But they have sails and masts and you sail them like sailships from my home world. Amazing!"

"Aye, Lord, Your word none that I doubt. But sometimes You say the strangest things. The only ships that I know of sail like those you saw the other night. Is there any other way for a ship to sail?"

"Surely," He replied, speaking through the voice translator, as He called it, and looking at me. "On my home world, people sail in wooden boats, using sails for power.

21

But they sail on large bodies of water and not in the air! How can a dirigible sail in the air? What do you use for buoyance?"

I shrugged, unable to answer My Lord. He spoke in strange words to me on many occasions. And I could never understand what He meant when He referred to His world. I could only think that perhaps other worlds other than the one we stood on were His as well. And to me, this made sense. Aye, it made more sense to me the longer I thought about it. Perhaps Our Lord had been too long on another of His worlds and had grown unaccustomed to our ways? We then, as His devoted followers, would have to be the ones to teach Him the ways of our people. I could see the truth in this standing beside Him. And so convinced did I become that I decided we would begin immediately teaching Our Lord the ways of the Northern Hungar! Turning to old Fidor, I motioned the others to draw closer.

"I believe Our Lord must be taught our ways again, lads. As the prophets have promised, He is like a newborn child in a man's body among us! We must teach Him everything we know and we must begin now. Fidor and Hagbash, hurry and construct ladders so that we can climb this old grandfather Yab'lal. Tallsus! Scurry up this tree and climb to the hulls above. See if any of them can be repaired. Bidgar and Tadan, you two hurry back to the old camp and bring everything down to here. We will stay in this spot until we have rebuilt one of the ships above. And you two will be the hunters for our food. Now hurry, we must begin teaching Our Lord our ways before something else befalls us."

The men nodded and scurried about to do my bidding. I turned and gazed upon His face. The language translator had decoded all that I had said to the men and He was looking upon my face with deep concern in His eyes.

"Magdar, I am no god."

"Aye, my Lord, You are," I corrected, grinning fondly at the bearded giant. "Believe me, You are. It will only take time to convince You of that. Our many old prophets have told us the Sa'yen would return to us in the disguise of a strange warrior professing not to be what he truly was. You are the Sa'yen, My Lord. The Promised One. Believe me."

"I am no god, Magdar," He said, shaking His head sadly and allowing the strange object that turned the language of the Gods into the language of mortals to talk to me. 'I am no god, Magdar. And sooner or later it will be proven to you. See, how can I be a god if I too bleed as you? Would a god bleed? Would a god feel pain? Could a god die like any other mortal, Magdar?"

He held up the back of His hand and revealed to me a long scratch He had received in the battle the other night. I nodded, concerned even by this small mark, but confident that His time among us mortals would yet run for years on end.

"My Lord, the prophets have told us that You would come to us claiming You were not what You actually were. I know You feel Yourself as not being the Promised One. So be it. It will eventually come to You. Until then, let us six be your servants, My Lord. Let us teach You our ways and serve Your needs. And in the end, You will soon see the truth."

He sighed heavily in resignation, rubbing His eyes with a hand. But then He smiled as He looked up at me and nodded. And then He looked up the towering Yab'lal tree and at the floating hulks of the black-hulls before peering at me again.

"You will be convinced soon enough, Magdar the Bull. You are as stubborn as I am, it seems. Well, my friend, never mind. But I will take you up on your offer to teach me about your world! And I would like to know everything about the dirigibles that are powered by the wind. Come! Show me these ships!"

And He jumped to the lowest limb of the giant tree and quickly was climbing upward before I could shout.

"My Lord! Be careful! This old tree is at least three hundred feet tall. Wait until Fidor and Hagbash have made ladders so that it will be safer for You to ascend to the ships."

"Nonsense, Magdar! Come on with me and we'll beat Tallsus to the top!" He said, smiling down at me like a kid eager for a race. But then He frowned as He glanced at my shoulder. "Ah, like a fool I forgot about your wound, my friend! Wait until the ladders are constructed, Magdar, and then meet me up on one of the ships!"

"My Lord! Take care of yourself!" I shouted, truly terrified at the thought of the Sa'yen scaling a three-hundred-foot Yab'lal tree alone.

Yet as I watched, He ascended the old tree with the ease and grace of a man born to such work. He rapidly disappeared through the branches of the towering trees and I soon found myself stamping around impatiently for Hagbash and Fidor to hurry with the ladder. It took hours to complete the work. We started up the large grandfather Yab'lal with rough hammers made of stone and leather thongs, using wooden pegs carved from limbs. At the two-hundred-foot level Hagbash quickly strapped together a large platform and we three rested there for some time. I was feeling weak and dizzy. But my wound had not opened and I was determined to climb to the top and be beside our Lord again. Urging Hagbash and Fidor on, we again began to ascend upward. It was late in the evening when we three finally broke through the upper branches of the giant tree, high above the forest, and climbed aboard one of the black-hulls. The sun was setting off in the west, at the mouth of the narrow, forest-covered valley we were in, and we found our Lord and Tallsus standing side by side, looking at the setting sun. When we appeared, Tallsus bowed slightly to our Lord and hurried to my side.

"Magdar, we are in luck! The far black-hull is barely damaged! All we need to do is replace the masts and spars, re-rig it and we have a perfectly good ship to sail."

I nodded, pleased at the report. I told him to help Fidor and Hagbash begin the repairs, then I walked up to stand close to the Sa'yen.

"My Lord, we are in luck. In a few days we will sail out of here in an Aggarian ship. A black-hull!"

"This is good?" He asked, turning to look at me with a lifted eyebrow questioningly.

"Aye, this is excellent! The Aggarian pirates build the best of the raiders. With such a ship we could run with the best of them, My Lord."

He said nothing as He turned to look at the sunset

again. I stood close to Him, and turned my eyes to look at the view myself. It was an interesting sight. The sun was a bright orange orb sitting between the walls of the narrow valley. High, thin clouds were of various hues of soft oranges while the high-walled valley was a dark, deep emerald green. Through the green blanket of the Yab'lal trees jutted giant slabs of gray-blue rock. The valley itself was a twisting, narrow affair that would have been quite hard to sail through in the best of times. We were a good thousand feet above the floor of the valley, stuck in the trees that grew from a large rock outcrop. Down far below, I could see the thin ribbon of a river twisting and turning as it traveled down the valley floor. I turned to look at My Lord, and He spoke as He slowly turned in place, viewing the entire valley from His ship's deck.

"Magdar, this is the most rugged, mountainous planet I have ever seen! Even when I descended down through the atmosphere in my Escape Capsule, the instruments showed a mountainous planet like no other I've ever seen. Is it all like this?"

"Aye, Lord. That it is. We are in some valley in the High Tors. If I am correct in my guess, we are about two hundred miles north of the city of Altalya."

I was frowning. Again the Sa'yen was speaking strangely to me. Escape Capsule? What was that? Shaking my head, I looked down at the planking of the black hull and wondered to myself what it meant. My Lord, of course, in His infinite wisdom, read my thoughts easily enough.

"Magdar, what puzzles you?"

"My Lord?" I said, smiling wanly at him as I tried to say something I knew not of.

"You are wondering what an escape capsule is?" He asked, smiling knowingly at me.

I nodded.

"Well, you assume I am a god, Magdar. If I tell you what an escape capsule is, would you believe me?"

"I never doubt the Sa'yen, My Lord!" I said, becoming pale over the thought of doubting my God's spoken word.

"Well then, Magdar. Let me explain to you where I

come from," He said, smiling as He looked up into the sky.

The sky had turned dark as we had talked, the sun disappearing through the mouth of the valley. Overhead, the stars shone brightly through the thin clouds, and as I watched my Lord, He took his time before finally lifting an arm and pointing with His finger at a certain dim, barely visible star.

"There, Magdar. There is where I come from," he said, looking up at that star with an odd smile on His lips before looking at me. "Can you see it?"

"Aye, My Lord. That I can. That is then the Halls of Sa'yen!"

"The Halls of Sa'yen?" He repeated, shaking His head sadly as He looked upon me with resignation. "No, Magdar, you are wrong. That is not your equivalent of Heaven. That small star is the Sun that my home planet circles. A sun much like the one that burns in your sky. I come from that far sun, Magdar. I come from a planet called New Earth, Magdar. A planet that was settled a thousand years ago by men and women from an even older world called Earth. Do you understand?"

"No, My Lord," I said truthfully, at a loss to know what next to say.

He smiled. There is something in His smile that makes one relax, feel at peace in the world, even though He speaks in strange words. He smiled and looked upon me with a sad look in His eyes and sighed loudly. But He continued speaking.

"Magdar, I fell to your planet almost a full year ago in a small ship that is called an escape capsule. I was traveling from that small star to that bright star there, Magdar. Do you see it?"

He was pointing to another star far to one side of the sky and I looked to see where His finger was pointing. I saw the bright light in the sky and frowned. Other worlds circling these tiny dots of light in the sky? His words were odd to my ears, but even more oddly, they were words that I found compelling to listen to. I could not imagine worlds such as mine circling these small lights in the sky. I had no clear idea as to what these lights actually were, our prophets somewhat vague themselves as to their explanations in this matter. Yet I did not doubt the Sa'yen's words. If He said He came from one of those tiny lights, then I was prepared to believe him emphatically. How could I doubt the words of the Promised One? Was He not the Sa'yen? Was I not but a mere mortal? I did not doubt the Sa'yen's words, but I found myself full of questions.

"My Lord, if you will excuse the questions of a poor servant, how do you travel from one point of light to another?"

"In a ship much like this, Magdar. But bigger. And made entirely of metal."

"And they use sails too, my Lord?"

"No, not hardly!" He said, booming with laughter at my question and putting His hand on my good shoulder fondly. "We use things that make our ships go very fast, Magdar. Very fast! The distance between that point of light and the other is so far it would be too much for you to grasp, my friend. Too much!"

"And this escape capsule is . . . ?"

"Ah, yes. The escape capsule!" He nodded, remembering the original line of our conversation. "An escape capsule is a much smaller ship one uses when the larger ship no longer can fly. Can you understand that, my friend?"

I nodded. It sounded odd to me to have a ship large enough to carry another ship within it but at least that sounded possible to me. The Sa'yen turned to face me fully as he tried to explain how He came among us.

"My large ship hit a very large asteroid, a rock that flies in space, Magdar, and it caused my big ship to cease flying. I had to use the smaller ship, the escape capsule, to come to this planet. I came in it and landed far up in the valley almost a year ago. I did not even have time to find out if anyone lived on this planet when I landed. My capsule's batteries were almost drained of power by the time I started my descent so I could not scan the planet with my instruments except just to get an overall view. You are, Magdar, the first living creature I've seen that can talk to me for over a year. And am I glad that you are here!"

He again touched me warmly with His hand and I felt

too much honor was being heaped upon me for no reason. I started to say something else, to ask another question but before I could, Hagbash's young voice yelled out into the night air suddenly and we turned hurriedly to find the boy. My Lord the Sa'yen drew His sword instantly as we bounded across the still body-cluttered deck of the black-hulled ships and I too drew mine. Leaping across the gap between ships, a gap such that if we failed to land on the deck of the second ship we would have fallen over a thousand feet before hitting the valley floor far below, we landed on the deck of the second ship and quickly found the young boy standing frozen in horror close to the stump of the ship's mizzenmast. The young lad stood there with such a look of terror on his face that I and the Sa'yen approached the boy with swords ready for instant work.

"My Lord, that, that dead man moved!" Hagbash shouted, pointing a shaking finger at a bloodied body sitting up against the mizzenmast with blood stains bathing his once light-blue toga to a dark ebony black color.

My Lord the Sa'yen moved to approach the wounded Aggarian pirate, but I stepped in front of Him and stopped Him. He looked at me with a lifted eyebrow in surprise but waited to hear what I had to say.

"My Lord, do not approach further, I beg you! This is a common trick of the Aggarians! They feign being wounded by smearing blood from a corpse onto their clothing and wait for an opportunity to strike back or to escape. Look, see the small green ring that is pierced through his nose?"

The Promised One looked, eyes narrowed suspiciously, and nodded when He observed the small ring hanging from the lower portion of the pirate's nose. I nodded and continued on with my story.

"That is a badge that shows his ranking, My Lord. This Aggarian pirate is a chieftain among his kind. He is well placed among the pirate chieftains! No doubt this was his ship that is ruined and he seeks revenge! Let Tallsus and Fidor dispatch this rogue quickly and heave his body over a railing!"

"What? Kill a wounded man, Magdar? Surely you mean not what you say!" the Promised One exclaimed, looking

at me with irritation before sweeping me to one side with
His hand and moving to kneel beside the pirate chieftain.

Aye, as I have said before, the Sa'yen's ways are strange
to us mortals. It has always, for as long as I can remember, been a practice among us Hungars to kill the foes
wounded and pitch their bodies over the sides of the ship.
What purpose do the wounded of our enemies shower
upon us? Especially the wounded of Aggarian pirates? We
cannot barter them for ransom, since the Aggarian
chieftains care little to pay ransom for their kind that fail
in their raiding adventures and Aggarian pirates are noto-
rious for being the worst slaves. And the Aggarians would
have quickly dispatched us to our untimely deaths if we
had failed to escape their clutches, so I was mystified in
my Lord's irritation at me for suggesting the obvious. Yet
I was very unhappy when Our Lord knelt down beside the
wounded chieftain and, with His free hand, began to examine the pirate's wounds. I stepped closer to the pirate
chieftain, anticipating the worst from the bearded rogue.
Keeping my eyes on the pirate, sword point close to the
warrior's throat, I was amazed at the deft, expert ease with
which the Promised One quickly examined the man's
wounds. The way in which my Lord examined the warrior
made me think of a few of the rare Hungar physicians I
had seen work on the wounded and the sick. Tall, gray-
robed monks of the Charolarl Sect were the best physicians and they were as delicate and as expert in diagnosing
the lame and the wounded as was my Lord. But Charolarl
priests are rare among the rugged mountain crags of
Northern Hungar, and I found myself both gladdened and
surprised that the Sa'yen, the God of War, would be a
skilled physician as well.

My thoughts were pushed aside when old Fidor and
Tallsus pushed their heavy frames up through the fo'ard
hatch, dragging a heavy-looking wooden chest with them.
Fidor, grinning from ear to ear and brow covered with
sweat, shouted excitedly to us, lumbering across the deck
with the big chest across his chest.

"Magdar! My Lord! Look! Look! Treasure! Treasure
beyond your wildest thoughts!"

And he dumped the contents of the chest onto the deck

beside the Sa'yen in his excitement. Out came large jewels
of a thousand colors, gold coins, gold necklaces studded
with jewels, and thousands of other coins of lesser value.
A massive treasure that equaled more than any other I
had viewed before. The riches that lay at the Sa'yen's feet
made Him a fabulously wealthy man. We all gasped. And
even the Sa'yen seemed stunned at this sudden access to
riches. But from this stroke of fortune came near tragedy.
That foul, bearded pirate, who had been apparently slumbering up against the stump of the mizzenmast, suddenly
swept his hand across the hilt of a large dagger stuffed in
his belt and pulled the wicked curved blade out with lightning speed. I had my eyes foolishly on the wealth lying at
the Sa'yen's feet and knew nothing of the Aggarian pirate's move until Hagbash yelled a warning. But it was too
late! By the time I turned and started to drive my sword's
point into the rogue's throat, his hand was slicing down
through the air, the tip of the dagger aimed at my Lord's
jugular vein. I knew I would be too late in killing the pirate but before I could push the sword forward, the Sa'yen
did the incredible. His hand was like a blinding flash as it
came up in a clenched fist and smashed into the wrist of
the pirate's blow with such a jarring smack, the dagger
sailed through the air harmlessly. And then, using the back
of the same hand, the Sa'yen slapped the bearded face of
the pirate so hard I too winced in pain involuntarily. But
I stepped forward, anger flowing through my soul at this
treacherous filth that had come so close to harming the
Sa'yen, and started to slash the man's head from his shoulders. But the Sa'yen stood up quickly, and His hands were
on my shoulders restraining my anger.

"Magdar! No! Everything is fine! I disarmed him; there
is no need to kill him!"

"But My Lord! He is a treacherous animal! He almost
took You away from us! He deserves to die!" I shouted,
rage filling me from the near deed.

"No! I forbid it!" the Sa'yen's voice sounded over the
shouting of us six, His voice like ringing trumpets blaring
into our ears.

Reluctantly, I stepped back and sheathed my sword.
There was a look of black hatred on my face as I stared

down into the grinning, though bloodied, face of the bearded pirate. All of us six stood glaring at the man, yet the pirate chieftain was brave. Severely wounded, yet still capable of trying to seek revenge even though it meant his instant death, the bearded pirate looked into our faces calmly with a sneering grin on his pale lips. The Sa'yen removed His hands from me and nodded. His gray-blue eyes viewed each of us closely and saw the rage and hatred in our eyes. There was, amazingly it seemed to me, a look of sadness on His face. Seeing this, the rage inside me cooled somewhat and I looked at Him questioningly. He saw my consternation and smiled at me.

"Magdar, my hot-blooded friend, you must learn to be magnanimous with the defeated. This man's reaction was to be expected, my friend! As you warned me, I was prepared for just such a move, old friend. Now, he realizes it is in our hands and can do nothing about it. So, I want to move him below in order that I may heal him. Do you understand?"

We all listened as the little object He carried with Him at all times changed His words over to our language so that we could understand Him. Looks of surprise registered on all of our faces when He said He wanted to save this fiend's life. Fidor and Tallsus looked at me questioningly, but I shrugged and motioned for them to carry the pirate below. Yet our surprise was nothing like the surprise that was clearly etched on the Aggarian's face. He was stunned by this sudden event, fully expecting to die at our hands at any moment. As Tallsus and Fidor roughly picked the man up, he reached out with a hand and touched me on the arm.

"Why is he saving my life?"

"Do not ask foolish questions, pirate. I do not question His motives."

"You use the High Language in addressing Him. Why? Is He your Lord?"

"Fool. He is my God! He is the Sa'yen!"

The bearded pirate blinked up at me in the arms of Tallsus and Fidor, color draining from the man's face. But he had been right. I was using the High Language every time I addressed Him. The High Language is always used by the Northern Hungar when addressing or conversing about religious matters. It was, to us all, a sign of our devotion when we addressed Him with the High Language. But frowning, I motioned for the two to carry the wounded pirate down below. They did, carrying a bearded pirate chieftain who had grown suddenly quiet, with a look of moody contemplation in his eyes. I turned to find My Lord and saw him slide over the railing of the furthest black-hull to begin the descent down the giant Yab'lal tree. Frowning, and suddenly finding myself exhausted, I motioned the tall, thin-framed, baby-faced figure of Hagbash to follow Our Lord down the tree. I then went below deck, found a small bunk that still had bedding on it and crawled into it to rest.

III

Trusting a Pirate

Although I and the five others that were the Sa'yen's devoted followers treated Our Lord with all the humble devotion that He deserved, there were things we wished to do He simply disallowed in His presence. He absolutely forbade us to kneel in His presence when we came to look directly into His face to address Him. He refused to allow only us six to do the menial chores of the camp. He constantly disappeared into the thick woods of the Yab'lal forest to hunt and fish, sending me into fits of sheer panic when none of us left to follow him. He became furious when one of us constantly tried to be with Him at all times. And over and over again He kept on insisting that He was not the Sa'yen. But every time he uttered these words we all would smile knowingly. Our Lord the Sa'yen was exactly what we knew He was. And He was reacting to his divinity exactly the way the prophets said He would react. So we would say nothing when He denied to us His divinity and moved a bit farther away in order for Him to cool from His rages faster. Yet for the most part, He took His situation gracefully and without complaint. The Sa'yen was a big man with a fine physique and with His blond-bearded face and cut hair, which He allowed Tadan to do twice a month, My Lord the Sa'yen was a magnificent presence to look upon! But He insisted that we treat Him like a mortal and not like a god! This posed many problems for us, but usually we reluctantly acceded to His demands. At nights we would sit on the deck of the best

33

black-hull around a strong fire with cloaks over our shoulders and He would speak to us about the many worlds He had been to. He explained to us that where He came from—again mystifying many of us as we listened to Him—men such as we traveled from star to star in long ships made of metal. With wonder we would hear His tales of other worlds and the customs of these peoples on other worlds. He said that a star He called Rigel had a world that circled that sun much like ours. The planet was high, rugged mountains covered with forests of tall green trees but there the people did not fly in ships like ours. Hagbash, the baby-faced youngest of our group, wondered how people traveled from one place to another in such rugged country. The Sa'yen replied that on this planet the populace had animals that could scale sheer cliff walls as easily as a man could walk in a straight line and carry a man on its back at the same time. We could only look upon Him with wonder at such a thing! But the Sa'yen spoke in strange words to us on many nights; some we could vaguely understand, some we could not grasp at all. Like the time when one cool night the black-hull we were repairing was almost complete in its refitting, we sat around the campfire and listened to His words about the planet He claimed was His home world. He called it New Earth. He said this planet was mostly rolling hills of green grass and deep blue oceans. We had to ask him what an ocean was since the Language of the Gods has words that the Language of Mortals has not. An ocean, much to our amazement, was like a lake in many respects. Except that the size was so vast that it would take weeks, even months, for a ship or boat to sail across it. We could not envision such a large body of water! The largest bodies of water I have ever seen, or heard talked about, were the Lakes of the Salt Peern far to the southeast of the High Tor Mountains we now found ourselves in. Yet these lakes, the largest called Lake of the Blue Mists, could be traveled across in two days by canoe or by ship. To take months, or even weeks, to travel across such a body of water seemed impossible to us. Yet for all of our amazement, the Sa'yen had even more astounding things to say to us.

The night He talked to us about His home world He

told us of the struggle He had found Himself in during His early youth that eventually forced Him to flee the planet for His life. A struggle to suppress greed and evil was how He explained it to us, a struggle that eventually destroyed all His loved ones and almost destroyed Him. We listened to His words in deep rapture, unable and unwilling to break the spell He wove around us. Yet, as He spoke of His home world and seeing His parents die in an attack that wiped out an entire city with one blinding ball of light and heat, vague stirrings of uneasiness stole through my mind. I grew worried. Could this God before me be a God to our eyes and only a mortal, a normal mortal, on other worlds? Were gods so powerful that on other worlds, even stronger gods made ours nothing but minute peasants such as we? Could my God, the Sa'yen, actually be nothing but a mere person, a mortal cast down upon this planet? A mortal with infinitely more knowledge and wisdom, but nevertheless still only a mortal? Pulling on my mustache, sitting across from my Lord, I thought over this dreadful idea in silence. I knew not what to think. Was my Lord a mortal? Or was He not the Sa'yen? When at last the hour grew late and we all broke from the campfire to bed down, I found myself throwing sleeping furs over my body, still in deep thought over the subject. I knew not what to say.

Yet, mortal or not, the Sa'yen was a being that far surpassed us all in knowledge and skills of combat. Two weeks of intensive work in rebuilding the mastless hull of the Aggarian raider had put us all in a state of raw, edgy nerves and all we could do in the last few days before the ship was ready was bitterly complain about each other's failings. The Master saw this symptom some days before I and, as was His trait, He thought up the perfect cure for our frayed nerves. A contest. A contest of skill that made us compete with each other. He even included the Aggarian pirate chieftain, Hakba Baru, in with our games. The pirate's wounds had not been so serious as they had appeared but he had lost much blood. Two weeks of rest with the Sa'yen feeding him daily the herbs and powders that He seemed so familiar with soon brought this dreaded pirate chieftain's strength back to him in full. Aye, I was deeply concerned about the Sa'yen's attention to this pirate. The name of Hakba Baru was known far and wide as the name of an exceedingly daring pirate. The daring and cunning of the pirate were almost a legend within themselves and now this same legend lived among us. Aye, although the Sa'yen frowned upon it, I nevertheless insisted this pirate was to be chained to his bed each night when we slept, with an armed guard at his front door. And while we worked during the day, this pirate chieftain was to be chained to the for'mast with food and water placed close to him so that he would not thirst or grow hungry. And although I protested loudly over it, the Master insisted on including this treacherous pirate prince in with the games He had planned us to compete in, in our diversion from work. We could only comply with the Master's wishes on this final point, none of us liking the decision, however.

We descended to the carpeted floor of the Yab'lal forest and found a large clearing to hold the games in. The games would include a foot race, mock combats using the sword, halberd and bow, wrestling and heaving of a large round stone. We all competed, including the Sa'yen, although we all knew that we, being only poor servants and weak mortals, could not expect to compete against a God on an even basis. But the Master insisted on His participation. It was like watching a phantom take to his wings and fly before us, the way the Sa'yen ran! Still the race was long and demanding, and as each of us stepped over the finish line, we dropped to the ground to gather our breath and all we could do was groan from our exertions. We could hardly stand on our feet, our breath loud, deep spasms of rapid breathing as we kneeled to the ground. But the Sa'yen, although breathing somewhat heavily and rapidly, stood on His feet grinning at us. To me He appeared to look a bit saddened that none of us had challenged Him more seriously in the race, but He stood before us, His beard and hair the color of dark gold straw, hands on His hips, smiling down upon several weak and exhausted mortals. I, gritting my teeth and forcing myself, came to my feet and announced that I was ready for the next contest. My Lord, the Master, wanted each of us to compete the hardest he could against Him and I was determined to do the best that I could! Using the toe of my boot, I roused the others and we stepped up to the next contest.

All through the day, the Sa'yen pushed us to our very limits of strength and endurance. I came within inches in the weight-heaving contest of beating the Master. And actually led the contest all the way up to the Master's last throw. But the Sa'yen heaved with all his might, each muscle in his body standing out from the flesh in the effort, and the large stone sailed through the air to land finally only an inch and a quarter in front of my stone! Disgusted, I did not heed to the cheers of my comrades as they congratulated me on almost winning the contest. Even the cold-hearted Hakba Baru, the Aggarian pirate, nodded his approval at my effort. The Sa'yen came up to me, put both of His hands on my shoulders and shook me fondly. I could see in His eyes He was very pleased with me. And seeing the warmth and friendship in His gray-blue eyes cooled my anger at myself somewhat and I grinned back to the Master ruefully. With one of His hands He rubbed the top of my head playfully, turned and announced the next contest was ready to begin.

Yet, there was little need to continue. The Master won with singular ease in the bow contest. He used His own bow, a long, heavy looking thing made from a limb from the Kakla trees that sometimes fringe the outer portions of the Yab'lal forests. We had, thanks to Hakba Baru, found several double-concave horn bows up in the black-hull we were refitting and we used them in the contest. But the Master allowed each of us to try His bow in the contest, which we all did. To our amazement, we found His bow to be almost beyond our strength to pull. Only I was capable of notching the arrow and pulling it back, but even then I could only make a quarter pull with it. Yet the Sa'yen, taking the bow from my hand, notched the arrow to the gut-string and pulled back the arrow clear to the wide blade of the arrowhead itself. And when He let fly, the bow string sung a loud, powerful song of power and the arrow flew swift and sure. Twice I saw the Sa'yen drive good, hard shafts made of Kakla wood through small trunks of young Yab'lal trees, much to our amazement. The Yab'lal tree is an exceptionally durable, yet light wood. We use this wood to build our famous ships because of its strength and light weight. I have seen grown men pick up an entire tree trunk that was eighty feet long, stripped of any limbs, and heave it onto their shoulders as if it were a sack of flour and walk away with it. Yet I have seen the heavy, slow moving stone balls hurled from our cannon careen off Yab'lal wood planking that was yet young and still green from its curing as if bouncing off a stone wall! But to see the Master hurl two shafts of hard, heavier Kakla wood through a yet living Yab'lal tree was astounding.

In the halberd and sword events, the Master clearly was the winner. I had the honor of facing the Master for the decision of champion, having defeated five opponents in a row to face the Sa'yen. Hakba Baru declined to participate in this event, claiming that his wounds were beginning to hurt him. Yet, as the Master sent Tallsus running to ascend up through the grandfather Yab'lal tree that our black-hull was moored to for medicine, I watched the green-robed pirate chieftain slowly recline on a small knoll of grass with suspicious eyes. He appeared not to be in pain. Yet I wondered why he did not participate. Hakba Baru was reputed to be one of the best swordsmen of the Northern Hungar, and so I found myself surprised that he did not leap to this challenge and try to best the Master. Of course, in the contest there would have been no unsheathing of steel blades. Even though the Master protested somewhat upon my insistence, I yet won the argument. I had Hagbash carve for us several stout mock swords, weighted with small stones for the proper weight of a true blade. I did not want to take any chances of the pirate prince having an opportunity to harm the Sa'yen. All our weapons were left up in the black-hulls, except for bows and arrows, and they were guarded by the dour face of Fidor when we competed. But the Aggarian pirate declined to participate in the contest, claiming illness, and the Sa'yen and I finally faced each other in mock combat.

Each of us carried the small, round shield so common to the Northern Hungar. Made of strips of Kakla wood

edged with a band of iron, this small shield in the right
hand made a defensive weapon extremely difficult to break
through. My father, an old Ha'valli warrior of the Ha'valli
Plains, had taught me the use of the shield and sword. My
father had been a good man and an excellent swordsman.
He had survived through one hundred fifty single combats
with the sword and shield. He was a master with the
weapon, and he had taught me well. Facing the Master,
yet even knowing that I would be in the end defeated, I
felt the closest to being on an even standing with the
Sa'yen in any of the contests. The Master and I faced each
other in a large circle formed by my comrades as we faced
each other, and even Hakba Baru came to stand beside
old Fidor as the Sa'yen and I first struck blows. I began
the action by exploring the Master's use of the shield. A
feint, a parry and then a swift attack to His lower left
were my intentions. The sound of the Kakla wood, slapping up against both the shield and wooden blade the
Master wielded, soon reverberated back and forth in the
small clearing within the Yab'lal forest. Straining, with
sweat soon rolling large droplets down my forehead from
the exertion, the Master and I fought with a fierce intensity. Stroke after stroke was neatly parried by the Sa'yen
and I soon found myself being barraged by the Master's
relentless, pressing attack. Soon the clearing sounded like a
thousand woodsmen madly chopping trees. My shield arm
was buffeted time and time again with bone-jarring blows
the Sa'yen launched. And I, with all my might, would
counter with blows that were met by the Master's shield
no matter where I tried to break through. Like maddened
bulls we two kept hammering at each other, neither yet
finding the opening that would allow our wooden blades to
slip through and register the killing stroke. I found myself
tiring rapidly, the sweat pouring from my body, each
breath becoming a ragged explosion for oxygen. Yet even
though the Sa'yen hammered with all his might, using both
shield and sword for weapons, He had not found a weak
spot in my defense. I was elated! I felt at last I was going
to defeat the Master. Suddenly stepping back from the
fray, lowering my shield a fraction, breathing hard
through my mouth, I grinned as I looked upon the Mas-

ter's face. He too was showing signs of combat. His shoulder-length hair was drenched with sweat, his beard contained large droplets of water, his breath came ragged and rapidly. And He too was grinning. Saluting me with His wooden blade, He nodded to me His pleasure in my swordsmanship, then lifted His shield to commence the combat again. I too grinned, pleased with myself, and lifted shield to step into the fray again. We stepped to each other, eager to resume. But the excited voice of Tallsus made us pause and turn to see the heavy-framed, wide-shouldered man waving to us high up in the giant Yab'lal tree.

"Ho, there! Beware! Beware! Yonder are ships of the Hakadians!"

I shouted in anger, threw my sword and shield down and raced for the Yab'lal tree. Hakadians! This far north that meant only one thing. They again were hunting for the Northern Passages. Racing to the grandfather Yab'lal, I leaped to the lower limbs and started racing up through the branches for the black-hulls above. Behind me I heard the others following me rapidly, yet I did not pause to wait for the Master. Climbing as rapidly as I knew how, I eventually got to the keel masts of the black-hulls and rapidly climbed to the upper decks. Racing to the aft quarterdeck of the ship we were refitting, I took the long-glass from Tallsus and lifted it up to look at the ships.

"Magdar? What is happening?" I heard the voice of the Master beside me.

"Hakadians, My Lord," I said, focusing on the two ships still far off down the green-walled valley and approaching slowly. "Hakadians this far north."

"What are Hakadians?" the Sa'yen asked, sounding puzzled as he stood beside me peering down the long valley of green forest.

In silence, I handed Him the long-glass and looked into His face. He took the glass from me, lifted it to His eye and looked. I knew what He would see. Two gold-hulled Hakadian warships, big Hakadian frigates with for' and main'sails set, both upper and keel masts, with pennants trailing from almost every mast. One of the pennants would be from the upper main'mast and it would be trailing out in the breeze for over forty feet. It would be a huge pennant of crimson with gold trim. I smiled ruefully as I watched His face steady the two ships far down the valley carefully. I knew the pennant that flew from the mast of the larger Hakadian frigate well. It was the pennant of the Hakadian Admiral Hasdrabul. I turned and peered down the valley in silence. As I looked at the two tiny objects floating lazily above the valley floor, the Master spoke to me.

"Who are the Hakadians, Magdar?"

"A powerful city to the far south, My Lord. The Hakadians consider themselves the rulers of the world, Sire. Their god is Shilra, the Goddess of the Moon. And they are again in the Far North hunting."

"Hunting? Hunting for what?"

"The Northern Passages, My Lord," I answered, not taking my eyes from the objects as they slowly grew larger in view. "For years they have wanted to dominate the trade routes of the lesser cities of the Zygar Mountains. Only these cities know the best routes through the Far North, and Hakadians, being naturally selfish and arrogant, wish to control these routes for their own treasures. They have for years searched in vain for the Northern Passages and, apparently, are again in search of them."

"And what will happen if they discover them, Magdar?"

"If they discover them, My Lord? Well, in a few short months at most, the cities of the Zygar Mountains, the city I claim home port included, will soon be dominated by Hakadian merchants and eventually would become a part of the Hakadian Empire." I answered, my voice sounding bitter.

"And this would be bad?" the Master queried, still peering through the long-glass at the ships far away.

"Aye, Lord, this would be bad." I answered readily enough, nodding as I thought about it.

"They seem to be approaching us, Magdar," the Master grunted, handing me suddenly the long-glass.

"Aye, Lord. They are. The wind is from the nor'west and it will be only one or two hours before they see our position."

"And when that happens?" He asked, peering at me with one eyebrow lifted questioningly.

"Then you may have the opportunity to see the hospitality of a Hakadian warship," I growled, peering down the long, narrow valley.

They came. Two gold-painted Hakadian frigates. With upper and lower mast mainsails set for a leisurely passage up the narrow valley, banners and pennants waving arrogantly in the afternoon breeze. The larger frigate, the flagship of the Hakadian Admiral Hasdrabul, had her guns run out on her port side. I counted thirty cannon. Her sails were a deep crimson red, each mast, both upper and lower, carrying main' and main'top sails to catch the breeze. Her huge rudders, both upper and keel, were bright blue, signifying with that color the presence of the admiral on board her. I watched through the long-glass, ruefully admiring the lines of the frigate and the way she was picking her way arrogantly up the narrow, twisting valley.

"They are beautiful, Magdar," I heard the Master say to me, His voice a soft, admiring rumble as He watched the ships. "Dirigibles with masts! Two masts on top with sails! And two masts on the bottom with sails! Amazing! Truly amazing!"

"Aye, Lord, If you say so," I growled, closing the long-glass with a vicious snap and looking at Him angrily. "But if they spy our position shortly, we all will wish that our ship here had a crew to man her."

"You mean they will attack a distressed vessel such as ours?"

"Ha! And with pleasure, Sire! Hakadians have no love for Aggarian Pirates either. They will come over us and throw broadside after broadside down into us without batting an eye. Aye, Lord! Never worry about the hospitality of a Hakadian. Their only move is to conquer. Their only desire is to rule."

The Sa'yen looked at me, then turned to view the ships still far down the valley. They reached approximately to the height where we sat in the trees on the upper wall of the valley. Except they floated lazily along at a sedate speed of five or ten knots and we lay among the treetops,

still aground and unable to flee. Judging from the amount
of sail they carried and the speed of the breeze, I gave
ourselves a little over an hour before they were upon us.
Turning, I gazed upon the Master's face. His bearded face
was a mask hiding His true feelings but I saw in His
gray-blue eyes a sharp light glowing brightly. Frowning, I
felt the skin on the back of my neck begin to tingle with
excitement and I turned to face the Sa'yen fully. Then I
saw a smile spread across His lips and He turned to look
at me.

"Magdar, can we sail this craft now?"

"Now?"

"Aye, now!" He asked again.

"Surely, My Lord!" Fidor broke in, he too suddenly becoming excited for no apparent reason.

"Aye! The sails are set, the masts are firm and rigged.
We can sail this ship!" Tadan shouted, clapping tall Tallsus on the shoulders firmly.

"Let's run with her, Magdar!" Hagbash shouted,
jumping up and down excitedly in front of me. "Come on,
we can do it!"

"Aye, and even I will assist, Magdar," Hakba Baru said,
his voice breaking into my thoughts as he stepped up and
nodded to me gravely. "We must do something quickly or
it will be too late for all of us!"

I nodded. I too felt the excitement surging through me.
We yet had enough time to use sweeps to push the black-
hulled ship out of the treetops and set sail. We would run
before the Hakadian frigates and lead them on a merry
chase. Nodding again and smiling, I quickly gave the orders needed to begin the chase. Hagbash shouted his approval, jumping up and down in his excitement as he
raced down the deck to man the sweeps, followed by
Hakba Baru and Tallsus. Tadan and Fidor and Bidgar
were scurrying up the mainmast to set sail and I soon
leaped into the rigging of the mizzen to set some sail as
well. And the Sa'yen! He raced to the for'mast and soon
was rapidly among the upper spars of the mast, dropping
canvas as if He had been born to the rigging!

We were going to run in front of the Hakadian Admiral
Hasdrabul! I did not have time to consider the conse-

quences. I was too busy setting sail, both upper and lower
masts, and helping the rest at the sweeps trying to disengage
ourselves from the trees. Yet what madness this was! Only
eight men to man an entire black-hull. A ship, a fast
raider that usually required a crew of sixty. Yet we
manned it as best we could. And we soon had all sail set,
the rudders turned hard to starboard as the breeze bellowed the sails into life and strained to pull us away from
the valley walls and the Yab'lal forest. I could feel the excitement pounding through my veins. It was an exhila-
rating feeling. And the Sa'yen again was leading us into
battle!

IV

Attack of the Golden-Hulls

I took the helm of the black-hull and whirled the large wheel to starboard. My Lord the Sa'yen was forward helping man the long sweeps the others were using to push us out of the trees. The upper mast sails were all set, straining in the breeze and looking like huge carved walls as they captured the wind and refused to release it. I turned to look over my shoulder and almost cried out in anger at what I saw! The golden-hulls of the Ilakadians had observed our plight! I could see the admiral's flagship running up a series of signals to the smaller ship, and even as I watched, the two ships just seconds before so serenely floating over the valley floor now adjusted their course and began to make more sail. I turned and started to yell for Tadan, the ship's gunner from the old *Princess Tagia*, to go below and man the stern cannon. But before I could yell, the black-hull shuddered underneath my feet and lurched to one side drunkenly! We were moving! Grinning, I yelled for the black-hull to move again and she heard my words! There was a ripping, snapping sound of the hull moving through tree limbs ponderously, and then the ship jumped forward, free from the clutches of the trees. Slowly, hesitantly, the long, narrow-beamed black-hull slipped out from the green wall of the mountain, leaning heavily to starboard from the wind. I screamed to the men forward to run to the keel masts and quickly set sail or we would roll over slowly and all of us would be thrown to our deaths to the valley floor below. Yelling for

Tadan to man the stern cannon, I was suddenly alone, standing beside the huge helm, my hands flying over the wheel to bring the ship full before the wind in order for us to make the best possible speed! Through the wheel I felt the sudden correcting effect of keel sails filling with wind and pulling the black-hull back to an even plane. Smiling, the helm answered to my demands and soon she was running with the wind like a racehorse. We were fleeing down the narrow, twisting valley, with each minute that slipped by picking up speed and soon putting distance between us and the golden-hulls of the Hakadians. I laughed with delight at the sight. Looking over my shoulder I saw the hundreds of crew members on the admiral's ship scurrying through the rigging of all the masts to make more sail. Turning, I lifted my fist up and shook it at them in delight. We were running with ease with the wind. I knew there would be nothing that could catch us. But as if to challenge my beliefs, I saw two large puffs of gray-black smoke appear in front of the admiral's flagship and then the twin booms of the cannon came to my ears. In the afternoon sunlight I watched the two cannon shot sail high into the air and arc downward. They went sailing behind our stern by a good quarter mile, dropping the thousand or so feet into the valley to finally splash into the river below us. I shouted obscenities in delight at the Hakadian gunners, delighted at the chase and the sudden flurry of action after weeks of refitting the black-hull. And the Sa'yen was with us! The God of War! I felt like shouting and singing with unbelievable happiness for my strange luck. Turning to the helm, I adjusted our course a bit and watched with little concern as the hull of the ship tore past a large outcropping of rock that jutted from the wall of the valley. We slipped past the rock outcropping with only a foot to spare. Laughing like a madman, I whirled the wheel to adjust our course as the valley bent to port, then turned to watch the fall of the shot as the Hakadian gunners tried again.

The shot went arcing high up, paused at the top of their path and then went plunging downward again. Again they had been short in their range and below, the river splashed two huge columns of water as the shot dived into the cold river. Then there was a roaring, crashing boom, followed by a dense cloud of black smoke that smelled of gunpowder, and the black-hull shuddered from the recoil of the stern gun. Tadan, the cannon master, was answering the Hakadian challenge! Turning, peering over my shoulder as I kept my hands on the wheel, I watched the arc of our shot go sailing high up into the air and begin its plunge downward. But Tadan was a master with the cannon. His aim had been good: suddenly there was a huge hole in the flagship's mainsail. I cheered with delight at Tadan's shooting and danced in ecstasy. I was so involved with watching Tadan's firing I did not see the Master come up on deck and run to stand beside me. I did not know He was there until He placed a hand on my shoulder and leaned toward me to speak.

"Magdar! Where does this valley lead to?"

"I have no idea, My Lord. This is unknown country to me."

"But what do we do if the valley is boxed in?"

"We will try to sail over the tops of the mountains, Sire."

"Can we?"

"If the mountains are not too high, My Lord."

The green-robed Hakba Baru suddenly appeared, running toward us, his bearded face looking grim, the small ring in his nose making his angular face look cruel and arrogant. He hurried to stand before us, nodded with respect at the Master, then turned to address me.

"If I may take the wheel, I will be able to steer us to safety, Magdar."

"Or you may heave us up on the face of a mountain wall, you pirate scum!" I shouted, anger suddenly flooding through my veins. "Why should we trust you, Hakba Baru?"

"Because I know this valley well, Ha'valli warrior!" the pirate yelled through the wind and the straining sounds of the rigging above us, glaring at me in rage at what I had called him. "And if you do not let me take the helm, you will surely pile up onto the rocks of this valley's walls!"

I started to say something again, but the Sa'yen stepped up and put one of His hands on my shoulder. We looked

into His face and noted a thin smile underneath His blond
beard and mustache. He was looking into my eyes, and
when He spoke, I did not hesitate at all to obey Him.

"Let the pirate chieftain take the helm, my friend. We
will need his expert guidance in this affair."

The pirate chieftain took my place, his face grim, his
eyes looking directly ahead as we sailed on down the twisting valley. I stepped to the stern railing of the ship and
joined my Lord and together we watched the duel between
the gunners of the Hakadian flagship and of Tadan, the
cannon master. Yet I did not feel comfortable allowing the
Aggarian pirate to take the helm, and I continued to
glance at the pirate chieftain as he twisted and turned the
wheel of the black-hull. I am, by nature, a suspicious person. I did not trust Hakba Baru at all and I vowed to keep
a very close eye on his every move. But at times I turned
to watch the cannonading growing slowly in intensity. I
sent Hagbash and Bidgar down to assist Tadan with the
cannons and they were doing an incredible job. The Hakadians were slowly eating up the distance between us and
edging closer with each hour we raced with the wind. And
the closer they came, the better their gunners fired! Taking
the long-glass in hand, I snapped it open and peered at the
large flagship. I counted four prow guns, and from their
size, I suspected they were eighteen-pounders. She had set
all sail, both upper and keel masts, and so close was she
now that I could see individual faces of the crew easily
with the glass. For a moment or two I watched through
the gun ports as the Hakadian gunnery crew worked fever-
ishly to load and fire their guns. With the staggering roar
of four guns going off one after the other, we watched in
silence as four cannon shot lofted into the air and went
screaming through the rigging above us! And then below
us two guns, that Tadan with Hagbash and Bidgar's help
were manning, erupted in flame and smoke with a sharp
crack, shaking the black-hull with their combined recoil.
For a heartbeat or two the stern decking was engulfed
with acrid, foul-smelling smoke of spent gunpowder but
the wind quickly blew it away just in time to allow us to
count two more holes in the upper sails of the for'mast of
the Hakadian flagship. The Master grunted His pleasure in

our gunnery, standing beside me with His arms crossed over His chest arrogantly, looking unconcerned with the closeness of the engagement about Him. I grinned, feeling honored and pleased that such a god had at last joined the mortals of this world to lead us again to the south. Turning, I glanced at the green-robed form of the Aggarian pirate standing at the wheel and straining with every muscle to adjust our course a fraction. And then looking ahead, I almost dropped my long-glass at what was before us.

"My Lord! Look! The traitor of a pirate prince has again tricked us!" I shouted, jumping forward and reaching out to tear the pirate chieftain from the wheel of the helm.

Ahead of us and towering above us for thousands of feet were the far mountains that boxed in this long, twisting valley. Black rock, bare of any vegetation, jutted up from the valley floor for thousands of feet, much too high for us to sail above. The walls of the valley on either side of us were still thick carpets of green Yab'lal trees, but without a full crew to man the ship's bellows and stoking fires, there was no chance to sail above the green walls to freedom. We were trapped! Furious at the treachery of the Aggarian pirate, I took him by the shoulder and pulled him viciously from the wheel. He was shouting at me, pointing ahead at something, but I paid him no heed. Taking the wheel myself, I threw him to the Master and started to turn the wheel to starboard in an attempt to save us. I heard the pirate chieftain talking rapidly and excitedly to the Master, and then suddenly the Master pulled me from the wheel and the Aggarian replaced me again. Stunned, I looked into His face for an explanation and the Master stepped up closer to speak over the roaring of the cannonading.

"Allow the pirate to steer the ship, Magdar! He is not betraying us."

"But My Lord! The wall before us does not have any passages through it. We will smash up against it in barely a half hour."

"Nevertheless, you will do as I have asked, Magdar!" He shouted back to me over the roar of the guns, looking very stern in His bearded face. "I trust the pirate chieftain, my friend. He will not betray us further."

The guns of the Hakadian flagship were now finding the range and were being loaded and rammed home as fast as their crews could arm them. And the smaller golden-hull Hakadian was also finding the range, her two smaller guns coming into action as well. Tadan below was still banging away with his two guns and as we watched, the damage he was doing was constantly being written onto the Hakadian flagship. But we were being damaged too. A sudden ripping sound was heard above us and looking up, we saw the main'mast topsail rip completely in two and begin to flap angrily like some mad bird's wings. Cannon shot was whirling past us and then the Hakadian gunners struck the black-hull squarely for the first time. A cannonball smashed into the railing close beside the Sa'yen, splintering the stout Kakla wood railing into a thousand pieces and throwing both of us to the deck. I landed on top of the Master and shielded Him from the wood splinters as they whirled past us. The cannonball hurled into the decking of the black-hull and tore a long, narrow channel down the deck for twenty or more feet before falling off the side of the ship. I came to my feet, helping the Master up as well, and found Fidor beside us, kneeling on one knee with several large, heavy-looking muskets in his stout arms. I handed one to the Master, taking one myself, and the three of us began loading the heavy-looking weapons and firing at the Hakadian flagship. I shouted at them to aim for the gunnery crews of the prow guns and, with any luck, we might hamper their effectiveness if we could shake their concentration. Aiming, I fired and watched wood splinter beside the head of the chief gunnery officer standing beside the number-one gun on the flagship.

The golden-hull of the Hakadian admiral was now only a few yards behind us, and still closing slowly upon us. I knew in a few short moments the fight would be over, and turning, I peered ahead to see how close the valley wall of towering black rock was. And I almost screamed from the sight. The wall was directly over us, rising up thousands and thousands of feet, and still I saw no crack that would appear to be a passage. I glanced at the green robe of

Hakba Baru and saw him bent to the wheel, trying desperately to spin the wheel to port. Shouting, I ordered the strong-armed Fidor to help the pirate, then turning, I picked up another musket and fired. Luck was with me and a Hakadian gunner fell across his smoking gun suddenly and was quickly thrown to one side roughly by his crewmates. I saw the Master fire twice, each time striking a Hakadian with his musket ball, and I shouted in delight. The roar of the guns, the whirling smoke from the cannonading, and the screaming of falling shot all combined to create a deafening roar. But I was not listening to the roar. Loading and firing muskets, the Master and I did our best to lessen the cannonading the Hakadians were throwing at us. I found myself in the fighting rage that grips me in such emergencies and I smiled savagely.

The decking of the ship below me heeled to port suddenly and I was almost thrown from my feet. But the Sa'yen caught me with one of His strong arms and held me tightly until I could regain my balance. And then Tadan and his two cannon fired and through the smoke we saw the Hakadian flagship's for'mast suddenly tilt to starboard and then come crashing down in slow, agonizing finality! Hakadian sailors went screaming to their deaths a thousand feet below as the mast fell forward, snapping all its rigging in the process, then went sliding off the deck itself and tumbled downward into the valley. I shouted in glee, noting the Hakadian slowed immensely with such a loss of sail, and then suddenly, the decking of our ship was no longer under my feet and I was violently thrown to the starboard. I hit the Master just above the knees and together we went rolling across the crazily tilted deck in one large ball of arms and legs. We untangled ourselves from each other, but before we could come to our feet again, the afternoon sun was suddenly torn from the sky and we plunged into gloomy blackness. The screeching, eerie roar of a hurricane, with winds as fierce and as strong as a tempest, gripped us and again we were thrown to the decking violently. I felt the strong wind tearing at me, slowly moving me across the wood planking of the deck and frantically I reached out to find something to hold onto. The Master's iron fingers clamped around my wrist, stopping my movement across the deck as the roar of the wind built up into unbelievable intensity. Looking up, I screamed in terror at the view. The walls of the black mountain were racing past our sides at an incredible rate only inches from us. The pirate chieftain had found the hidden passage through the mountain wall. But such a passage! The wind was like nothing imaginable through this narrow passage, and so strong it was hurling our ship along with it as if the black-hull were nothing but a straw being tossed about in the winds of a powerful storm. I turned and looked into the face of the Sa'yen. He had wrapped an arm and a leg through what remained of the stern railing, His other arm outstretched and holding me onto the ship's madly tossing deck.

Then, as suddenly as we entered the passage, we shot out into bright sunlight and clear skies. The roaring of the hurricane winds died almost as quickly, and stunned, we found ourselves floating along in silence under a bright sun and clear skies. Too weak to move for some time, I lay on the deck in mild shock, numbed at the thought we had survived such an unbelievable ride. But we had with the Presence of the Sa'yen! His help had been the guiding light through such a harrowing adventure, and I rejoiced again for the hundredeth time that He was among us. The God of War was among us again! I felt like jumping up and shouting my praises to Him. But I found myself too weak to speak even in a low whisper. Tired, I closed my eyes and told myself that I would give thanks to the Master the moment I recovered my strength.

V

Our Lord's Mysterious Chariot

My Lord the Sa'yen stood beside the stern railing, gazing out over the port side, His face filled with bright surprise. He was, as He told me, amazed at the sight below. Standing beside Him, I said nothing and took His words with quiet calm. The Sa'yen, as the prophets had foretold, would be like a newborn child in a man's body when He first comes among us; and aye, He was as excited and impressed at seeing the high mountain city of Triisus as if a small child, for the first time, looked upon the white towers of the city.

"Magdar, this is a beautiful sight! I have been to many alien planets and seen truly strange things before which I have described as beautiful. But this city so high up off the valley floor is truly astounding."

I frowned at His words. He was talking about other planets again and visiting them, as I would have talked of my travels among the cities of the northern ranges of the mountainous Hungar. Again, over the last few days, I had found myself having doubts about the Sa'yen, even though everything He said or professed not to have knowledge of had been foretold by the prophets of our ancestors. I knew what the many legends of the Sa'yen were. Was I not a Ha'valli warrior? And were not the Ha'valli noted for being a people who looked upon the Sa'yen as their special deity? Aye, I knew I was having doubts about the Master, doubts I found shameful to think about, yet doubts that persisted and would not leave my mind. And yet, I could not pinpoint exactly what made me doubt that the man standing beside me was the Sa'yen.

My ancestors' prophets, over the burning campfires of the Ha'valli tribes, for years had told the legends of the Sa'yen. Of how He would come back among His people such as we were in the body of a mortal. Of how He would come falling out of the sky in a burning chariot. And how, with such suddenness, He would appear before His selected chosen that were destined to follow Him to the ends of the world. I could remember my father's devotion, the campfire flames dancing shadows across his craggy, sun-burned face, his eyes alit with a light I found akin to madness, softly talking to me about what it would mean to have the Sa'yen again leading us to the south. Aye, my father was a child to the Sa'yen! I remember the nights sitting beside the campfire listening to him and to the legends about the coming of the Master. The prophets had foretold all. The Sa'yen would be among the mortals of Hungar for a brief visit of a few years in the guise of a mortal. He would feel all the woes and hardships we mortals would feel and He would have no divine powers except one. None knew what that one power might be. He would, in battle, be undefeated. He would, while He stayed on Hungar, be like a child in a man's body. He would profess not to know the customs of our ancestors. and He would speak in riddles on occasion which none would understand. And, as the prophets had forewarned, He would always deny that He was indeed the Master.

I frowned at that, never feeling comfortable over that last prophesy. Why would a God deny that He was indeed a God? Why would a God come among His people in the guise of a mortal, and allow Himself to feel the pains, the emotions, the weaknesses of His people? Aye, I knew all the standard answers to these questions. The Sa'yen, even though the God of War, was nevertheless a compassionate deity. When He comes among His people, He comes to feel and understand the woes and terrors that sometimes makes His people grow weak in their devotion to Him. And in order to feel the many tribulations of the true mortal, He comes in the disguise of a mortal, leaving behind the powers of His deity. All His powers except one.

and none knew what that power might be. Aye, I knew the standard answers to the questions in my mind, yet I could not accept them fully. I had trouble accepting the idea that a deity such as the Sa'yen would need to delve into such complex disguises just to be among His people.

And yet, how could I doubt Him? Had He not appeared before me and the five who survived the massacre of the old *Princess Tagia* miraculously? And had I not seen with my own eyes the resting place of His fiery chariot? Aye! That was a sight to behold! The Master had made a request, after successfully fleeing from the Hakadian ships, to return to the same valley a few weeks later so that He could journey back to the sight of His chariot. I had protested vigorously concerned that again we might be drawn into battle with the Hakadian ships but this time might not be so fortunate. Yet Tadan and Fidor pointed out to me that in all likelihood the golden-hulls of the Hakadian ships would be gone from such a lonely and out of the way valley by then, and we could journey safely. And what if the Hakadians were there? Was not the Sa'yen among us? Did we fear the Hakadians seeking combat with us with the Master to lead us? Aye, I had no argument for that, and we turned about, to return to the High Tors valley, with me grumbling all the way. Yet, as we approached the resting place of His chariot, I stopped my grumbling. The prophets of the past had said He would fall among us in a fiery chariot. And as we all stood beside the port railing looking downward, there were no doubts in our minds that He had indeed fallen in a mighty chariot of burning flame. It was staggering to behold! The blackened, charred land below us had been consumed by a furious, intensive heat. For miles as we traveled up the valley, the once mighty Yab'lal forest of the valley was barren of all growth, its ground desolate and charred to a blackness, short, blackened stumps jutting up from a barren ground where Yab'lal trees had towered into the air. Miles and miles of this burnt desolation! And even though my Lord had professed to us earlier that He had lived among the wilds for almost a year before we were rescued by Him from the Aggarian pirates, yet nothing of new growth had started to appear in the ravaged, blackened valley floor. We were speechless at the sight. Yet as we watched, soon we came, floating our black-hull over the resting place of the Sa'yen. Furling sails, we quickly threw out mooring anchors and after some difficulty we had heavy ropes tied to stout mooring stakes that were driven with mallets deep into the blackened soil below us. And directly below us was the chariot of the Sa'yen.

Such a strange object! I had always thought that the chariot the Sa'yen would descend down to us in would be *that*—a typical chariot. But below us, looking massive and disturbingly foreign, was a huge object that was made of gold. Gold! Gold discolored from the intensive heat and in places blackened from the conflagration that had consumed the forest around us, but nevertheless most of the chariot gleamed a dull gold. A huge object, looking like a ball half severed, with a slightly curved plate of gold with a blister in the center of the surface. It had buried itself deeply into the charred ground, leaning somewhat to the starboard as it sat in the soil. Around the chariot were large, twisted pieces of metal—large pieces almost the size of the chariot itself, the metal twisted and charred a deep black from the fire and littering the area for some distance around the chariot. I estimated the chariot was a good thirty feet high and perhaps that length in diameter. In silence, Fidor, at the Master's urging, threw over the side the heavy rope ladders, and we descended to the ground below. In silence, filled with awe, we meekly followed Our Lord as He stepped up to the gold craft before us. We watched Him as He lifted a hand up to a strange little bump on the curved wall of the chariot. And then suddenly we heard something like air escaping through a thin crack and a door appeared as if by magic, opening from the once-solid gold wall of the chariot. I, with the others, jumped back some feet away from the opening door as it slid out in silence. Hagbash, being yet a young boy, yelled in terror and dropped to his knees, repeating over and over a common prayer of forgiveness to the Sa'yen. Irritably, the Master told young Hagbash to rise to his feet and stop his gibberish, and then He stepped up onto the lowered door and turned to motion us to enter His heavenly craft. After much discussion among us, only I and the dour-faced, strong-willed Fidor entered the Master's heavenly craft. And we entered with our mouths dry, our knees weak from the honor of it, and our eyes wide with near terror. But the Master gruffly told us to forget our terror; there was nothing inside His craft to be afraid of, and He even smiled at our fear. We, being men coming from fierce and proud ancestors, tried to recompose our normal selves as we followed the Sa'yen through His heavenly craft but neither of us could overcome the humbling awe of standing in such a holy place. It was strange, yet I found that the Sa'yen's heavenly craft reminded me of a small ship, with cramped, tiny compartments packed with strange objects of glass and multicolored wires whose use I couldn't guess. But to old Fidor's and my surprise, we found four rooms within the Master's chariot. In one tiny closet room we found four bunks; sleeping bunks, stacked one above the other. On the top bunk was the bedding where the Master had slept, sheets wrinkled, now covered with a fine, soft coating of dust from disuse. In silence, we followed the Master up a cramped, narrow spiral staircase made of steel to the two upper compartments to help the Master carry some of His belongings from His chariot to our black-hull riding motionless, moored to the stakes, overhead. As we watched, the Sa'yen opened a few small doors built into the bulkheads themselves and pulled out several large, black leather cases. Frowning, old Fidor and I exchanged questioning glances, then we turned again to look at Our Lord. The Sa'yen handed each of us two large cases, each case surprisingly heavy. The bearded, golden-haired Sa'yen grinned His pleasure at us, then turned again and withdrew something that was long and narrow, much like a portion of a lance and shaped roughly like the killing point of a lance tip. But this strange object was made of some metal that was grayish white in color, with handles of dark coal black jutting at a ninety-degree angle from the main portion of the thing. One end tapered down to a fine point while the opposite end thickened and finally bent to form a large Y-shaped end. The cup of the Y-shaped end was rounded and it occurred to me it would fit nicely a warrior's shoulder if one held it up in such a fashion. I was obviously right, for My

Lord read my thoughts, grinned at me in pleasure and held the thing up between us for Fidor and me to look at more closely.

"This is to be in your care, Magdar. You are to carefully preserve this for me. And never, under any circumstances, is anyone allowed to touch this object unless you have heard it from my lips directly. Can you do this for me, Magdar?"

"Aye, My Lord! It will be just as you say while in my keeping."

"Good. I knew you would say that." The Sa'yen nodded, smiling through His golden beard. His gray-blue eyes fell upon the strange object He held in His hand for a moment. Fidor and I saw Him frown in deep thought before speaking again. "This is a weapon, my friends. A weapon that has been beside me for years and years. We have fought many engagements together, this weapon and I. I would feel strange if it were not beside me again."

"A weapon, My Lord?" Fidor asked, his dour-looking, weathered face looking at the strange object with suspicion mixed with awe and then at the Master questioningly.

"A weapon, Fidor, my friend. A weapon with such power as you have never seen before. A weapon that, with one shot, could cut the largest ship that you know of in half like a hot knife slicing through butter. Eh? You do not believe me?"

"It is not that I do not believe you, My Lord." Fidor hastily put in, paling at the last words the Sa'yen had uttered to him. "It is that, that. . . ."

"That you cannot imagine such a weapon. Eh?"

"Aye, My Lord. It, it sounds so impossible to me."

The Master smiled at old Fidor, a smile I thought had the look of sadness, a sadness that had been earned after years of experiencing knowledge we knew nothing of. He nodded, looked at the weapon He held in His hand and paused a heartbeat or two before speaking again.

"Yes, I can understand your disbelief, my friend. Listen, both of you. You have given me the honor of thinking of me as your god returned to you. And I admit, there are too many legends that explain away what the actions would be of an alien cast among you by accident. I shall have to examine these legends more to ascertain the truth to that thought. But that is not the point I wish to make. What I am trying to say, my friends, is that I am not your god. I am a mortal like you, who, in the end, will eventually die either from old age or from battle wounds. Yet, what you cannot realize is the one important difference that separates me from you. And that is I come from a different planet, a different world! But this world is so far ahead of yours in science and technology that, as of yet, the best minds you have could not grasp the gap of knowledge that separates our cultures. And this, this in my hands, is but one example of what you cannot understand. Aye, I am just like you two, my friends. I live, I eat, I breathe just as you do. And I will die, in the end, just as you will. But try to understand, try to grasp what I have to tell you. The world I come from is so far advanced compared to yours that the knowledge I take as commonplace, the things my race uses every day without a second's thought, your race will consider magic. Or the powers of gods. Come; come, I will show you what such a weapon can do and perhaps you may grasp some of my meaning.

We followed the Master out of his heavenly craft and stepped out onto the scorched, blackened soil again. Overhead, the large mass of the black-hull floated, straining against the mooring ropes. The black-hull, her keel masts only a man's body length above us, appeared to me to be eager to leave this blackened, desolate scene. And reluctantly I conceded to myself that I too wanted to leave this place. Yet, keeping my thoughts to myself, I followed the Master out to stand below the ship and watched the Sa'yen as he stepped to one side and lifted the long, gray-white, rod-shaped object to His shoulder. Glancing up hurriedly, I noticed that the others were leaning over the railing, looking down at the Sa'yen. Hakba Baru, in a green robe, was to one side of the rest of the men, his darkly bearded and cruel looking face just as interested in what the Sa'yen was ready to show us as the rest were. Turning my eyes back to the Master, I watched Him as He lifted the thing to His shoulder, paused for a second, and then pressed His finger to a bright red button built into the black handle at the rear portion of the object.

I was not prepared for what was to happen next. I had no idea that such things could exist. There was suddenly, overpowering us, a deafening crack of thunder. There was a glaring green light, so bright that I had to throw an arm up, dropping one of the Master's cases in the process, to cover my eyes. The glaring, dazzling green light was so intense I saw old Fidor beside me, an arm up to protect his eyes as well, standing directly in the midday sun nevertheless fully bathed in the unnerving light. There was a high-pitched hissing sound, like the sound of snakes in the dark but a thousand times louder, and suddenly I found myself gripped with unimaginable terror. Above, faintly, I heard young Hagbash's voice screaming, joined surprisingly by two or three others, and I too felt like screaming. But I fought to control my natural emotions, and forcing myself I kept my eyes on the object that the Master had pointed to just before lifting the strange weapon to His shoulder. It had been a large stump of a Yab'lal tree, perhaps forty or fifty feet in diameter. Charred and blackened from the conflagration that had swept through this area like a curse, the stump rose from the ground only to the height of four or five feet. Yet as I watched, my eyes burning like hot coals as I peered at the green light coming from the thing at the Master's shoulder, I saw the giant tree stump absorb the green death, and then after throwing off large sparks of bright white and yellow fire, the stump disappeared in a cloud of white smoke.

As suddenly as the blinding green light appeared, it was no longer with us. As if I had stepped out of a bright sun into a dark cavern, I found myself momentarily blinded. I found my mouth dry and parched, my mind unable to comprehend what I had just witnessed, my ears still echoing the sharp crack of thunder that had sounded the instant the green light appeared. I felt myself stagger to one side, my knees weak, and I had an overwhelming desire to sit down and rest. I did so. Turning, I saw old Fidor down on his knees, his face lacking color, thoroughly shaken from the exhibition of power we had just witnessed. I said nothing. I cast my eyes upon the face of the Master. He stood a few yards away, the strange weapon in one hand down at His side, His face looking into mine with sadness. I could not understand that—the constant look of sadness every time He tried to convince us of His mortality. Or that he originated from another world much like ours, yet very much different from ours. With such command of vast power, and with all the weapons I was familiar with, why should the Master look saddened? I said nothing as I helped the dour-faced Fidor to his feet and collected the leather cases the Sa'yen gave us to carry for Him. Yet I felt uneasy at the look I saw on the Sa'yen's face. Or perhaps I was more uneasy at the feelings I myself was experiencing, feelings that, if known, would be called blasphemy.

I stood beside the Lord at the stern railing, our eyes cast down upon the site of the mountain city of Triisus. The city was situated some fifteen hundred feet up from the valley floor, on a large ledge that ran for miles on the eastern wall of the mountains that made up part of the valley below. Triisus was, by comparison, a small city. I told the Master that I did not think the city had a population of more than fifty thousand, but in my mind, that fifty thousand were fierce, proud people, proud of their city and very proud of the ships they were noted for. And indeed, the sky above Triisus was busier than that of many cities her size. Large, single-mast (per upper and keel) grain transports littered the sky. From the rooftops of several landing towers we could see the hulls of many ships, sails furled, their masts sporting banners of bright colors, their crews on leave with only a handful on board each ship to maintain the buoyance fires in their fire holds. Dotting the sky above and below us, their crews scampering up and down the rigging, ships made sail to leave or worked to take in sail in preparation for mooring. The sky was a rainbow of colors. The hull of each captain's ship was a color he preferred, with sails of different colors as well. I was always pleased to see such a sight. Triisus was the city I had adopted and I was proud that such a small city would have such renown. Triisus was noted for its shipwrights, considered by many to be the best in the business. It was also a thriving farming community. At the base of the mountain range that held her aloft and stretching off for miles up and down the valley floor, we could see the checkerboard squares of cultivated croplands.

The city itself sat on the ridge, clinging to the side of the mountain like a barnacle. The majority of the buildings were the stubby, three-storied fortress towers of merchants. Here and there among the roofs of the thick-walled small towers, a rich merchant had imported marble and built towers of tall, tapering, graceful lines. Such merchants liked to hire artisans to carve designs into the walls of the white marble, to be inlaid with gold or silver. There were also the towering, rounded towers of the landing platforms for the ships. These were the most plentiful, since landing towers facilitated trade. Far to the south, at the end of the ridge the city sat on, was the only road that led down to the valley floor below. It was a sharply twisting, narrow road of roughly hewn stone. Where the road pushed out onto the valley floor we could, in the distance, barely see the walls of the fortress that guarded the city's gates. It was constantly manned by the city's meager but well-trained troops. The road itself, sharply angling up from the valley floor to the city, was, despite its severe twists and turns, nevertheless heavily used by the peasants who farmed the valley floor. To the north, another road twisted and turned as it climbed upward to the top of the mountains where, guarded by another powerful fortress, a road had been constructed over a narrow mountain pass to connect with the valley on the other side of the mountain range. From the tops of many towers, and from almost all ships moored to the landing towers, banners and flags of all sizes and shapes danced in the morning breeze below us, adding gaiety to an already colorful scene.

The Master was quite pleased to see such a spectacle below us, and He had many questions to ask me about the city, its customs, and the customs of the people that lived in this region. I answered everything He asked, conveying to the best of my ability the information He was seeking. I was pleased with the Sa'yen immensely. After weeks of constant tutoring, the Master had discarded His strange-looking talking device that had helped Him understand what I said to Him. I had, quite frankly, felt somewhat uneasy with such a strange thing having the ability to speak words, even though it did nothing but translate the Language of Man into the Language of the Gods. Now He stood beside me, conversing easily with me in the language I could understand with only the slightest of accents that would indicate to others He was perhaps not from this world. Actually, I was doubly pleased with the Sa'yen. As He began to comprehend better what I said to Him directly, He demanded that I show Him the black-hull we now claimed as our own from one end of the craft to the other. And He demanded that I treat Him as a child, explaining to Him everything about the ship from the simplest to the most complex. Pleased and somewhat expecting a request such as this, since the prophets had foretold the Sa'yen would eventually ask, I plunged headlong into teaching the Master the intricacies of a Hungar skyship. We began first down in the bowels of the ship, in the fireholds of the buoyance tanks. The Master had often said to me He could not understand how such a ship, a dirigible as He called it, could float in the air, powered by sail, and yet tack back and forth and even sail into the wind. I explained to Him, as we crawled through the cramped corridors of the ship down to the fireholds, the Sacred Stones of the Pictii.

The Pictii were a Sacred Brotherhood far to the south that commanded the trade of the Sacred Stones. And, because of their control, their brotherhood was the most powerful religious order on the planet. They inhabited the high mountains to the south of the Ha'valli plains, mountains so high that no man had been known to climb them. Mountains so high that at their peaks there was no air to breathe, only emptiness. From somewhere in the depth of these mountains, called The Halls of the Mountain Kings, came the Sacred Stones.

As we finally stepped into the firehold, I held a torch high to show the oddly dark red stone blocks lying side by side and stretching down the length of the firehold directly under the buoyance bags, and the Master looked closely at the stones and started to reach out and touch one. I grabbed Him quickly and pulled Him back to safety, since He did not yet know the power of the stones. Surprised at my reaction, He stepped back and looked at me questioningly. I hurriedly lit two or three torches that sat in their stone holders on the sides of the bulkhead; then I casually tossed my torch onto one of the stones. There was the crackling, cutting sound of power and destruction and for some seconds, lightning danced back and forth across the surfaces of the stones, the lightning concentrating around the wooden torch. To our nostrils came the strong, acrid odor of sulfur, which the Sacred Stones emitted any time they were disturbed, and they danced with lightning. To many old hands of the skyships of Hungar, the Sacred Stones were living beings; and down in the firehold, many common sailors would be found on their rest periods, whispering silent prayers to the Pictii and to the Stones themselves.

The Sa'yen was quite surprised at the lightning emitted from the Stones. I explained to Him what the Stones were used for. Below was a long trough, lined with common dirtstone; the crew of the firehold filled the trough with Kakla woods, where then fire consumed the wood, its heat rising to heat the Sacred Stones. The fire caused the Stones to give off intense heat as no other stone could. The heat from the fire and the Stones then rose above, flowed around the buoyance bags that were the central part of the ship, adding much power to the lifting ability of the bags themselves. The Master was quite intrigued with the Stones of the Pictii, and grudgingly I told Him I had always been curious about them too. They had strange powers. I told Him that once heated by fire, the Stones had the ability to absorb and give off much heat for weeks to come, even if the fires had been extinguished for some time—as with the black-hull we now commanded. The firing trough had not burnt Kakla wood for some time, yet the Master and I both could feel the heat emitted from the Stones. The Lord asked me many questions about the Sacred Stones, and to the best of my knowledge, I answered Him quickly and accurately. I told Him, among other things, never to approach the Sacred Stones with a

sword or an iron-tipped lance. For if He did, the Sacred
Stones would become angered and would strike Him a
mighty blow with a bolt of lightning. Men had been
known to die from the wrath of the Sacred Stones and
none of the crew that worked in the firehold would use
any kind of metal near them. Also, but rarely, when a ship
was caught in a strong thunderstorm that was heavy with
lightning, the Sacred Stones of that ship would sometimes
become angered and spew forth bolts of lightning themselves. It was not uncommon to hear of good ships and all
their crew being destroyed in such storms from the angered Sacred Stones ripping the ship apart with their own
lightning bolts. It was for this reason, I suspected, that
slaves were used to man the fireholds of most ships, although a few captains preferred freemen, devotees even of
the Pictii and of the Stones, to be their firehold crew.

I found my Lord in deep thought after my words, but
He waved me on to continue my discussion of the ship's
workings. And as I continued my talk, I would at times
see Him glance back at the Stones, His eyes narrowed in
contemplation. But I did not stop in my talk. Pointing up
to the large, clear bags that were the buoyance tanks, I began to explain to Him what they were. I told Him that the
knowledge and control of the gas that made the ships of
Hungar lift into the air were in the hands of the merchants in any city. In Triisus, two of the wealthiest merchants of the city were the suppliers of the lifting gas.
Somewhere high up in the mountains, unknown by all except to the merchants and their most trusted captains,
were the mines that the gas came from. To my surprise,
the Master asked if the gas would burn if flames licked at
an open hole within the bag itself. I told Him this did not
happen and the Lord nodded, as if pleased with my answer. Confused somewhat by such a question, I nevertheless went on with my lecture. The bag itself, or the
material of the bag, was something controlled by various
merchants of the city. It was a product of some type of
plant extract for which only the Cloth Merchants, as they
were known, knew the formula. But the bags in themselves
were almost indestructible. Fire and heat did not harm
them at all. I had no idea how the gas was inserted into

the bags and then the bags sealed shut, for that knowledge was also a trade secret closely guarded by the caste that alone guarded this knowledge. It went without saying that the Cloth Merchants and the Caste of Cloud Walkers, as they were called, worked closely together in maintaining their trade secrets. There was no way to harm the bags that I knew of. Sharp blades and even arrows would not penetrate the special cloth. The bag was even impervious to the round shot of cannonfire. I was, I confessed to the Lord, at a lose to explain further such a phenomenon. The Lord nodded, His eyes yet filled with curiosity but now watching the bags themselves, and we continued on in our examination of the black-hull.

I told Him that other captains had tried to use stones other than the Sacred Stones of the Pictii to heat their buoyance bags. And all had failed. Not only would common stone not give off the heat the Stones of the Pictii would but the ships using other stones could not sail upwind at all and were seemingly helpless except when the wind blew in the direction the ship wished to sail. The Lord nodded at this statement and suddenly smiled as if at a revelation. He saw my puzzled look and told me He thought He might have an answer to the mysteries I had explained to Him. But, He cautioned, He would in the next few weeks have to examine the Sacred Stones more closely before revealing anything of His thoughts. And until then, He very much wanted to learn about the rest of the ship. Reluctantly, I could see the wisdom in this reasoning, and with a heavy heart, for I too much wanted to know why such things were the way they were, I led the Lord on through the ship and explained to Him everything I knew.

The Master was very much surprised to hear that the cannons the ships of the Hungar carried were made of Bak'li stone. On the starboard gundeck of the black-hull we stood looking down the deck, the five Bak'li cannon sitting in their heavy Kakla frames, the wheels blocked motionless to the deck, heavy rope lashing the cannon to the bulkhead securely. Bak'li stone is a dark green in color and is very strong. When first hewn from the Bak'li beds where it comes from, the stone is wet and moist and very pliable. The cannon, when the stone is yet very moist and pliable, is molded by the hands of craftsmen, its barrel even carved with intricate designs. The Aggarian black-hull that was now ours had ten superbly carved cannon for her main armaments. Each cannon's muzzle ended in the open mouth of a mythical mountain ghoul, the face of the ghoul part of the cannon's barrel and fully animated and lifelike in appearance. Even the carriages of the cannon, made of hard and heavy Kakla wood, were carved by loving hands and deeply polished, showing bright in the torchlight. I had Tadan, who was a master gunner, with us as we stood on the gundeck, allowing the gunnery master to answer the questions the Lord asked. Tadan was a man of very thin frame yet with hard, wiry muscles. He was losing his hair and had big, thick ears. But his dark brown eyes were clear and sharp, and he was given to smiling quickly and easily. He was, to my knowledge, one of the best gunnery masters that I knew of. And what he did not know of the art of making cannons and all its accessory arts there was no need to know. As I stood silently, holding the torch over our heads, I listened to the two men talk about the cannon. Somewhat to my surprise, the Master seemed to be quite familiar with the art of mixing the chemicals needed to make gunpowder—knowledge that is fiercely protected by the Caste of Gunmakers of Northern Hungar. I saw in Tadan's face his surprise, as well, at the Lord's knowledge, but the gunmaker said nothing. Tadan and I were surprised again when the Lord wondered out loud why cannons were made of Bak'li stone and not of bronze or cast iron. Cautiously, Tadan cleared his throat and said that the Caste of Gunmakers and the Merchants of Metal, with their attending Caste of Metalsmiths, were bitter enemies. Metals such as bronze, iron and especially steel were very rare commodities on Hungar and came only at premium prices. There had been experiments using cast iron and even bronze to make cannons in other cities a time or two in the past, but each time a hardy member of the Caste of Gunmakers had tried, the Merchants of Metal and the Caste of Metalsmiths had revolted within the cities and had applied enough pressure to force the hardy Gunmaker experimenting with metal to be hurled from the ranks of his own caste! And even barred from living in the city! With downcast eyes, filled somewhat with tears, Tadan's voice broke once or twice as he explained to the Lord the shame his father had known when, as a youth, he was denounced by the elders of his city and barred from the Caste of Gunmakers for undertaking just such experiments. Now, as the son of an outcast Gunmaker, Tadan was practicing the trade of his father and forefathers as an outlaw, though until that moment, only I and no one else other than Tadan himself knew about it. Yet, as Tadan confessed, he felt he could not serve the Lord with such a secret between them, so he confessed his father's crime, head bowed, prepared to accept whatever justice the Lord wished to render him. As I watched the bearded face of the Lord, I saw compassion for Tadan's shame run through His eyes. Frowning, the Lord stepped to the tall, thin Gunmaker and clasped the man by both shoulders. Shaking the Gunmaker firmly yet gently, He told the man to look up into His face. The Lord said to Tadan that He was proud to have such a man as the tall, somewhat bald Gunmaker at His side and as a trusted friend. He told the tear-streamed face of Tadan that if there was a crime committed, the crime was committed by the elders and the Caste of Metalsmiths and the Merchants of Metal for denouncing his father as a vile criminal. In the words of the Master, the worst crime of all, as far as He was concerned, was in the creation of the Caste system as a whole—barring fellow men and women from attaining whatever goal they wished by forever keeping them in a closed, crippling system of bondage that was, to his mind, barbaric and horrible. I was stunned by the Master's words. Here, the Sa'yen was denouncing one of the most ancient of traditions of Hungar! He was denouncing the hierarchy of the Castes! Somewhat speechless, I would have shouted blasphemy and protected myself by kissing my hand and touching my forehead with the tips of my fingers, a sign of humbling oneself to all the Gods of Hungar. But I did not because the Sa'yen had been the one who uttered such blasphemy. To my ears, the God of War had uttered His displeasure at one of the basic foundations of a Hungar's life. Looking at Tadan beside me, I saw the

tall, thin, bald-headed Gunmaker wipe tears from his
cheek, his face filled with happiness. He dropped to his
knees, took one of the Lord's hands and kissed it fer-
vently. Growling His displeasure at such a show of emotion, yet quietly tolerant, the Master told Tadan to stop
such nonsense and come to his feet again. Tadan obeyed
instantly, his face still beaming as if the Lord's words
meant salvation. The Lord asked Tadan a few more questions concerning cannons and cannon making, and the
Gunmaker answered unhesitantly. A few of the questions
sought information the Caste of Gunmakers would have
killed to keep secret, yet Tadan did not blink an eye in answering the Master. I was just as surprised at Tadan for
giving his information freely to the Lord with someone
who was not of his Caste standing beside him and listening
to the conversation. But the tall Gunmaker acted as if I
were not there when he gave the Master the answers he
asked for. In silence, I looked into the Lord's face. I saw
the face of a golden-bearded giant of immense strength
and deep kindness I had not, until then, even thought existed in Him. It was like looking into His face for the first
time and for the first time seeing the true strength and
purpose in Him. A surge of electric excitement made me
shiver as I stood beside Him, holding a torch up for us to
see down the deserted gundeck. The Sa'yen! All praise to
the Lord! Suddenly I could feel Tadan's excitement flooding into me and, like the tall Gunmaker, I too wanted to
shout for joy! I could not then and cannot now explain the
surge of joy and the thrill of the power of the Sa'yen. It
was like being swept away with a jolt of lightning from
one of the Sacred Stones. Yet, instead of pain from such a
jolt, I felt ecstasy; I felt overwhelming happiness. I wanted
to shout the praises of the Sa'yen!

Hakba Baru, the Pirate Prince of the Aggarian Mountains, was ushered into the presence of the Master on the
second day after our arrival in Triisus. I stood behind and
to the right of the Lord, my arms crossed, watching the
bearded face of the pirate closely, I still could not trust
him. His fame for being the boldest of the bold, the Master of Cunning, was too much to set aside. He had asked

for a meeting with the Sa'yen, and the Lord, being the generous Master that He is, had granted the interview immediately. I had already, at the Master's bidding, made arrangements for the pirate prince to be returned to his black Aggarian Mountains and his pirate den. Much to my displeasure, I had made the arrangements only hours before and had but just informed the Aggarian pirate of his gift of freedom. And now he wished to see the Sa'yen. The Master was seated in a high-backed chair of finely carved Kakla wood with deep, red leather cushions. He was dressed in a plain brown jerkin with matching trousers; high, brilliantly polished black boots that ended just below His kneecap; and strapped to His waist was a heavy, studded leather belt that held the long, thin-bladed rapier He seemed to be so fond of. As the pirate prince stooped to enter the Master's quarters, old Fidor closed the door behind the bearded, cruel-faced pirate and watched in silence, as I did. Neither Fidor nor I trusted the Aggarian pirate. But our feelings did not matter. The Sa'yen wished to free Hakba Baru and send him on his way back to his kind. The arrangements had been made, and soon the pirate would leave us.

I watched the robed pirate step up to the Master and stop only a few feet away from Him. A glance at me, then a casual glance over his shoulder at the silent, scowling face of Fidor behind him, and the bold pirate turned to look at the Master with a thin, sardonic grin. Then he gave the Master a respectful bow before speaking his mind.

"My Lord, I have come to give you my thanks, and perhaps to give you a warning."

"As to your thanks, Hakba Baru," the Master began, His voice rolling out of His chest in a deep, controlled boom of thunder that I so much enjoyed listening to, "it should be ourselves thanking you for your assistance in rescuing us from the Hakadians. It was your knowledge of the High Tors that allowed us to escape from an otherwise assured death."

"You are so kind, My Lord," Hakba Baru said, bowing again before resuming. "Yet, out of gratitude for saving me from death when you first found me, and now for giv-

ing me freedom again, I should in all sincerity give you a
warning of imminent peril."

"You threaten the Master after all He's done for you,
pirate?" I growled, stepping forward in anger and clench-
ing my hands into fists of fury.

"Hold on, friend Magdar! Let the pirate captain have
his say before we make accusations," the Master said, lifting a hand to restrain me.

Hakba Baru did not seem in the least concerned for his
health or my anger. He still held that narrow, sardonic
grin, watching me in an amused fashion and then turning
to look upon the face of the Master. Dressed in a dark
blue robe and belted around the waist by a wide belt of
green leather, encrusted with many jewels, the pirate
prince was now armed with a long, wide blade equally
jeweled. Reluctantly, I quelled my anger and silently
stepped back to wait for the Sa'yen to question the pirate
further. But for some time the Master sat in His high-
backed chair, His gray-blue eyes watching the pirate's face
minutely as He casually kept tugging on His blond beard.
I knew the Lord was thinking upon the pirate's words, and
scowling, I waited in silence. One word from the Sa'yen
and old Fidor, who was just as displeased with the pirate's
arrogance as I was, and I would have tossed him over the
port railing, bound and gagged, without the slightest pause.
Yet the Master said nothing to me and for some time kept
silent altogether as He watched the pirate prince. Finally,
He cleared His throat and His voice again rolled out in
booming, yet controlled tones of authority.

"You spoke of warning me, Hakba Baru. I appreciate
your concern for me. Of what, may I ask, do you warn
me?"

"Ah, My Lord, there be two dangers I, in all faithful-
ness, must warn you about before my departure. And one
is just as serious as the other; aye, perhaps they are too
much for even you to master if both should attack you at
the same time."

"Since none of us are the masters of our fate, Hakba
Baru, but only players on the much larger stage of life, we
can only do the best our roles will allow us to do. And
now, what was it you wished to warn me about?"

"My Lord, you overwhelm me with your wisdom. But first, allow me to inform you that this, your ship, was once mine only a few weeks past. She was called *Black Falcon* by my crew, and she was made in the yards of Baril Mac-Cak of this fair city of Triisus. I have no doubts that you will treat her with the same reverence and confidence that I and my crew did before our untimely demise."

The Sa'yen nodded after I quickly whispered into His ear that Baril MacCak was the most renowned Building Master in the far north ranges of Hungar. A ship by Mac-Cak was a major investment, bound to last almost forever, and the fastest of its class without exception. I was not surprised at the pirate's statement. I had suspected this ship had been his when we first boarded her and found him gravely wounded. That it was from the yards of Baril MacCak I was not surprised to hear either. The pirates of the dark Aggarian mountains took for their own anything they pleased and their swords could procure, but when it came to their black-hulled ships even they, when they were rich enough to afford it, paid a Building Master gold freely for a good ship. And I suspected that Hakba Baru, as his fame reputed him to be, was one of the richest pirate chieftains in the Aggarian Mountains. Only the best had been used for his ship. As it should have been for a feared black-hull.

"Now, as to the warnings I have mentioned. I must inform you that the appearance a week back of the two golden-hulls of the Hakadians was not sheer accident. The two Hakadian ships were there by plan and we were the ones who accidently stumbled upon them."

"By plan you say?" I growled, narrowing my eyes suspiciously. "And when did an Hakadian pilot learn to navigate so far northward, pirate?"

"Why, when a Triisusian pilot held the helm of the Hakadian Admiral's own ship, friend Magdar! That is when!"

"That is impossible, Hakba Baru!" I retorted, shouting in my anger at such an accusation. "A Triisusian pilot would never show a Hakadian the northern trade routes! They would cut his tongue from his mouth before a pilot from this city would reveal such secrets!"

"Aye, in most cases, that is true, friend Magdar!"

Hakba Baru nodded, smiling evilly, standing with casual ease as he continued speaking. "But in this case the Triisusian pilot was sent to guide the Hakadians northward on orders from his prince."

"Heh, what's that you say? A prince of Triisus sending a pilot to guide the Hakadians northward? You say this treason knowingly?" Fidor shouted, stepped menacingly forward toward the pirate chieftain with hatred and anger etched on his wrinkled, weatherbeaten face.

"Aye, that is exactly what I tell you, Fidor! A prince of Triisus, a jewel of the Far North, in league with the hated Hakadians of the South! I know this to be true, my friends, for I paid much gold to my spies both here in Triisus and in the far palaces of Hakad to hear of such news."

"But why? Tell us why, pirate! Why would a Triisusian prince wish to be in league with the Hakadians?" I yelled, cooling my anger somewhat but still furious at the pirate's vile accusations.

"For an empire, Magdar! For an empire! The prince of this fair city offered to the Hakadians Triisus for their most northern base of conquest after he becomes the acknowledged ruler, in exchange for the prize the Triisusian prince most desires. A Royal Marriage to the Princess Saphid of Hakad, the third daughter of the Emperor Hassad of Hakad!"

I felt the anger drain from my body at those words. Saphid of Hakad to be married to one of the princes of Triisus! Saphid was reputed to be the most beautiful woman in the Empire of Hakad! To marry her to a prince of far Triisus meant that the rulers of Hakad saw the importance of having Triisus under their domination. Growling in anger, I clenched my hands into hard fists at the thought of an Hakadian princess sitting on the throne beside her husband in the High Halls of Triisus as joint rulers. This was outrageous, yet the pirate's words rung with the sound of truth. I knew the Hakadians had, for hundreds of years, searched in vain to find and control the trade routes of the Far North. And Triisus had, as the largest city of the Far North, led in the fight to keep the

Hakadians and their fleets from finding the northern passages. The cities of the Far North were few in number but extremely fierce about controlling their trade routes. Triisus, for over two hundred years, had grown rich from the profits she made by her ships plowing through the high mountain passes she guarded as her own. The high mountain passes were the most important possessions a city controlled and to lose them meant in many cases the city died from the strangulation of trade. And the Hakadians of the Far South, arrogant and warlike, wished to control all the passes and thus all the cities of Northern Hungar! I started to speak, my anger under control, but the Master came to His feet and stepped in front of the pirate chieftain. The Master, in His magnificence, towered a good head taller than the pirate, and with His long hair and beard, of a golden color rare in a Hungar male, He appeared to me like the god He was.

"Hakba, yet you fail to tell me the warning you said you had for me. I do not understand why such fierce hatreds should be shown for the Hakadians, yet I blame myself and my lack of knowledge of this strange planet. But what, pray tell, are the dangers that I face from this tale? Can you tell me that?"

"Aye, that I can, My Lord," the pirate chieftain said, nodding his head and then bowing slightly. "The treasures that you found in the holds of this, once my own ship. The vast treasure of gold coins, jewels and necklaces of rare stones and metals. All the treasures that a man could ask for and never be able to spend in one lifetime. Do you not wonder how I came to possess them before your arrival, My Lord, or to whom they once belonged?"

"No, Hakba Baru, I never once wondered. You are a pirate, my friend, and a pirate comes by his gold in only one fashion. I did not need to ask how you came about it. Nor did I care who once owned it before you. Is that important?"

"Aye, My Lord, it certainly is. For no doubt the Hakadians will soon learn that my ship was captured by a strange man who calls himself the Sa'yen. And that he and not I possesses the dowry of the Princess Saphid."

"The dowry of the Princess Saphid!" I shouted, startled and deeply shaken by the pirate's words. "Why that is impossible! The Hakadians would send a fleet of their mightiest ships to protect the princess's own dowry. How came you by it, pirate?"

"Aye, that they indeed sent, Magdar!" Hakba Baru nodded, his eyes alight with an evil delight as he looked at me with pride. "A fleet of twenty of their best frigates, Magdar! A fleet no navy could defeat in open battle and all those ships escorting a slow Scud that held no gold, no treasure in her holds. A dummy, my friend! A ruse to hide the comings and goings of the real treasure ship carrying the princess's own dowry. And I, only I, thanks to the gold I paid to my spies, knew which ship was the real treasure ship. I took the treasure ship, Magdar! I took it as it sailed alone, unguarded, only a few hundred miles from the towers of Hakad itself."

"Any why would the Hakadians allow the dowry of their princess to go unescorted into the passes of the Far North, pirate? Tell us that if you can," old Fidor growled, yet his growl sounding like that of a man who more believed than disbelieved the pirate's tale.

"I shall tell you the reasons for that, Fidor my friend," the Master said, smiling into the face of the pirate chieftain as He pulled on His beard thoughtfully. "Because the Hakadians wished to protect the identity of the Triisusian prince. A fleet dispatched as a ruse would be followed whereas a single transport, unguarded, sent on its own would have a better chance of succeeding in both delivering the treasure and keeping the identity of the Triisusian prince out of the hands of prying spies. Am I correct, friend Hakba?"

"Competely, My Lord." The pirate bowed, showing his pleasure at the Master's knowledge of such intricate intrigues as the Hakads practiced with consummate skill.

"And I suspect you would know the name of the Triisusian prince who wished to become a Prince of the House of Hassad as well, would you now, Hakba?"

"Aye, My Lord, that too I would know thanks to my spies."

"I suspect then," the Lord began, smiling knowingly, "that the two warnings of peril you come to me with are indeed quite real. One, is it not, is that the Hakadians will wish to take the treasure back from me and seek possible revenge for your mischievous deeds?"

"Aye, My Lord, that is exactly what I came to warn you about."

"And the other, would it not be, was the danger the Triisusian prince would cause me for taking the dowry of the princess promised to him?"

"You read my mind like an open book, My Lord. I stand before you completely revealed."

The Lord chuckled to Himself in amusement at the pirate's words, but I saw nothing to chuckle about. On one side the Hakadians would soon launch a massive hunt to find the black-hull that had stolen the treasure of the Princess Saphid, and on the other the prince that sought the hand of Saphid would be equally eager to seek revenge for the theft of his promised one's dowry. Yet the Master seemed not in the least concerned with the perils facing Him. To confront the Empire of the Hakads alone, with only the craft of a black-hull, seemed too preposterous even to contemplate. And yet we had still to hear which prince of Triisus would soon be our sworn enemy. Grimacing, I stepped forward and spoke the question that hung on my lips with ill-concealed dread.

"And you could not guess, Magdar? A native of Triisus? Shame on you!" Hakba Baru chided, lifting his head and laughing at me. I held my tongue but rage flowed through me at the pirate's derision. "Why, the prince is of the House of Kandar! The oldest son of Babur Kandar, called The Cruel by some!"

"Bahir Kandar!" Fidor and I shouted at the same time, angrily.

"Aye, the one and the same. Beware, My Lord, of Bahir Kandar! His wealth will soon buy spies that will tell him all he will be seeking. And his household troops are the finest blades gold can buy."

The Lord only smiled at the words of Hakba Baru! I felt myself grow weak from the words, but looking quickly into His face, I felt strength return to me. I could easily see much danger lurking ahead of us. Yet, I knew the Lord would guide us through with His hand and calm assurance, though hardly could I guess the dangers that we were destined to experience.

VI

What Only The Priest Knows

The cobblestone pavement reverberated with the sounds of our boots as we walked up the sharply inclined street. I, old Fidor, Tadan and Tallsus, the Sail Master of our ship, followed the Sa'yen as we showed Him the city for the first time. The Master wore a heavy cloak around His shoulders, for the mountain winds become exceedingly cold once the sun drops below the far peaks, and underneath was the plain attire of a simple warrior. Strapped to His waist was the long, thin blade of the plain-hilted rapier, a weapon that I knew He could wield with a deadly pattern of impenetrability. Each of us was equally wrapped in a heavy cloak for warmth. Around us the squat, square-shaped gray stone buildings of the city hugged the side of the streets like sulking giants huddling close to each other for warmth against the bitter cold of the mountain winds. Few people were out in the narrow, twisting streets, for the promise of the first snow-blowing storm of the season hung in the air. As we hurried up the street to find a small inn that old Fidor knew well and had good ale to drink, dogs barked and from dark windows I saw faces peering down at us suspiciously. I did not like the feeling of being spied upon from every dark alley we passed, and I found myself constantly looking over my shoulder as we climbed the steep street up farther into the older part of the city. So far the *Black Falcon*, the name of the black-hull, which the Lord wished to keep as the name of His ship, had been moored to a common landing

tower for three days. With His permission, I had begun
the task of hiring a full crew for the ship, paying good
copper and silver coins for the best hands available. After
long discussions with the Lord at night, we finally agreed
not to reveal that the Master was the Sa'yen returned. It
was I who first broached this subject, and the Lord was
somewhat surprised. Smiling at me, He pointed out that
He had all along claimed not to be the Sa'yen, a point I
quickly acceded to. Yet, as I explained to Him, I knew
Him to be the Sa'yen, as did the rest of His crew. But high
up in the Zhygar mountains where the city of Triisus sat,
the Sa'yen, the God of War, was looked upon as a minor
divinity. And in fact, among the followers of the Pictii, the
Sa'yen was looked upon with suspicion and even open hostility. The city of Triisus was a stronghold of the Pictii,
and the God of War, the Sa'yen, was laughed at by many
as a poor god, a weak god that could command little respect and much contempt. So it would be to our ad-
vantage, as I pointed out, to keep the Lord's true identity
a secret until the appropriate time came to reveal Him
properly. The Lord agreed with an amused nod of His
head, and nothing was said by myself or by the original
five of my crew of the Sa'yen's divinity. But, looking into
the future, in hiring the crew of the *Black Falcon* I hired
only those who were devotees of the Sa'yen or who cared
little for any deity whatsoever. I knew many good hands
in Triisus, and it was not hard to select the ones I thought
would be the most loyal and the best. Some of the best
hands hired were men who could not have cared less for
any deity. They were not atheistic, yet each professed not
to be a follower as well. These men I knew I could trust.
Most of them were transplanted warriors from the far
plains to the south, as was I. I hired Mul'gar and Ha'gar
warriors, enemies of the Ha'valli, the tribe that I and my
father were born into. Yet so far north and high up into
the Zhygar mountains, such old ties and enmities did not
count for much. I hired men who were good shipmates,
good hands with sail and helm. I was not concerned with
their ancestry. In hiring such men who had come from the
far southern plains for one reason or another, I knew I
was getting men who had no loyalties to anyone or any-

thing in the city of Triisus. I had a feeling that as the days would pass, their views would soon change. I expected them to become as devoted to the Sa'yen as I and the original five were now, so I wished to hire men who were not of the mountains themselves.

Yet, for all my caution, my planning went asunder. I had the uneasy feeling that the city had heard the first rumors concerning the Master. I had little evidence to go by to base my feelings, but that dark night as we strode up through the twisting cobblestone streets in the growing gloom of twilight, I was sure the Sa'yen's identity had been whispered from the lips of many of Triisus's citizens. And as we hurried on, the Lord's blond-maned head was held high and brightly illuminated by the torch Fidor held up over our heads to light the way, and I dropped to the rear of the group. I feared that we were being watched by prying eyes. The dark shadows of alleys were havens for eyes seeing, yet to be unseen. Turning up a narrow side street, I lingered for a moment at the corner, my ears alert to the sound of footfalls of whoever followed us. I was rewarded for my diligence. I heard the steps of someone following, only two steps, but enough to convince me that indeed my fears were not groundless. Smiling secretly under the hood of my cape, I turned and swiftly ran to catch up with the merry crowd of laughing men. Yet I followed, my cape only loosely wrapped around me, my hand close to the hilt of my long, plainly made rapier.

Fidor threw open the inn's door and stepped inside, yelling loudly for the proprietor, an old friend of his. I entered, the last of our group, and closed the door behind me. The inn was large, high-roofed, with fresh straw on the floor. A long bar, hewed from a massive Kakla tree, ran the length of the long hall to one side, and at the far end, a huge stone fireplace roared and snapped cheerfully with a warm, brightly burning fire. There were several tables empty, but by far the larger portion of the tables were occupied by common-looking peasants and sailors. Following the rest of the group, I pulled a plain wooden chair up to the table and sat down at the left of the Sa'yen. The proprietor of the inn was a jolly-looking bald man with a bright red nose and a stomach large enough

for six men. Wiping his hands with the apron tied around
his girth, he moved through the evening's crowd to our
table, yelling a gruff yet warm greeting to Fidor. Soon the
fat, laughing owner of the inn and a few of his young servants were wading through the crowd, carrying over their
heads platters heavily laden with stout tankards of good
mountain ale. When the platters reached the table, hands
reached to take the tankards and I followed, though
slowly. My eyes were glued to the far door of the inn. I
was expecting the mysterious unseen follower who had
trailed our party to enter through the inn's door at any
second. Several times I was asked questions on one thing
or another but my mind was elsewhere, and I had to be
asked repeatedly before I could tear my attention away
from the door. In the middle of one of my comments, the
door to the inn opened and a gray-cloaked figure quickly
stepped in and closed the door behind him. His entrance
captured my thoughts and it took a great effort to bring
myself back to the group. As I watched, he turned his
back to me and started to throw his cloak off. I felt the
Lord lean close to me, and over the roaring of our drinking companions, He spoke to me quietly.

"You seem very interested in that stranger yonder, Magdar. Is anything amiss?"

"Eh? Amiss? Perhaps, Master, perhaps. We were followed, My Lord, as we journeyed from the *Black Falcon*
to the inn."

"Followed?"

"Aye, Lord, followed. Yet methinks we were not followed by that person," I said, nodding my head toward
the tall figure at the far end of the hall who was now
hanging his gray cloak upon a wall peg.

The Master looked down the hall at the far figure for a
few seconds before looking at me again. He saw a man
with very shortly cropped, dark hair, a sharply hooked
nose, and dressed in a plain gray robe. He had high
cheekbones and shoulders of wide breadth, suggesting controlled power. Around his waist was a piece of dark rope
and, to the Master's surprise, the man was unarmed. He
looked at me and I could see the questions in His face.

"And you say he was not the one who followed us, Magdar?"

"Aye, Lord, that is what I said."

"And what makes you believe he was not the one?"

"Our follower wore boots, Master. I heard his boots slap against the stones twice before he stopped and allowed us to move on. That man yonder wears no boots, My Lord. He is a Charolarl Priest, and priests of his sect wear only sandals of soft leather."

The Charolarl Priest took a chair beside a small table in one far corner of the drinking hall. By all appearances the man moved with the firm grace of a warrior and I was pleased. Charolarl Priests were odd creatures, rare among the mountainous paths of Hungar. Yet they were generally a gentle sect, learned in the many knowledges few others shared. They were trained in the arts of Healing and Soothsaying, and it was said that the higher orders of the Charolarl Priests knew magic as well. Among the Ha'valli, the tribe of my fathers and forefathers, such men of the gray cloth, as they were sometimes known, were welcomed with pleasure among the campfires of the many Ha'valli tribes. They brought much news to the campfires of the Ha'valli, and their knowledge of healing and sickness would have of itself made them welcomed guests. Among the Ha'valli, these strange priests who counted no one as their enemy were nevertheless known to have many enemies. I could never understand the reasons why men of other tribes could look upon the Charolarl sect with animosity. There were always rumors about the priests and their secrets. They professed to worship no particular god, which for many was hard to understand since they indeed were some form of religious sect. They made no distinction between tribes and would freely come among all men and teach all their knowledge without exception. Yet even in Triisus, even in this large, crowded inn I could see faces turn to look upon the Charolarl Priest with suspicion and contempt.

"You say we were followed, Magdar. By whom then?" the Master asked, looking at me again with His strangely arresting gray-blue eyes.

"Aye, we were followed, My Lord. But by. . . ."

The door to the inn opened again and in walked two figures, which made me pause as I spoke to the Lord. Even He grunted in surprise when he saw the new arrivals. Such opposite extremes I had never before viewed in my life! Entering first was a bent man with long, bony arms and legs, and a face that was a mask of ill-concealed evil. A huge hooked nose and thick lips made the man look ugly. A scar, ragged and still purple from being freshly healed, ran from the middle of the man's forehead around his left eyebrow and down the left side of his face to end just below the jaw line. He was dressed in dark brown, dirty peasant's clothing with a stained, mud-splattered black cape thrown over his bent shoulders. Heavy leather boots covered his feet and strapped around each heel were large iron spurs. Strapped to his waist was the wide, heavy blade of a mountain *fadih*, an extremely heavy blade that required much skill and in the right hands, a weapon that could crush the defenses of a warrior wielding merely the light blade of a delicate rapier. His face was darkly tanned, almost black, etched deeply with lines of animal cunning. As he stepped into the inn, he swirled off his cloak with one hand and hung it on a wall peg. Turning, his eyes fell upon the gray-robed Charolarl Priest. And it was not the look of a man of tolerance.

Entering after him was a tall warrior, finely dressed with a cloak of dark wine red hanging from wide, strong shoulders. He wore a dark blue velvet blouse with white silk sleeves. Underneath, at his wrists, I could see the dull gleam of chain mail and around his waist was a belt of white leather laden with many bright, expensive jewels. A rapier of exquisite design with a jeweled hand guard of silver and gold inlay was his sword, and he had the look of a swordsman. On the upper right shoulder of his dark red cape was an emblem I recognized instantly. The coat of arms of the House of Kandar. Smiling thinly, I recognized the warrior and leaned toward the Sa'yen to speak.

"We were followed by the first man, My Lord. I know not who he is, but I am sure that was the man who followed us."

"And yet both men view the gray-robed priest with

much hostility, Magdar. It appears strange to me," the Lord answered.

"Aye, Lord, that strikes me as strange as well. Perhaps they were not following us, eh? The priest entered soon after we did, My Lord. Methinks perhaps the Charolarl Priest came to the inn the same as we and it was he they followed and not us!"

"Ah! Very possible, Magdar! Very possible!" the Lord nodded, His blond face breaking into a pleased smile with this new thought. But then His eyes clouded over, and as we both watched, the two men stepped up to the bar and accepted large tankards of steaming ale. He leaned again to me, "And who may be the tall man with the sharp eyes and the look of arrogance on his face, Magdar?"

"That man I know! His name is Thordak, Captain of the Household Troops of the House of Kandar, Master. And one of the city's finest swordsmen."

"Hmmmm," the Lord growled, as He looked suspiciously first at the two men and then to the gray-robed figure of the priest sitting alone at his table. "Magdar, you have said to me in the past that these priests know much of the planet at large and much of the past?"

"Aye, Master, 'tis true. The Charolarl claim no particular god as their own but recognize all of the deities. Yet the Charolarl are devotees of studying ancient writings of the past, Lord. And each priest actively searches the dusts of the past to seek out more knowledge. It is even rumored, Lord, that the Charolarl know more of the secrets of the Ancient Kings than even the Pictii do. And if that be true, then they must know much."

The Lord nodded and continued pulling thoughtfully on His beard. I had told Him much of the legends of the Ancient Kings. Far in the dim mists of time, so far back that nothing remained of their existence, the Ancient Kings ruled all of Hungar. The powers, the knowledge, the magic the Ancient Kings were said to control were all rumored to be beyond any race now possessed. Yet, as the legends oft repeated, it was this immense power so casually dispensed by the Ancient Kings that led them to their downfall. And when they fell, in a series of vicious civil wars that consumed the entire planet with forces of evil power clashing headlong with equally powerful forces of good, all of Hungar was ripped asunder. It was said that Northern Hungar as it now is, almost entirely mountainous and covered by huge forests of Yab'lal and Kakla, was once broad flat plains of rich, dark ground. It was said that the only mountains in Northern Hungar when the Ancient Kings ruled were the central ranges of the Ha'kad peaks. Yet when they fell, the power of their destruction was so immense, the Ancient Kings completely reshaped Hungar into the twisted, rugged remains of what it was now. The Lord and I discussed often the many legends of the Ancient Kings, and the knowledge of the Charolarl Priests. The Sa'yen seemed very eager and curious to meet such a priest, and this seemed perhaps the best opportunity. I started to suggest this, but He spoke first.

"Magdar, I do not like the looks of those two men yonder. They look to me not to have much love for yonder priest. I think it would be wise if we could perhaps invite the priest to our table and offer him food and drink. Go, ask the priest to join us in friendly conversation about his journeys and tell him I wish to talk much of his knowledge about the Ancient Kings."

"Aye, Lord!" I grinned, pleased as I got up.

It did not take me long to work my way through the heavy crowd of loud, boisterous, drinking men and approach the priest's table. I saw his dark brown eyes watching me with curious politeness. He seemed not in the least worried about his trackers standing only a dozen feet away from the table and even may not have been aware of being followed at all. I bowed, glanced sidelong down the inn and saw the two men at the end of the bar frowning at me severely. And the warrior with the cruel, arrogant face and dark, wine-red robe over his wide shoulders appeared to be the most annoyed at my intrusion into his hunt. I was pleased that I annoyed him, and looked at the Charolarl Priest humbly.

"Greetings, gray-robed friend. I bring you felicitations."

"Thank you, warrior, for your words," he answered in a voice with deep tones of strength and patience and bowed his head.

"My Lord yonder," I said, indicating the table where the Sa'yen and the rest of our crew sat, "is a fellow traveler of the woods and mountains, gray-robed friend. Yet He is not of the cloth as you are. But He shares the same love of the past and wonders if perhaps, at your convenience, He could persuade you to join us over a tankard of ale to converse on the subject of Ancient Kings and other points of interest."

For some seconds the Charolarl Priest did not answer but viewed me with keen interest. Turning to look at the Master, the priest studied His face for some seconds. Then he smiled warmly up at me.

"You are not of the mountains, warrior?"

"For the last fifteen years I have been, traveler. I am of the south originally, south of the ranges of the Hungar."

"Of what tribe?"

"The Ha'valli."

"Aye, only the Ha'valli address all the gray-robed priests of my kind with respect and restraint. Something, unfortunately, few of us of the gray-robes find nowadays among the mountains of Hungar."

"This is a sad fact, traveler. But something that only the Ancient Kings can relieve."

"Ah, how true." The priest nodded, smiling sadly as he watched me with his brown eyes afire. "You speak of your master strangely, warrior. In the use of the word 'lord' you used the tense usually reserved for one of the deity."

"Did I?" I said, grinning sheepishly and feeling like a fool for such a slip of the tongue. "Uh . . . I am but an uneducated warrior, gray-robed friend. I still carry much of the ignorance we of the plains have in our youth. Think nothing of my speech."

The priest smiled fondly at my words, his eyes still bright lights of brown curiosity as he looked up at me. Then he took his tankard in his hand and stood up wearily. For a moment, I saw a look of pain cross his strong, high-cheeked face, but it quickly disappeared and he smiled weakly at me.

"It has been a long journey through the mountains for me, warrior. A long journey. Yet, I grow curious to speak to your master. There are few of the mountains who seek knowledge of the Ancient Kings. And fewer still who have displaced Ha'valli warriors in their service. Lead me to your master, warrior, and pleased am I of your invitation."

I bowed, and led our way through the crowd, opening a path for the tall, gray-robed figure. Twice I saw him wince in pain when a careless elbow or a drunken patron bumped into him. I suspected something more than mere weariness as we approached the table of the Sa'yen. The Lord stood when we approached, as did the rest of the men at our table, and all eyes were on the priest.

"My Lord." I bowed, and suddenly realized that again I had slipped and used one of the deity greetings! "This is the Charolari Priest, the gray-robed. . . ."

"Kadeesh, my lord."

"Welcome to my table, friend Kadeesh," the Sa'yen growled pleasantly, His gray-blue eyes dancing with fire. "Please be seated and let us refill your tankard."

"My thanks, noble . . ." the gray-robed priest began, sitting down painfully and pausing for one of the party at the table to reveal to him the name of the Sa'yen.

"Kadeesh, humble servant of all the gods," I began, addressing him hurriedly and thinking quickly at the same time, "I present to you the lord. . . ."

"You!"

We all jumped, for the word was a command of imperial decree and given with such authority that all in the inn ceased in their noisemaking. A deathly silence hung suddenly around us in the inn. Not a sound stirred and faintly, I became aware of the pounding in my chest of my own heartbeat. I glanced at the Lord and noticed He had His eyes fixed on a position just behind and above me. Grinning like a fool, for it occurred to me I had recognized the voice, I turned in my chair and laid eyes upon the arrogant form of the red-cloaked Thordak, Captain of the Household Troops of the House of Kandar.

"Priest, you are to come with me. I have orders from my lord, Bahir Kandar himself, to bring you with me to Kandar Palace at once! Attend to me, heretic!"

For a few seconds again the oppressive curtain of electrified silence hung about our ears as all eyes turned to

look at the drawn, pale face of the Charolarl Priest. I saw
him smile in a sad, knowing way, as did all of his kind, it
seemed, when confronted by enemies. Charolarl Priests
were strong, gentle people, gifted with much knowledge
and were willing tutors to any who wished to learn from
them. They traveled about the woods and mountains of the
planet fearing no one and asking nothing in return, generally content to seek to solve the many mysteries that
weave spells about us all. And for their meekness, which
was mistaken for cowardice by all that did not know
them, they were hounded, condemned, held in contempt,
and looked upon with the foulest suspicion. It was not uncommon to hear one called a heretic as Thordak of the
House of Kandar had done just now. I must confess I was
at this point consumed in red rage at the arrogant warrior,
and I started to rise, hot words ready to spring from my lips,
my hand ready to unsheathe my long sword! But the Lord
put a restraining hand on my arm and held me firmly in
check. His gray-blue eyes lit up with that odd fire that
shone when He went into battle, and I rejoiced. The
Sa'yen would defend the priest's rights! I sat back in my
chair to be a spectator in the coming fray, and savagely
held no pity for Thordak of the House of Kandar!

"As I understand it, you wish to speak to the priest that
sits at my table, is that right, warrior?" the Sa'yen questioned, His voice amazingly quiet and as cold as glacier
ice.

Thordak lifted an eyebrow haughtily and looked down
his classically shaped nose with an expression of distaste as
he viewed the Master. Unaccustomed to being questioned
at all in the city of Triisus, he plainly intended for a moment or two to disregard the Master's question. But
Kadeesh, the gray-robed priest, started to rise and broke
the silence about us.

"Thank you for the invitation to join you, my lord. But
apparently this warrior wishes to escort me to a dungeon
for questioning. And I would never consider having my
problems involve you as well. So, please excuse me."

The Lord settled His gaze upon the face of Kadeesh the
priest, and it was of such intensity that Kadeesh paused in
his move to step away from the table. The Lord's eyes are

magnets to the souls of men. With powers that can compel
men to do His bidding without ever a word needing to be
said! And such was the case with Kadeesh. When the
Sa'yen motioned with a hand for him to resume his seat,
the priest did so without uttering a word. But Thordak
chose that time to become the imperial caller of the House
of Kandar, and as he stepped closer to our table, his face
angrily red, I could see that the crossing of swords was
only a few seconds away!

"Peasant! Do you know what you do? I am Thordak,
Captain of the Household Troops of the House of Kandar!
Dare you stand before me in my duty to bring this heretic
before the Prince of the House of Kandar?"

Hearing him call the Lord a peasant, I was almost up to
my feet again with hot words barely contained! But I
heard the deep, amused roll of laughter come out of the
chest of the Master, and I saw the Sa'yen sitting back in
his chair, his amusement clearly written on his face. I
smiled, knowing full well what this laughter would do to
the vain Thordak. All of Triisus feared the man, knowing
that in his uniform and taking the pay of Bahir Kandar a
merciless killer walked the streets. His reputation as a
swordsman in Triisus was legendary. It was reputed that
he had met seventy men in individual combat and had
killed sixty-seven of them. All feared him or hated him
with a passion. Yet it was more the power of Bahir Kandar than of his own sword that kept the man alive. Bahir
Kandar had converted his father's household troops into a
band of well-trained, yet savage, shock troops. And Bahir
Kandar, oldest son of Babur Kandar, would not hesitate to
unleash his troops to plunder and ravage the city if he felt
it would accomplish his goals. That he had not in the past
meant nothing. All in Triisus knew how ruthless the oldest
son of Babur Kandar was.

"Tell your lord, warrior, that he may come to my ship
and question the priest there. My ship is the *Black Falcon*,
and tomorrow you and your lord may come aboard her.
Or if your lord so desires, a day may be arranged in the
near future for seeking an audience with the priest.
Whichever day your lord chooses will be convenient for
us."

"What? You stand before me and against the will of Prince Bahir Kandar? Fool! Do you know what insanity you propose? Stand aside so that I may escort this heretic to his just rewards!"

I paled and saw the Master come to His feet slowly with a deadly, mocking smile. His gray-blue eyes were flashing fire, and so fierce was His look that even the vaunted champion of the House of Kandar stepped back in haste and confusion. All the inn had grown deathly silent and all eyes were on the Lord. One could have heard the scurry of mice in the loft through a carpet of straw, so intense was the silence. My eyes went back and forth from the Lord to the face of the arrogant, red-robed warrior who regained the confidence he had momentarily lost when the Lord came to his feet smiling. Squaring his shoulders, the brown-eyed warrior disregarded the Lord and looked down on the ashen face of the Charolarl Priest in a fierce gaze of hatred.

"Heretic! Rise and come with me! And I warn you. None of this rabble will come to your aid. If they do then the wrath of the House of Kandar will fall upon them with a heavy hand!"

The Charolarl Priest made no attempt to rise from his chair. The rest of us sitting around the table kept our eyes on the Lord, for we knew what was soon to happen. Frustrated in his attempts to stun us with his imperial commands, the arrogant warrior again faced the Sa'yen. And in his rage he made the mistake we knew he would make in the end. Lifting a mailed fist, he drew back to strike the Lord viciously. But woe to the fool that did not know whom he faced! With a blinding motion too swift to follow by mortal eye, the Sa'yen swept the mailed, large-boned warrior from his feet, and lifting him high over His head, the Sa'yen threw him across the inn itself! With a crash and thunderous roar, the red-robed warrior smashed through a heavy wooden table, sending a large bottle of wine and tankards of ale flying through the air. The table's occupants barely had time to dive from their chairs to safety. There was a roar from many within the inn who witnessed the Sa'yen's immense strength, and even I was stunned. But before any of us could regain our voices, so

stunned were we, from the splintered remains of the table
we heard the enraged roar of a furious warrior, and suddenly before the Lord stood the wide-shouldered captain
with sheer fury and passionate rage in his eyes!

"Peasant! Fool! For that little trick you shall pay dearly.
You die tonight, peasant! And none will mourn your passing!"

The warrior then slashed viciously with a sweeping blow
at the Lord's head. But the Sa'yen danced to one side,
jumped effortlessly upon the top of a wooden table, and in
His hand was the long, thin blade of the rapier He favored
so much. Mockingly, He lifted His weapon up to His face
in a salute to the warrior facing Him, and then brought
the blade down with a snapping flick of his wrist. Infuriated past reason, the red-caped, wide-shouldered warrior
jumped to the attack, heedless of the Sa'yen's already
demonstrated strength and agility. Their blades touched
once, twice, then a score of times as the Captain of the
Household Troops of Kandar attacked furiously. The song
of steel touching steel in deadly combat came to our ears,
and never before had I looked upon such a devastating attack from a determined opponent. The ring of steel reverberated throughout the stout walls of the inn, and all were
pressed away from the two warriors, giving as much room
as possible for the opponents to fight freely and unhin-
dered. I saw the Lord laugh, toss back his shoulder-length
blond hair and meet every attack from the blade of His
opponent with an ease and swiftness that was blinding to
the eye. Leaping from one tabletop to the next, the Lord
wove such a defense around His body that nothing could
penetrate it. Furiously, the Lord's opponent drove in to
finish the duel regardless of the time that was being consumed and the drain on his strength. The song of steel was
fast and furious as we watched the duel and moved away
from the two antagonists. I heard men in the inn shouting
bets back and forth, and as the duel continued furiously
before our eyes, I heard the betting swing more and more
to favor the Lord. I saw faces clearly amazed at the Lord's
prowess. And as I swept my eyes around to view the
crowd, I at last saw the form of the man who had entered
the inn with the warrior the Lord now faced. He stood in

the corner of the inn, on top of a table, an evil mask of black hatred on his twisted face. And in the stooped man's right hand was a curved, flat blade of an Hakad throwing knife, and the hook-nosed man was lifting his hand as if to throw the knife at the back of the Sa'yen! With a shout of rage I leaped to the seat of a chair and pulled from my wide leather belt a half-moon-shaped throwing knife so commonly found among the northern mountains, and threw it with every ounce of strength I could command at the bent figure of the lurking assassin. A piercing scream cut through even the sound of steel clashing against steel, and eyes turned away from the fight to see what else had happened. In agony, the stoop-shouldered assassin with the hook nose stood on the top of the table, his right arm pinned to the far wall with half of the flat, steel blade protruding from his forearm. Frantically he was twisting and turning in agony, yet with each move the double-edged weapon cut more deeply into his bloody arm. Pleased with my aim, I stepped down from the chair, folded my arms and again turned my attention to the fight before us.

In the flutter of an eyelid, the fight was over. Tired, dripping with sweat, the captain of the House of Kandar guards made the mistake of lowering his guard for only a heartbeat. With a cry of triumph, the Lord stepped in and ran His blade into the man's throat all the way up to the cupped hilt of His sword. Pulling His sword out, the Sa'yen stepped back and watched the caped warrior fall to his knees, clutching his throat with blood spurting from between his fingers.

"You will not die, warrior, from this wound. But then again, neither will you ever speak to others with the arrogance and contempt you did in the past. Be glad that you yet live!"

Fidor, Tadan, Tallsus, and Hagbash leaped to their feet shouting, "Ala Sa'yen! Ala Sa'yen! Ala Sa'yen!" Even I could not keep my lips sealed. Shouting praises to the Sa'yen, we surrounded the Lord and danced happily, like children, before Him. So thrilled was I over the Lord's victory that I did not notice the disappearance of the Charolarl Priest. But after we all calmed down, for the whole inn exploded into a spasm of cheering and celebrating at the defeat of the Captain of the Household Troops of the House of Kandar, we found the priest gone. The Lord bid us quickly search the streets and alleys around the inn, fearing that perhaps others had whisked away the priest from under our eyes while we celebrated. But even though we searched for some time through the streets and alleys close to the inn, yet did we fail in our endeavor. Nothing could be found of the Charolarl Priest. At last, in the early hours of the morning, we journeyed back to the *Black Falcon*, each of us wondering about the disappearance of the strange, tall Charolarl Priest.

VII

The Lore of the Ancient Kings

Like a swift tide, the word spread through the city of
Triisus. The Sa'yen was among the living! The Sa'yen
lived! One could feel the sudden ripple of excitement and
see the mixed expressions in the faces of those who heard
of the Sa'yen's return. To many, the return of the Sa'yen
meant little. The mountain folk of Northern Hungar do
not look upon the Sa'yen with longing as do the many of
the southern reaches of the northern hemisphere. But
within the high walls of Triisus, sitting like some stone
jewel on the ledge high above the valley floor which it
hailed as its own, many heard the news of the Sa'yen's return and rejoiced. For the followers of the Sa'yen knew
what it meant to have the Lord among us again. It would
be the Wha'ta! The Holy Pilgrimage! For hundreds of
years the many prophets of the Sa'yen had been promis-
ing, prophesying to His followers, that He would return to
lead His devoted through the Halls of the Ancient Kings
and into the lands of the Southern Horde. And now, burning on the lips of His followers, the news spread like a
raging fire throughout the city. The Sa'yen lived! I heard
these rumors, felt the excitement growing in the city and
the tension mount in those who looked upon the Lord with
eyes of suspicion and even hostility. I knew that the Pictii,
the Lords of the Sacred Stones, as they sometimes were
known, would take the arrival of the Sa'yen with little
warmth in their hearts. The Pictii, the strongest, most or-
ganized of the religious orders, viewed the other religions

and deities with contempt and disinterest or with looks of hatred and scorn. And the Pictii had no love for the followers of the Sa'yen. Back in the dim past, as the legends said, it was the Sa'yen and His followers that broke the iron hold the Pictii had forged upon the southern tribes before the walls of the Halls of the Ancient Kings. And shattered, the Pictii almost disappeared from the face of the planet while the horde that followed the living Sa'yen found the mystic Gate through the Hall of the Ancient Kings and descended into the plains of the Southern Hemisphere. And the Pictii never forgot the defeat at the hands of the Sa'yen! From the ashes of defeat it took thousands of years to regain their stature and strength among the peasants of Northern Hungar. And from their most sacred fortresses deep within the high crags of the Halls of the Ancient Kings, the Pictii controlled a following that made other religious orders seem pale and insignificant in comparison. Yet I knew that deep within the hearts of the higher orders of the Pictii, no love existed for the Sa'yen or His followers. And I expected trouble to erupt in the city between the growing order of followers of the Sa'yen and the followers of the Pictii.

The Master made it almost impossible to keep the excitement from generating into a fever pitch among His followers. When asked if He was indeed the Sa'yen, the Master would deny ever being anything else but a mortal. And this made His followers shout with delight. For all the hundreds of prophets down through the ages had foretold that the Sa'yen would forever deny that He was indeed who He was. Somehow, the tale of our rescue from the Aggarian pirates was told and was whispered over and over again to any that would listen within the city. So intense was the excitement of the Sa'yen's arrival that crowds formed at the base of the landing tower the *Black Falcon* was moored to and they lingered day and night and slowly grew in numbers. It made it almost impossible for the crew of the *Black Falcon* to move back and forth to the streets of the city below without being deluged for more news of the Sa'yen.

And yet, as each day went by and I listened to the Master receive groups of important personages of the city's

royal families and politely deny any claim of being truly
the Lord, I grew more and more doubtful myself. At
nights aboard the ship, floating serenely above the towers
of the mountain city, eating the evening meal with the
Lord in His cabins, I would listen to His many tales of visiting other worlds and wonder at what He said and, with
disturbing uneasiness, grow more convinced that He was
truly not the Sa'yen. Aye, I knew that all His deeds up to
now could only point to His being the Promised One. And
He did truly act as the prophets said He would while
among us mortals of Hungar. Still, I had my doubts. And
they grew with each passing day. I found it hard to sleep
at night in my bunk, lying awake and wondering what
would happen to Him if He indeed was not the Sa'yen.
For in the past there had been those who claimed to be
the Promised One. And when they had been revealed to
be false, mere usurpers of the true Sa'yen, they were torn
to pieces by the enraged who had so eagerly followed
them. And I knew that if this happened to Him, I would
be the cause of His death. For it had been I who had convinced the others that this strange man before us, who had
saved us from sure death at the hands of Aggarian pirates,
was the Sa'yen. It had been I who had first thought of
Him as the Sa'yen and yet now I was equally unsure
whether the strange being from the stars was not or perhaps truly was the promised Sa'yen. Yet what could I do
if He was not the Sa'yen? And if He was the Sa'yen, there
was nothing I need do. Mystified, I lay awake nights in my
bunk, listening to the many sounds of the ship as it tugged
and strained at its mooring ropes and floated serenely
above the city. My doubts grew, and yet I found myself
wanting to believe. I found a deep emptiness inside that
urged, even demanded, that I believe in the Sa'yen. And I
told myself it would be easy to believe. For the man I first
claimed to be the Lord was indeed a person who was truly
a godlike figure.

The Lord further enhanced His image as the Sa'yen by
the many projects He was interested in while we floated
above the city, moored to the landing tower. Two projects
seemed to consume Him. One was the study of the Sacred
Stones—the fiery, wrath-filled stones which fed the ship's

fires to give us lift and buoyance. For hours on end, He
tinkered with various materials down in the depths of the
ship, and in His tinkering, He made the Sacred Stones
dance excitedly with massive bolts of thunder and lightning. So intense was the Lord's interest in the Sacred
Stones there were many times when the *Black Falcon*
rocked back and forth on her mooring ropes and shuddered and groaned dreadfully with each thundering crash
of lightning from within her. And when the Lord played
with the Sacred Stones, we of His crew would, almost to
the man, descend from the ship and mingle with the
crowds below and crane our necks upward to see the
Black Falcon bobble and weave ferociously from the
wrath of the Sacred Stones. Aye, the peals of thunder that
rolled from the bulkheads of the *Black Falcon* at times
were so intense their roar would echo out across the towers of the city, forcing the city's guards to come to the
base of the *Black Falcon*'s mooring tower and demand
that the Lord's tinkering with the Sacred Stones cease immediately. As the Lord's chosen Second in Command, I
had to ascend the tower and enter the ship to pass the
word on to the Lord.

The Master's other interest, for which He constantly
sought more information, was in the Ancient Kings and
their artifacts. My knowledge of the Ancient Kings was
limited, as I was no scholar or philosopher. But I told Him
all that I knew of the Ancient Kings of the dim past. Yet
it took the small shop of an armorer to fire the imagina-
tion of the Lord and send Him searching for more and
more knowledge of the Ancient Kings.

Tallsus, the ship's gunner, mentioned one day to the
Lord that Triisus had within her walls one of Hungar's
most noted makers of fine steel blades. An old man by the
name of Fadah, whose blades were reputed to be the finest
in the world, had a small armorer's shop in the oldest section of town up a narrow street that was a dead end. The
Lord, being what He was, found this news most interesting
and together with Tallsus and myself journeyed from the
Black Falcon to find the shop of Fadah the Armorer. It
took some effort to disguise the Lord in rags and smear
His face with soot to make Him appear a common

peasant wood stoker, one who supplies the ships of Hungar with cut wood for the fireholds of the Sacred Stones. In this way we were able to leave the large crowd of devoted Sa'yen worshippers behind us. After succeeding in this ruse, we stopped at an inn for the Lord to wash and dress Himself more appropriately and then journeyed on into the city to find the armorer's shop. After some searching, late in the afternoon we discovered the street the shop fronted on, and we slowly drifted through the heavy crowds that filled the Street of the Armorers to find the shop of old Fadah. It was Tallsus who opened the door to the small shop, allowing the Lord to enter first. We found ourselves in a small shop that was a mass of tables overflowing with weapons of every conceivable type. Swords, battleaxes, spears, halberds, suits of armor, various pieces of armor, all packed the shop tightly. So tightly that it was with some difficulty that we moved farther into the shop. Four large torches were all that lit the shop, and their light was dim and filled with shadows and smoke. Dust coated most of the weapons and pieces of armor with a fine layer, and the shop smelled of dust and oil, and hot odors of an armorer's forge and white-hot coals. Somewhere in the back of the shop we heard the slow, methodical pounding of a hammer beating on a piece of steel. I saw the Lord's eyes dance with excitement as He stepped from one table to the next, examining weapons and pieces of armor. Several long, thin rapiers He tried, feeling the balance and nodding in satisfaction. He inspected two suits of fine chain mail, examining the mesh of each steel loop, and was equally impressed with the craftsmanship of this merchandise. As Tallsus and I stood side by side, we watched the Lord in silence as He walked through the shop, stopping here and there to look at something or other. Finally, after some time in the shop without old Fadah presenting himself to help us, I touched the elbow of Tallsus and whispered to him to seek out the shop's proprietor and bring him to the Lord. Tallsus nodded and disappeared behind a curtain of beads, leaving the Lord and myself alone among the tables of weapons and armor. Only a few moments passed before Tallsus returned, escorting the legendary armorer before him. I saw the eyebrows of the Lord lift in surprise to see such an ancient, wrinkled old man enter the shop. Fadah was perhaps the oldest man I had ever laid eyes upon. His face and bare arms were a mass of wrinkles, splotched with brown, his head devoid of hair. The armorer was a small-framed man with delicately thin bone structure. He moved in sliding, halting steps, and one hand was always out for support. Tallsus hovered close to the side of the old armorer and was prepared to catch him if he stumbled. But the old man shuffled along from one table to the next, his dark eyes looking onto the face of the Lord with an odd bright light in the ancient eyes as he moved.

"My Lord, the armorer Fadah, of Triisus."

"Eh? Is this the Sa'yen? The Sa'yen!"

The Lord looked at me with a sigh of resignation, then turned to take the outstretched hands of the old man in both of His. Fadah the Armorer shuffled forward and shook visibly with the thrill of touching his god! The Sa'yen frowned at the man's obvious ecstasy, cleared His throat, and spoke in a gentle voice.

"Master Fadah, whatever you have heard of me is only poor lies. I claim to be no god. And certainly not your God of War!"

"So? As you are supposed to answer, My Lord! As the prophets have foretold to all of your followers, Lord. Ala Sa'yen!"

"Ala Sa'yen!" Tallsus and I automatically repeated, the litany of devotion to the Lord as ingrained into us as it was into the old bones of Fadah the Armorer.

"The Sa'yen! Here, in my humble shop! Ah, truly have the gods smiled on me, My Lord. In all the years that I have served you, never did I think the Lord would come in my lifetime. And if He did, not once did it occur to me He would grace my poor shop with His presence. Lord, let me take your hand and press it to my lips. Long have I wished that the Sa'yen would return to us again and lead His devoted in another Wha'ta!"

The Lord did not resist as the old man took one of His hands and pressed it firmly to his lips, He was clearly irritated that He had again been taken and accepted completely as the Sa'yen. Finally, the old man stepped back, his wrinkled face stained with long tracks of tears running down his cheeks, yet a large, happy smile was on his gray lips. The Lord smiled upon the old man and with a gesture of His hand, addressed the old man as if He were but a mere mortal addressing another mortal.

"Master Fadah, I am truly impressed with the arms and weapons of your shop. You are indeed a master of this trade. And, with your permission, I wish to purchase a sword and some mail that I have seen."

"Purchase? Purchase? The Sa'yen, My God, purchase weapons from Me? Never! My Lord, I am humbled in Your presence. Anything, anything that pleases You, take with my deep pleasure. To serve the Sa'yen faithfully is all that old Fadah the Armorer can ask. Please, what do you wish from my poor shop?"

"Why, this blade here and this suit of fine chain mail please me the most, Master Fadah. Yet, please humor me. Let me leave after paying in full for these objects. Even a devoted follower of the Sa'yen must eat."

"Eh? This sword you say, Lord? And this mail? Hah! My Lord, allow me to say that this is but common trash to be offered only to the average warrior of little skill or training. Sire, allow me to show you truly the best of my craft."

The Lord looked at me, then turned His gaze to Fadah. I glanced at Tallsus and saw the tall gunner smiling, pleased at the old man's words, and it occurred to me that Tallsus knew more of this old man than he had mentioned to us. But the Lord looked upon Fadah and voiced His desire to see the best of the old man's weapons. Happily, the old man nodded his head and asked the Lord to follow him. And slowly the old armorer moved back through the curtain of beads and stopped at the base of a long, narrow flight of wooden stairs. Looking up at the Lord, the old man shrugged his shoulders and smiled a toothless grin.

"In my youth, My Lord, I experimented with many formulas to perfect my technique of making fine steel. Once, a long, long time ago in my youth, I journeyed far to the east and sought out an old man who lived high up in a mountain cave. A Charolarl Priest, My Lord. One of the White Sash."

The Lord looked at me for clarification. I whispered into His ear what a White Sash was for a Charolarl Priest. For that sect, the White Sash was the ultimate goal. One could not go higher, and only the Charolarl Priests knew who their White Sashed elders were. Yet it was rumored that there were not more than ten such high officials of the order. For Fadah to find such a priest in his early youth must have been an unprecedented experience. He continued his story.

"This ancient priest, My Lord, knew the lore of the Ancient Kings and he taught me much. I stayed with him for years, My Lord, and was honored in being taught much in the mystical arts of mixing liquids together to cure fine steel. This priest was an old, old man, and he was near to death. Aye! Even a White Sashed Charolarl Priest dies, My Lord. So as death approached, he wanted to teach me as much as he could, and together we experimented in making steel with formulas handed down by the Ancient Kings themselves. We made rapiers of steel so flexible and resilient that one could take it in a mailed glove and bend the blade double without breaking it! Yet the edge of such a weapon always held. We made weapons, Lord, that could cut through armor plate and yet not lose their razor's touch. We made chain mail that was impervious to any arrow or sword thrust. The formula was long and complex. Too long for a mortal mind to remember alone. He gave me an ancient scroll that was aged and brown from long years. And it had the processes written on it. For years after the death of the priest I followed that formula in making my weapons. And then, disaster struck me! A shop I owned far to the south, in the city of Kadash, erupted in fire and burned to the ground while I was out on business. My family, then young and unknowing, fled to safety, but left behind the scroll with the secret formula. It was consumed in flames and lost forever!

"I was never to copy the excellence of steel that the formula gave to me again. As much as I tried, I could not remember all that the formula said, and even to this day, I yet rack my mind in trying to remember the many steps that had to be taken in an ordered manner to make the steel of the Ancient Kings. But alas! I can only remember so much of the formula. But not all. Sadly, I used as much of the formula as I could remember, and from those fragments, I made a reputation of being the best armorer on Hungar. But the formula of the Ancient Kings made me look like a child to them, Lord. Aye, I made fine weapons never before seen by mortals with the formula that I could remember. And I grew rich and famous. Out there, in the ground floor of my shop, My Lord, are the weapons I make from the formula that I yet remember. But up these stairs, in a private display of my own, I have an assorted collection of the best chain mail and edged weapons I made using the formula of the Ancient Kings. The full formula! Come, My Lord! Allow this old, ancient figure to ascend these stairs and show you what the Ancient Kings fought and died with!"

The Lord nodded, smiling in pleasure at seeing the old armorer's best. And then on an impulse, He made a gesture that would add to His already large legend as being a strangely kind and gentle god of war. He bent down and suddenly swept up in His arms the bent, ancient figure of the old armorer, and holding him like a baby, flew up the narrow, steep flight of stairs with such a speed that Tallsus and I had almost to run to keep up with Him! But to the best of our ability we followed the Lord through a small door the old armorer pointed to. We entered a small room, richly carpeted with fine tapestries and a deep, richly thick, dark red carpet. In one corner was a rough iron tripod on which a large iron kettle hung from a chain. Below the pot, and on a block of wide granite slab, was a small fire. Within the pot bubbled hot brew of fine horse tea—an ancient, almost forgotten relic of the past that was once a standard ritual of all who worshipped the Sa'yen. I remember my father's large, wide wagon of the Ha'valli. In his wagon would be found the iron tripod with the chain and the kettle filled with horse tea. My father was one of the ancient followers of the Sa'yen. And for him, the ancient ways of worshipping the Sa'yen were the best. Seeing the pot and the tripod, with the small fire keeping the hot tea simmering, I was flooded with a sadness and a deep longing. It had been years, so many years, since I had last seen my father. Reluctantly, and with much effort, I pulled my thoughts away from my dead father and looked upon the face of the Sa'yen. And seeing that He stood in the middle of the carpeted, tapestried room with glowing eyes of surprise, I turned to look the room over myself. I was startled at what I saw! Along one wall, a wall hidden by a large tapestry of a wild hunting scene on a snow-capped mountain, were life-sized mannequins dressed in full armor and fine, expensive clothing. My eyes were immediately captured by two full sets of plate armor, completely enclosing the figures, and sitting on a life-sized replica of a Mountain Hiirli, with lances in one hand extended as if charging at a foe. They faced each other, lances down as if to charge, and looked so fantastically real that I had to reach out and touch them. I found the Mountain Hiirli to be a stuffed animal so cunningly made as to appear genuinely real! Amazed at such a sight, I turned and looked upon the face of the Lord and smiled.

"Aye, a fine example of the taxidermist art, eh, warrior?" remarked Fadah. "But come, let me show My Lord a truly exquisite pair of weapons that can only be for Him. Come, My Lord, come!"

Fadah the Armorer stepped to a far corner of the room, and from an unmounted mannequin's hands he took the long, heavy blade of an unusually designed rapier and handed it to the Sa'yen.

"Try this, My Lord. An old design for a rapier, it is true, Sire. A design perfected in the city of Hakad years ago. Yet, made with the steel of the Ancient Kings. There is no blade on the entire planet finer than that one, My Lord!"

I saw the Lord take the weapon from the old man's hands and heft it in His, then smile and shout in delight. Pleased and excited, the Lord took up the classical stance of a fencing master and made two blinding passes with the sword at an imaginary opponent. And the smile on His face broadened with infinite pleasure at the weapon's feel. Nodding at seeing the Lord so pleased, I did not see the old armorer approach me with a similar sword in his wrinkled old hands, until he spoke.

"Here, warrior, try this one. It is the sister to the one

the Lord has in His hands now. A matched pair I made in my youth in a cave high up in the Black Pillar Mountains, far to the east of us. Here! Try the feel of this weapon and face the Lord. Touch swords with the Lord and experience their balance. You both will never feel better balanced, lighter weapons in your lives!"

Stunned at this unexpected honor, I took the weapon from the armorer's hands and almost shouted myself with delight. Such a long, heavy looking blade, yet so incredibly light in my hand! And so finely balanced that it seemed to have been made for my hand and my hand only. Smiling, I stepped up and saluted the Lord with a wide grin on my lips. The bearded Master returned my salute, smiling at me, and we touched swords. We parried with each other in our happiness at the weapons we held. For a few heartbeats we danced back and forth, the song of steel sounding pleasant and soothing to our ears. Such incredible weapons. The sword fairly danced in my hand! Pleased and delighted, we stepped back, sweat on our brows yet happy as children at finding something precious and wonderful.

"Aye? Have you ever felt such a weapon, My Lord? And you, warrior, you with the heavy shoulders and thick arms. I have never seen a mere mortal handle a blade as you do! If this were not the Sa'yen standing here with us, I would say you were the finest swordsman my old eyes had ever beheld!"

"Aye, Master Fadah, truly a wonderful weapon. And wish I that I could afford such a beauty," I said, smiling and a bit embarrassed at the old man's flattery.

"Eh? Afford such a weapon? It is yours, warrior! Being in the entourage of the Sa'yen is the price you pay, warrior. And wish I that I were young enough to follow the Sa'yen southward. Aye, that is the second best blade I forged. The sister to the weapon that the Lord holds now in His hand. It is yours, warrior! Wear and use it with pride! Now, as to the mail you may need, My Lord. That I have, of such light weight You will never think that You wear mail at all. Here. Here it is. Let me strip this mannequin, and You may try it on."

The old man's hands stripped the figure of a light mail

and handed it to the Lord. The Sa'yen took the mail and, following the old armorer, disappeared into a small room to dress. Looking at Tallsus, I grinned and tossed him the sword. He caught it by the pommel and hefted it up to feel the balance of the blade. He smiled, nodded at me, and tossed the weapon back to me.

"A wonderful thing, that blade. Fadah is truly the best armorer in the world, Magdar!"

"Aye, I think that is the truth, Tallsus. But tell me, how is it that you know so much about Fadah the Armorer?"

The tall cannoneer glanced at his feet and his complexion turned a bright red. There was a sheepish smile on his face and, looking up, he started to answer. But downstairs we heard the beads of the curtain separate, and then the voice of a woman spoke the old armorer's name. Tallsus and I stood still as we heard footsteps come up the narrow stairs. The woman called twice old Fadah's name, and then she entered the small room we stood in. She first looked at me, and I saw fear in her eyes as she swallowed a startled gasp. But Tallsus stepped up and touched her arm gently, and when she turned and saw him I saw something else replace the fear in the young woman's eyes and I smiled. She was tall for a woman, young, with short-cropped dark brown hair. Her eyes were large, almond-shaped, and she had a boy's figure. She was dressed in rough peasant's trousers and a blouse of plain gray cloth. Her skin was smooth and unblemished and, in a boyish way, she was lovely to look upon. I smiled. This was Tallsus's betrothed. He had spoken of her to me often. Yet he had not mentioned she was related to Fadah the Armorer. I bowed to the young woman who now looked at me curiously as she stood in the arms of the tall ship's cannoneer.

"Magdar, this is my betrothed, Jamilia, great-granddaughter of Fadah the Armorer. Jamalia, this is my friend and My Lord's Left Hand, Magdar, called the Bull by his friends and foes alike."

"I am honored to meet the Sa'yen's Left Hand and equally pleased to hear he is the friend of my love as well. Welcome, Magdar, to my grandfather's humble house."

I bowed again, smiling. She had a voice that was like wonderful music, like a fresh running brook to listen to, and well could I understand Tallsus's devotion to her. I started to say something, but the armorer suddenly pulled a curtain back and stepped into the room again, holding the curtain to allow the Lord to enter. Old Fadah did not see his great-granddaughter standing beside Tallsus. Jamilia started to speak to her grandfather but then the Lord stepped into the room in His bearded magnificence, tall and wonderful to look upon. She let out a scream and dropped to her knees, head bowed in fright. The Lord indicated the young woman on the floor, and looked at me for an explanation. I smiled, stepped up to His side and quickly explained.

"The great-granddaughter to Fadah the Armorer, My Lord. And she is betrothed to our Tallsus, the lucky devil! Soon to be wedded, I fear. And yet, I would grudge him not."

"So? Marriage to such a pretty thing, is it? Well then, we must expect a few things from your wife here, Tallsus." The Lord grinned, looking down at the supplicating form of the woman at His feet. "And the first is this. I cannot tolerate people kowtowing before me, young woman. Stand up and let me look at your face!"

And the Lord bent down and helped the young woman to her feet. Jamilia, the great-granddaughter to Fadah the Armorer, was speechless as she came to her feet, one of her small white hands firmly grasping the hand of the Lord. She could not look up into the eyes of the Sa'yen. The Lord took one look at the young, boyish face of the woman, and then smiled at Tallsus.

"Ah, you are a lucky man, Tallsus! Such a lovely face. And I'll be losing my best ship's gunner."

"My Lord, no!" the girl suddenly said, looking up into the face of the Master with serious, wide brown eyes of innocent beauty. "We have decided that even after we marry, his responsibility is to be at Your side, commanding the *Black Falcon*'s guns. And I would not have it any other way, Sire!"

"Then twice am I a lucky man, my dear. I'll keep such a valuable comrade as your Tallsus is to me, and he will be a most happy man in my command because of you.

That will mean that the *Black Falcon*'s guns will be well served."

The boyish face of the young girl beamed up at the Lord in pride and pleasure as the Lord turned and faced me. He had on the long, single-piece suit of chain mail that covered Him from the shoulders clear to His knees. It was a fine, light suit of mail, each small round ring of steel superbly linked to other rings. Each link was small and compact yet the whole suit allowed complete freedom of movement for the wearer and offered protection for every vital and vulnerable portion of the body. I nodded my approval just as old Fadah broke the silence and touched my arm.

"Warrior, I give you, too, a suit of mail such as you see the Master wearing now. The Left Hand of the Sa'yen should be well protected so that he may protect the Master faithfully. Therefore, take this with my humble blessings. May the sword and this suit of mail preserve and protect you so that you may serve the Lord always!"

Neatly folded in his arms was a suit of chain mail much like the one the Lord wore. And he handed it to me with a toothless wide grin on his wrinkled old face. Not knowing what to say, I took the suit of mail and merely nodded.

"Ah, Magdar!" Tallsus said, smiling broadly at me as he held his beloved close to him. "With such a sword and such a suit of mail, no one except the Lord will be able to stand before you! Ala Sa'yen, to you!"

"Ala Sa'yen, Tallsus." I nodded, at last finding my tongue and speaking.

Fadah clapped his hands and beamed up at us. Then, tilting his head sideways, he looked at the Lord and made a strange little sound. We all looked at him, and saw him nod his head and turn on his heels, crooking a finger at us to follow as he spoke.

"Sire, I wish to show you my most prized possession. Come! Come! Let me show you a genuine suit of armor actually worn by the Ancient Kings. Come!"

The Lord and I exchanged glances, my face clearly revealing my bewilderment and excitement at seeing such an ancient and sacred thing. A suit of armor worn by the Ancient Kings! How old would such a suit be? A thousand

years? Five thousand years? Ten thousand? No one knew!
The Ancient Kings lived so far back in the dim past that
not even the most wise of the Charolarl Priests knew when
the last of them walked this planet. So old the suit would
be and, if known among the populace of Triisus, so highly
prized, that it would be immediately enshrined in a
temple built just for it. And Fadah, the ancient Armorer,
claimed it as his own! Excitedly, we followed the old armorer across the room and into one dimly lit corner. The
armorer bid Jamilia to bring forward a torch so that all
might see better. She did and the old armorer stood beside
a tall object draped and hidden by a heavy black cloth of
fine silk. With brightly burning eyes, he turned and faced
us, rubbing his hands together as he again began to cackle
with his old, screeching bird-like voice.

"I told you of my stay in the cavern up in the Black
Pillar Mountains with the White Sashed Charolarl Priest. I
have said that this priest knew much of the lore of the Ancient Kings, did I not? Ah, but did I mention that the
priest knew the whereabouts of an Ancient King's fortress
yet intact and complete? Aye! A fortress of the Ancient
Kings! And not ransacked or destroyed by defilers. And
from this fortress the priest obtained much of the
knowledge of the Ancient Kings. And such knowledge,
Lord! This priest told me of things that had lights and
talked strange languages. Of machines that would write on
paper reams upon reams of a strange language. And deep
within the bowels of this fortress, the priest said, pulsed
the power and heat of a thousand suns! And this White
Sashed priest knew the languages of the Ancient Kings.

"Aye, I did not know whether to believe him or not, My
Lord. But this was a Charolarl Priest talking to me. And
such men do not lie! This old priest was dying and wished
to impart to me much knowledge he had learned. And
then one day, one rainy day, the priest brought from out
of the depths of his cavern this suit of armor, My Lord.
And he gave it to me. To Fadah, the Armorer, he gave a
genuine suit of armor worn by the Ancient Kings! The
priest told me to keep it always hidden and not to tell anyone but my most trusted friends of its existence. He told
me that perhaps someday someone would come and tell

me how to unleash the secrets this strange suit of armor yet held within it. For the priest quickly warned me that somehow, some way, this suit of armor worn by the Ancient Kings had the power to unleash such devastation as had never before been seen by us poor mortals of Hungar! And such a monster of a suit, My Lord. No mortal my eyes have looked upon could ever wear such a suit. Even you, My Lord, are much too small to fit into this suit. Such a strange suit, My Lord. A suit, I think, that possesses a life of its own. A suit of the Ancient Kings!"

And with these last words the old man took hold of the black cloth and whipped it away from the tall figure underneath it. I could not help but yelp with surprise and genuine fear at what lay underneath the black cloth. A mannequin, some ten feet in height, covered from head to foot with a thousand tiny lights that winked on and off continuously. Fine gold wires, or what I took to be gold wires, created a crossed pattern that wove into a thick net around the form of the mannequin, and thousands of tiny points of light blinked on and off continuously within this net. Astounded, speechless, I stepped back and looked upon the face of the Lord. I saw the myriad of lights of the suit glow on the face of the Sa'yen, and I had a deep conviction that the armorer's words rang with truth. This suit of the Ancient Kings possessed a life of its own! In the gloom of darkness in his corner of the room, this mannequin dressed in the armor of the Ancient Kings glowed and pulsed with a life that seemed vaguely evil. And the size of the armor! It towered over our heads by a good four feet! Lights of every color continued to wink at us mockingly, taunting us as we stood before it, with awe and genuine fright in our hearts. That is genuine fright in the hearts of myself, Tallsus, Jamilia and even the old form of Fadah the Armorer! For even though he had preserved this gigantic and ancient relic for all his adult life, the armorer had yet to come to accept it without a sense of awe and suppressed terror. And truly, the sight before us was terrifying. To think the Ancient Kings were men standing ten feet tall! Towering over our heads by a good three or four feet or more! Yet, as I watched the Lord, I saw that look come into His face of one who knew exactly what He faced. The Sa'yen knew of the powers of this relic of the Ancient Kings! Stunned, I inadvertently touched the shoulder of the Sa'yen, concerned at the paleness and white mask that was part of the determined look on His face. As if not noticing my hand, the Lord continued to look upon the thousands of lights as He addressed the ancient armorer beside him.

"Fadah, you say this is of the Ancient Kings? This is what the Charolarl Priest gave you?"

"Aye, Lord. This is what the priest said was the armor of the Ancient Kings."

"And the old priest found this in the fortress of the Ancient Kings?"

"Aye, Lord, years before I joined him in his cavern up in the high crags of the Black Pillar Mountains. He told me he found this deep within the ancient fortress, in a pile of dust and bones."

"And did the priest give you anything else, Fadah? Any other artifacts he claimed were of the Ancient Kings?"

"No, My Lord, he did not. He said that only this I could have. Yet his cavern was filled with many strange things that were from the fortress. Things unknown to me, except that the Ancient Kings used them."

"And you say this cavern of the old priest is where, Fadah?"

"Alas, My Lord, it is no more. It was once up in the highest crags of the Black Pillar Mountains. But on the night the priest died, he told me to pack my belongings and to take this gift and descend to the base of the mountain. I did as he bid, though reluctantly. It took me three whole days to make the journey down to the valley floor below. And when I finally reached the valley, I heard a roar of thunder from the mountain and, looking up, saw that a ball of white light had consumed the entire top of the mountain with fire and heat. Such a roar of noise, My Lord, I have never before heard. Then, after the explosion, only minutes later, a blast of searing heat threw me to the ground, burning my clothes from me, and the roar of the wind was such that Yab'lal and Kakla trees were uprooted and hurled for yards. So frightened was I, Lord, that I could not speak or eat for days afterward. The entire top of the mountain had been ripped to pieces. The cavern, the priest, the whole upper third of the mountain had completely disappeared, Lord. I could not believe what my eyes saw. Gone! All gone!"

Tallsus and Jamilia muttered disbelief at such a story, but the face of the Lord had not changed from that hard, determined look I knew so well. The Lord believed the armorer! The old man's words were truth! I found myself gaping in wonderment. What force could be so strong as to rip asunder an entire mountain? What power the Ancient Kings controlled I could not imagine. Yet the Lord knew of such and seemed unafraid! Licking my lips, for my mouth had turned suddenly dry with a vague form of dread, I waited for the Sa'yen to speak again.

"Did the priest tell you where the fortress was, Fadah?"

"No, My Lord. He gave no hint as to its whereabouts. I only assumed, without any real proof, that somewhere within or around the Black Pillar Mountains was the fortress. Yet I had no idea where."

"He never took you to it?"

"No, Sire. He refused to even talk about it on most occasions. The priest, Sire, seemed to be holding a great secret back. And I had the impression that even he was fearful of the ghosts that inhabited the dead halls of the fortress."

For some minutes the Sa'yen continued to watch the blinking lights of the gold-netted armor. On His face was a look of deep thought, of fierce determination, and somehow I had the feeling that the Lord was intimately familiar with the thing that draped the lifeless mannequin before us. Yet I said nothing. I continued to watch the Sa'yen's face, waiting for Him to say something or to move. We all stood before the monstrous mannequin dressed in the gold net and blinking lights, our eyes on the Lord. Finally, after some minutes, the Lord tore his eyes away from the figure and looked at me. And I paled under his stare. For I knew what the Master wished to do. We would soon search for the dead fortress of the Ancient Kings! Yet I said nothing and waited for the Lord to speak first. He did so immediately.

"Magdar, how far are the Black Pillar Mountains by the fastest route?"

"I know of only one route, Lord. And that is through the high pass of the Hakad Mountains. And barring any intervention from the Hakadians, we could sail to the Black Pillars in seven, possibly eight, months."

The Lord nodded, thought a moment, then turned to the ancient armorer. Smiling down at the toothless, wrinkled old man, He pulled from within the heavy cloak He had around His shoulders a large leather bag I knew was filled with double weighted gold coins. Taking the wrinkled, ancient hand of the armorer into His, He placed the bag into the old hand and firmly, yet gently, closed the old man's fingers around the bag as he spoke to him.

"For the gifts you gave us, friend Fadah. And more importantly, for the information concerning the Ancient Kings. For that alone you should be paid double what I have given you!"

"But Sire! I do not ask payment from the Lord! I am, even though bent with age and toothless, nevertheless a follower of the Sa'yen. I cannot take gold from my God!"

"Aye, but you can! Especially if I tell you to take it, eh?" The Lord grinned, turning and bowing to Jamilia and Tallsus. "And when, pretty lady, do you and my gunner plan to wed?"

"The night of the Feast of Flowers, Sire," Jamilia answered in a quiet, soft voice.

"Ah, then on that night your wedding will be on the main deck of the *Black Falcon*! And after the wedding I shall throw a feast such as your eyes have never seen!"

"Thank you, My Lord!" Tallsus said, grinning hugely with the pleasure and honor of the Sa'yen's gesture.

The Lord smiled and then moved to the door of the small room and disappeared. I quickly stepped up to Jamilia, took her hand and gently kissed it.

"To your happiness, lovely woman, May a thousand blessings of the Sa'yen fall upon you!"

"Thank you, friend of my husband and the exalted Left Hand of the Lord."

I hurried out of the room in pursuit of the Lord. Tallsus lingered only a second or two and quickly joined us in the

street in front of the armorer's shop. For some seconds the
Lord stroked His heavy beard with His hand, in deep
thought. And then He turned to me quickly, His eyes hard
and glittering with determination and purpose.

"We must obtain as much information as possible
concerning the Ancient Kings. Pay gold for information,
Magdar. Do not quibble over the price as long as the information is good and new to us. I must know all there is
to know about the old ruins of the Ancient Kings, Magdar! Can you do this for me?"

"Aye, Lord! It can be done. But the price might be
high."

"More than the treasure that is aboard the *Black Falcon*?"

"No, Lord! There is no way we will ever be able to
spend that treasure in our lifetimes, Sire!"

"Then disregard what it will cost us, Magdar! I must
find that fortress of the Ancient Kings! The key to my
possibly being rescued may lie within the walls of that
fortress. We must find it, Magdar! We must!"

And the Lord moved off into the crowded street scowling fiercely. One glance at Tallsus and I saw the puzzle-
ment in his eyes as well. The Lord's rescue? What did that
mean? Frowning, I hurried to catch up with the Lord in
the crowded street. With Tallsus flanking the other side of
the Lord, we hurried through the streets of Triisus to return to the *Black Falcon*.

VIII

A City Divided

A month passed and much gold was spent to buy every possible bit of information concerning the Ancient Kings. And with each passing day the crowds below the floating hull of the *Black Falcon* grew and grew. And Triisus, the jewel of the North, simmered into a hotbed of rumor and counter rumor concerning the Sa'yen. For the most part, the Lord stayed on board the *Black Falcon* while I separated the gold-seeking liars who knew nothing of the Ancient Kings from the few who did. And the gold from the dowry of the Hakadian Princess Saphid paid for other information as well. For to my ears came rumors that Bahir Kandar was forging an alliance with the Pictii within the city with the aim to crush the growing tide of followers of the Sa'yen. With the defeat of Thordak, the Captain of the Household Guards of the Kandar House, who was the most feared swordsman in the city, the populace had been growing more bold in their defiance of the Kandars. It was the Year of Kings for Triisus, when a new ruler for the city would be chosen from among the nobility by the people. Triisus, unlike other cities of Northern Hungar, preferred to elect kings on a five-year term from among the city's many houses of nobility. The House of Kandar, being the largest and by far the most wealthy, had nominated Bahir Kandar to run for the throne. In an election year even Bahir Kandar, normally a figure who controlled and commanded unlimited power without regard to others, dared not antagonize the populace of the city if he cared to succeed in his bid for the throne. Yet, as the gold I paid freely to those who brought me accurate news informed me, the Lord posed to the House of Kandar and particularly to Bahir Kandar serious pitfalls to his winning the throne. For daily the crowd at the base of the landing tower of the *Black Falcon* grew as more came to join the ranks of the believers.

I feared for my Lord. He, in His golden-maned magnificence, did not appear concerned at the news I brought Him regarding the growing intrigues the House of Kandar was plotting against Him. The Lord was more concerned about what made the Sacred Stones act the way they did and with controlling the awesome power they possessed. And even that created dangers for Him. For the Pictii, the High Order of the Brotherhood that controlled the market and sale of the Sacred Stones, heard of the Lord's experiments on the *Black Falcon* and denounced Him as a defiler of the accepted order and a heretic. And as each day passed, the city I once loved so deeply began to divide its ranks clearly to be either for or against the Sa'yen.

And I knew not how to save the Lord from this imminent threat of destruction. I feared war would erupt within the city. I feared the rugged, gray-towered city of Triisus would be torn asunder in the ravages of a civil war. I could see the hostility growing among those who did not believe in the Lord. Daily I heard of clashes between believers and nonbelievers on the city's darkest streets. Fierce clashes that made blood flow freely. Yet, no matter what tales I heard from reliable spies concerning the growing hostility to the Lord, and which I duly reported to Him, the Lord wished only to learn more about the Ancient Kings. And learn we did, thanks to the gold in the coffers of the *Black Falcon*'s hold. By piecing the bits and fragments of all that we heard of the Ancient Kings together, we eventually formed an overall picture of the true powers of the ancient race that roamed this planet far in our dim past. And a mighty race it was! The Ancient Kings, as we called them now, had only one government that ruled the entire planet, instead of each city ruling its own small kingdom as it was with us today. The Ancient Kings had power that was too immense to comprehend. That is, none

of us on the *Black Falcon* could comprehend it except the
Lord. He would sit in His favorite chair in His cabin, with
the stern gallery windows open to the night's cool breeze,
listening to my daily account of what the gold had paid
for, and He would nod silently, pulling thoughtfully on
His beard as I talked. At times, long moments of silence
would go by as He sat in His high-backed chair of finely
carved Kakla wood and red leather upholstery, as He
thought to Himself, with me standing in front of Him,
waiting to see if He had any further orders for me. And
the only sounds that would filter into my mind were the
quiet, soothing sounds of the ship as she tugged and
strained on her mooring ropes above the city; of wood
creaking softly in the night breeze, of ropes rubbing
against each other, of the slow, measured step of the crew
above us on the quarterdeck as they made their rounds.
Sometimes, with the stern windows thrown open, the smell
of an approaching fall thunderstorm drifted in with a stout
breeze and to me, the aromatic odor was pleasing to sniff.
Yet such pleasures would be interrupted as soon as the
Master came out of his reverie and cleared His throat to
speak to me. He had, in the last few weeks after the defeat
of Thordak, the paid killer in the employ of Bahir Kandar, become more reclusive. Rarely did He venture from
the deck of the *Black Falcon*. And, after examining the armor once worn by the Ancient Kings themselves, the Lord
became even more ill at ease. In vain would I attempt to
pry out whatever it was that had soured His heart. All that
I accomplished was to seal more resolutely His silence
about His burden. With a growing feeling of despair in my
heart, I did as my Lord bid me. I sought information concerning the Ancient Kings and recorded all that was
brought before me and covertly paid equally as well for
news that might affect the Lord in any fashion. It was
while seeking word about the Ancient Kings that I first
heard news concerning the mysterious Charolarl Priest we
had encountered in the inn.

It was late in the Thieves' Watch, just before sunrise,
and I was lying in my bunk restless and without sleep. The
ship bobbled and dipped as she floated above the city, a
desire running through her hull to escape into the clouds

and flee with the wind. I could hear the hum of the wind through the rigging and feel the keel-masts vibrating with a lust for freedom that grew as the wind increased. The ship's whispering desire to escape was affecting me, and I was eager to leave a city filled with rumors, filled with excitement as well as hatred; and lastly, filled with a religious fervor that I found most threatening of all. Lying in my bunk, with the sword the old armorer had given to me lying in its scabbard on the chair close to me, I lay staring up at the cabin's ceiling without thinking. My body was attuned to the sounds of the ship, and I was trying desperately not to think of my fear that the Lord had no regard for what His presence was doing to the city of Triisus. Yet I heard the watch officer shout out a warning and heard dimly a reply. I heard feet run across the poop deck and another voice ring out into the windblown night. Aroused, I swung my feet off the bunk and quickly slipped into my heavy boots. More feet were running to the port side of the ship, and as I threw the stout leather belt over my shoulder which held the sword close to me, a knock impatiently sounded on my cabin door. I opened it and found the wide, sour face of Fidor looking at me, his eyes filled with a concern that made me uneasy.

"Magdar, one of your informers has been brought aboard gravely wounded. He will not live to see the sunrise. He says he has information of the greatest importance for you, and will not talk to anyone but you!"

"Where is he now?"

"I have him under the stern canopy. He has been stabbed several times, Magdar. I doubt that he'll even be alive by the time you reach deck!"

"Then let us hurry!"

"Shall I arouse the Sa'yen?"

"No! The Master needs His rest first! Let us see what this rogue has to say before we disturb Him."

"Aye!"

With Fidor following, I hurried up to the stern of the ship and stepped out into a wild night of a windblown sky filled with clouds scudding across a large full moon. Under the brightly striped canvas we had spread above the stern to give shade in the day to the helm and watch, I saw a

large group of the crew standing beside a figure lying on
the deck. Pushing my way through the crowd, I told the
men to return to their duties, and then knelt down beside
the dying figure. He was a street urchin, a beggar that I
had bought for a few silver coins as a source of information within the city—for information not of the Ancient
Kings but of the comings and goings of the political fac-
tions within the city's wall. I held no faith in the House of
Kandar, nor of many other houses of the nobility within
the city. And I certainly placed no faith in the Brotherhood of the Pictii. Kneeling beside the man, with Fidor
standing behind me, I took the outstretched, bony hand
extended to me and held it firmly. The beggar, dressed in
perhaps the dirtiest rags of the foulest smell and grime I
had ever experienced, lay on the polished deck of the ship,
bleeding profusely. He had only minutes to live, and as I
watched, he tried to whisper to me.

"The. . . . priest! Charolarl . . . priest! He, he is to be
. . . be arrested by agents of Bahir . . . Kandar. The . . .
priest has been . . . asking . . . questions concerning the
Master! He seeks out the Master's . . . armorer! You must
. . . go . . . now. . . ."

"Why does Bahir Kandar want the priest, beggar? Do
you know the answer to that? Quickly, speak!"

"Hakadians! Golden. . . . ships. Hundreds of . . .
them. The priest . . . somehow . . . saw hundreds of
ships . . . of the Hakadians. You must go to the shop of
Fadah . . . save . . . the priest!"

Thin fingers squeezed my hand in a vise of pain and
then suddenly relaxed and finally slipped from my grip altogether. The beggar let out a soft sigh and died on the
deck of the *Black Falcon* in the midst of many strangers.
Coming to my feet, I took a deep breath and let it out
slowly. Looking out across the brightly lit city, I thought
over the words the beggar had gasped with a frown etched
across my lips. Hakadian golden-hulls and Bahir Kandar!
So the words of Hakba Baru were right! The House of
Kandar was in league with the Hakadians. But how did
this mysterious Charolarl Priest come to know this? And
why was he eager to speak to Fadah the Armorer? I did
not like the possibilities that came to mind with the priest

involving the old armorer and his granddaughter, and quickly I knew what I had to do.

"Fidor! Quickly, find four good men. Good swordsmen! We must hurry to the shop of Fadah the Armorer as quickly as possible."

"Aye, Magdar!" Fidor nodded, stepping forward and sliding down the ladder to the main deck swiftly.

I hurried down the open hatch and stepped to the cabin door of Tallsus, the lover of the woman that was Fadah's great-granddaughter.

"Tallsus! Tallsus! Awake and come to the deck at once!"

Tallsus opened his cabin door, pulling his trousers up at the same time. There was sleep in his eyes and his hair was a ragged mop, and I had to smile at his wild, unkempt look. But I grabbed him by an arm and almost dragged him to the poop deck.

"Tallsus! I and Fidor and a few men are hurrying to Fadah's shop to rescue the Charolarl Priest we met at the inn a few weeks ago!"

"What? Jamilia! What of Jamilia!" Tallsus shouted, fear coming into his eyes as we stepped out onto the poop deck of the small black-hull.

"She is safe, my friend!" I lied, for I knew nothing yet of her fate. "But you stay here and we'll return shortly with them all! Arouse the crew and be prepared to cast off the moment we return. Bahir Kandar will want our hides if we pluck the priest from his grasp a second time!"

"Where is the Lord, Magdar?" Tallsus uttered, looking around and confused in his actions still.

"He is below. He yet sleeps, as He should! There is no need to arouse Him now. If we hurry, we may yet remove the priest, Jamilia, and Fadah from the hands of Bahir Kandar's agents before they arrive. Give us until the beginning of the Virgin's Watch before you tell the Lord anything, Tallsus! If we have not returned by then, it will be too late. But do not fear! All will be well! But you must stay and prepare the ship to flee. Load cannon and run them out. We may yet have a glorious fight before the day ends!"

And I found myself grinning with delight at the thought

of a fight. I am, basically, a warrior, and little of anything I fear. I may sing and lust while cooling my heels in a port, but at heart I prefer a good fight and stiff danger to nothing at all. I am a poor man for this, I know. And foolishly, I shall never change. That is the way of the Ha'valli—the tribe of my ancestors.

I shook Tallsus firmly by one arm and smiled into his face. He watched me with a long, worried face as I jumped from the poop deck to the main deck and waved to Fidor and his four stout-looking men to follow me. We six quickly descended the gangplank from the ship and entered the tall, common landing tower the *Black Falcon* was moored to. Hurrying down the spiraling stairs, with four of the men holding above our heads brightly burning torches, we descended the tower and stepped out into the dark streets of the city.

The street below the tower was empty. Not a soul could be seen where thousands had milled only hours before. It was an unnerving sight to see the street empty of the Sa'yen's followers, and I saw the looks of surprise and fear come into the faces of the four warriors chosen by Fidor. I did not halt long enough for the fears of the men to subdue them and the absence of the Lord's followers to work upon their minds. Motioning for them to follow me, I quickly began hurrying through the dark and deserted streets of Triisus to Fadah's shop on the Street of Armorers in the heart of the city.

Twice we stopped to catch our breath, and on each occasion I thought my ears heard the sounds of steel scraping against stone behind us. We were being followed! I held no doubts for I had expected it from the moment we left the *Black Falcon*. Hurrying on, the long, heavy-looking blade old Fadah had given me in my grasp, I expected at the opening of each alley we came upon to be assailed by lurking assassins. We moved rapidly through the street, with the men behind me heavily armed and clutching gleaming weapons in their hands as well. That we were not jumped worried me more than if we had been, but I did not allow my fears to keep me from hurrying through the narrow streets and reaching at last the Street of the Armorers. Coming to the mouth of the street that opened onto the wide Avenue of Thieves, I raised a hand and the men halted behind me. The Street of the Armorers is a narrow, cobblestone one that leads away from the Avenue of Thieves and ends only three blocks away at the stone wall of a huge landing tower owned by the noble House of Mykar. For a thousand feet this landing tower rose above our heads. By a bright full moon that regularly was shielded from our view by angry, fast moving clouds which were hurried on by the growing wind of an approaching storm, we could see several large skyships moored to the tower's landing balconies. The Avenue of Thieves is a wide thoroughfare that runs like a lance from one end of the city to the other and, for the most part, is lined by the estates of nobility. But in the heart of the city, where we were now, several ancient streets and the oldest part of the city lines its sides. The Street of Armorers is one, and as I stepped around the corner of a large warehouse, I found myself peering down a narrow, dark street of stone warehouses and shops draped in evil-looking shadows. The shadows created by the clouds moving across the face of the moon seemed a bizarre, unnerving sea of phantoms dancing, whirling on the walls of the buildings and the street itself. The wind was nearly at the stage of a tempest, and the heavy cloak I wore snapped in the wind angrily. Gripping my sword firmly, I stepped into the middle of the narrow street of shadows and motioned for the men to follow me. With the wind howling in our ears and the clouds above us fleeing across the full moon, the five men followed me up the Street of Armorers, swords drawn and determined, hard looks upon their faces.

Halfway up the dark, threatening street the long, piercing scream of a terrified woman came to our ears. I waved to the men to hurry, and then I broke into a fast run headlong up the narrow, blackened street. The woman screamed again, a high, dreadful sound that almost froze the determination in our hearts, but then the crashing sound of tables and furniture being smashed and broken came to us in the wind. I started to move on, certain that the troops from the House of Kandar were tearing the shop of old Fadah to pieces. But suddenly torches lit the street ahead of us immediately in front of Fadah's shop, and we saw many armed warriors in the livery of the House of Kandar dragging the struggling form of a woman from within the shop. There was no doubt within me as to who it was. The fiancée of Tallsus. Jamilia! Anger intense and supreme flushed through my body, and I turned and hurriedly whispered orders to Fidor and the men behind me. Quickly and silently the five men disappeared into the shadows close to the walls on either side of the street, leaving me alone facing the armed warriors of the House of Kandar. A smile played across my lips as I gripped my sword and began moving slowly down the street toward the armed warriors. Only a few steps had I moved when one of the warriors in front of me held up a torch and yelled out a challenge.

"Who slinks about on a night like a thief? Halt and identify yourself, warrior!"

"I seek Fadah the Armorer and his granddaughter Jamilia. Is this the old man's shop?"

"Aye. That is, it *was*, warrior. Step forward and let Thordak, the Captain of the guards, look upon your face!"

Thordak! The Captain of the Household Guards of Kandar commanded these looting troops! Smiling even more in pleasure at a good fight soon to begin, I stepped boldly into the light of the torch the warrior held above his head. One look at me and I saw he recognized me. Turning, he yelled for his captain to come and look at what had crawled out from the shadows like an insect. Among the fifteen or twenty of his kind, this warrior from the House of Kandar felt safe. Safe enough to be arrogant and cruel. The House of Kandar Troops moved to surround me, nevertheless giving me a large space when they saw the cold steel I held in my hand. I smiled at their arrogance tempered with caution as they surrounded me, holding my smile even though the struggling figure of Jamilia, held in the merciless grip of two burly Kandarian warriors, appeared before me. The boyish face of Jamilia, wild fear in her brown eyes, looked upon me from between her two captors and she ceased struggling. Her red lips parted in surprise and terror at seeing me but she said nothing. The many warriors around me were talking and pointing at her, their voices and their words none too pleasant to listen to. Evidently, from hearing what they had to say, Thordak had generously given Jamilia to the troops to use as they saw fit, and they were eager to see what pleasures she had to offer. Their talk was rough, obscene, and I seethed in fury at the degradation they had subjected her to. But I kept my anger in control and was soon rewarded by the appearance of Thordak himself as he stepped through the crowd of his troops and faced me.

"You! Dog of a whore! What has your master done with that old fool called Fadah the Armorer?" Thordak hissed in a deep, coarse whisper of hatred and dripping evil.

I was surprised at the voice that spoke to me. Once a powerful, booming voice of vibrant strength and clarity, a voice that made many a man quiver in fear and terror when it spoke to them, it was now nothing but a vague shell, a menacing shadow of what it once was. Yet, hearing it, I could feel the tendrils of undeniable evil and strength hiss from it, and as I looked upon the twisted, scarred face of the man, I knew that in his heart was nothing but an evil, cruel monster filled with hatred at what had happened to him. I looked at his neck and saw for myself the pink scar of where the Master had run His sword through the throat of this man and it pleased me. Pleased me so much that I lifted my head a little and laughed carelessly into the face of the wide shouldered, strongly built warrior in front of me.

"Ah, Thordak! My Master sends you greetings and salutations. He bids me to inquire about your wound. He wishes to know if you would like a surgeon to look at the wound, hearing that you had been misguided and sent to have a butcher from the Street of Meat Cleavers to sew you up."

I heard his men gasp in surprise, mingled with sharp cries of rage, at my words to their captain. I saw the color in Thordak's face drain and watched his hands ball into fists as he stepped closer to me.

"You will die for that, son of a dog! Die a thousand deaths before your soul leaves you this night! And I will be the one that makes sure that you die properly. Sieze him and bring him along with us!"

"And when did the noble Thordak and his even more noble master, Bahir Kandar, begin stealing through the night like common criminals to seize defenseless women from their beds? I did not know that Thordak and his master were the ones who stole women in the middle of the night for their pleasure," I shouted before hands could be laid upon me.

"This female is a traitor to the city of Triisus, you dog!" Thordak hissed, pointing to Jamilia with one finger and shaking a fist at me with the other. "As apparently you are too! In league with that heretic Charolarl Priest that seeks to hand the city of Triisus into the clutches of the Hakadians. Well, tonight we shall eliminate two traitors from our midst. And as soon as we find that weak-willed, cowardly priest and the old fool of an armorer, two more traitors will die as well."

"This woman, a mere girl, is a danger to our fair city? Thordak! Never did I figure that you were a comedian! Ah, but how you make me laugh!"

And again I lifted my head and started laughing with a casual ease I knew would infuriate the proud, arrogant warrior in front of me. And I succeeded in making the deadly man before me throw away all restraints! Jumping back with startling speed, Thordak unsheathed his long rapier and stepped in to attack with death in his eyes. In the torchlight, the exposed blades looked deadly, as if they thirsted for blood as I parried several vicious thrusts. The men around us held their torches up high so that their captain could see better. And in their faces I saw they had no worries that the famous Thordak, the most feared blade in Triisus, would not eliminate me shortly. I smiled, parried another fierce thrust, and laughed into the scowling man's face.

"Thordak! Are you playing? Or is this the best you can do? My goodness! I thought you were a swordsman! Perhaps I am wrong, eh?"

The wide-shouldered, arrogant Captain of the Kandar Troops spit out a snarl of rage and leaped in at me again with another fierce attack. My sword, the gift of old Fadah, danced in my hand with wicked delight. My blade parried each thrust with ease, the sound of steel true and clear to our ears. Circling, I saw large beads of sweat rolling down the warrior's face and his breathing was labored. I saw looks of concern on the faces of a few of his men, and even Jamilia, innocent and sweet face that it was, seemed startled that I had stood up before the famous Thordak and survived so long. It pleased me to see that all of his men had gathered around in a large circle to witness my demise. I knew that in a few short seconds Fidor and my men would create havoc when they suddenly attacked from the depths of the shadows, allowing us to escape. All I had to do was stay alive just a few seconds longer. Lifting my sword, I saluted the assassin in the pay of Bahir Kandar and smiled easily. The sword in my hand felt light and comfortable to me, as if it was part of me. I was both confident and surprised. Confident that I could indeed survive this match with such a renowned warrior and surprised that Thordak was hardly the deadly swordsman he was reputed to be. Easily side-stepping a slashing blow, I lifted the point of my sword and ran it across the exposed portion of his left arm. A long, thin line of blood leaped to our eyes and the warrior jumped back, wincing in sudden pain. Some of his men shouted in surprise and rage, and I smiled and lowered my sword's point.

"Ah, Thordak! You disappoint me! And I had looked to have such a hard-fought battle with you, too! Be that as it may, if you and your men will drop your weapons to the street and release the woman yonder, I will yet allow you to withdraw from the field with your lives."

"Our lives!" the tall man shouted, hatred and rage dripping from his voice. "Why, you incipient fool! Do you think you will walk away from this alive? Look around you! You are surrounded!"

"And you, my dear Thordak, are no swordsman," I replied calmly, brushing his words aside with a bored wave of my hand. "I suggest you take up another profession. Perhaps a weaver of baskets or a spinner of cloth, eh?"

For my answer came a scream of rage, and the warrior leaped to the attack with such a fierceness that for a few moments I was hard pressed to keep his sword from laying me low. But the sword in my hand was like a living being. It danced and leaped to my defense with an ease and

swiftness that was amazing to observe. And then, as if
with its own power, the sword given to me by the old armorer Fadah slipped through the web of steel of Thordak's defense and knifed through the heavy chain mail the
warrior wore under his livery and sunk to the hilt into his
chest. His men gasped at seeing their leader mortally
wounded, and as Thordak's lifeless hand dropped the
sword, from the shadows around us came an unholy roar
as my men attacked like frenzied demons of the night.

Confusion reigned immediately. Surprised, the men who
had been with Thordak and who were now leaderless
turned to meet the attack as individuals and not as a
trained body of men. In the melee that followed, my
sword crossed steel twice and left two more bodies behind
me. Men all around me, both those of the House of Kandar and my own, were shouting and bleeding. The clash of
steel created a stupendous din in the dead-end street. I was
positive all the city would hear our melee and be aroused
from their deepest slumbers. With the flat of my blade I
knocked cold one of the men who was grasping the young
girl's wrist, parried the thrust of her other captor and
nicked him a severe cut on his cheek. The man dropped
his sword, turned and ran for his life. I grabbed her wrist,
smiled and bent down to yell in her ear.

"We meet again, young woman! A pleasant surprise!"

"A timely surprise, Left Hand of the Lord!" she yelled
back, putting both of her delicate white hands on my arm
and tilting her head up to look into my eyes. "Most happy
am I to see you!"

I nodded, turned and dealt with another warrior in the
livery of the House of Kandar, placing the beloved of
Tallsus, our ship's gunner, behind my back for safety. The
warrior sunk to the cobblestone street with a wound in his
sword arm, making him useless. I took the delicate wrist of
Jamilia in one hand and began fighting my way through
the crowd, shouting to my men to rally around me so that
we could fight our way out of the street. Fidor was soon at
my side, and I was pleased to see that all of the men the
dour-faced bull of a man had selected were still with us
and still capable of fighting. In a few short seconds we
were clear of the men opposing us and we quickly hurried

from the Street of Armorers and entered the Avenue of Thieves with none of the survivors of Thordak's troops following us. Moving swiftly, yet not running, I told Fidor to keep the men together in a tight group, weapons drawn and ready, in case we were attacked again. I then bent to the hurrying figure of the girl beside me and asked her about her grandfather.

"I have no idea, Left Hand of the Lord. He left just after the stroke of midnight in the company of a strange priest, and I have not seen him since. I am afraid something has happened to him."

"Left with a strange priest, you say? A Charolarl Priest, perhaps? A young one with a hook nose and long brown hair?"

"The one exactly! Magdar! Is my grandfather to be harmed?"

"Eh? Not by the priest, methinks, sweet child," I growled, turning swiftly up a side street that twisted and turned in the direction I desired. "The priest is a Charolarl, girl. Their kind do not harm innocent people such as your grandfather. But why would the priest want to see old Fadah?"

"I heard them talking in low voices down in the main part of the shop. The priest had come seeking information about the Ancient Kings. Somehow the robed figure had heard that my grandfather possessed articles once owned by the Ancient Kings. I know not how, but peeking through the beads that separate the shop from the rest of the house, I could see that grandfather was very surprised the young priest knew his secret."

I stopped suddenly, hearing sounds of pursuers. My men turned and peered down the darkened street we had just passed over, their swords yet in their hands. Dimly behind us we saw the flicker of light from a torch reflecting off dark walls. And then came the sounds of many men hurrying. Grimly, I took the hand of the young girl again and started up the street swiftly. We had much distance still to travel, and I wished not to stop! Hurrying on we kept to the shadows and paused only long enough to catch our breath. Yet at each pause we could hear the men who pursued us both coming closer and growing in numbers.

Fearing that we would not reach the *Black Falcon*, I decided to lead our trackers off into a merry chase. Beckoning to Fidor, I quickly outlined my plan. I told him to take the girl and the men and hasten to the *Black Falcon*; I would take a torch and wait for the pursuers to catch a glimpse of me before disappearing up an alley. The dourfaced old man protested ·violently, but I silenced his protests with a wave of my hand. I took a torch from one of the men and bid them to hurry on. They wished me well, the large brown eyes of the young girl looking up into my face tearfully. I smiled, nodded, and turned my back to them and waited for the men behind us to step into view.

I heard Fidor lead the men and young Jamilia off into the night and suddenly I found myself completely alone. Holding the torch over my head, I stepped quickly to the mouth of a foul-smelling alley that opened into the street and watched a large rat scurry from a garbage heap and disappear into the depths of the alley itself. The stench was nauseating. The filth was piled in large heaps and the light of my torch drew waves of flying insects as I passed by. One glance down the alley told me nothing and I hoped the alley would be open to escape for me. Yet I had no time to explore for from down the street came the shout of men's voices, and the clatter of heavily armed men breaking into a mad dash to capture me. I waved to them cheerily and then dashed off into the stench-filled alley.

And it was a merry run! Twice I had to scale rough plank fences, the pack of howling men always snapping at my heels. Several times the twang of a crossbow bolt glancing off stone walls came to my ears, and once a bolt from a marksman passed cleanly through the heavy cape I wore, only inches away from my body. Yet I held the men to a good distance as we hurried through twisting, smelly alleys and plunged into the darkness of narrow streets that led to parts of the city I was only vaguely familiar with. Behind me my pursuers, I soon discovered, were remnants of Thordak's little party joined by the dark robes of Pictii priests. The Pictii, being a religious order, were barred from carrying the blades of swords or knives, as these weapons were reserved for the Caste of Warriors only. But in the hands of each Pictii I could see the heavy cudgel with long iron spikes for added killing power or the iron-spiked ball of a heavy war mace. And I knew that in their hands these were terrible weapons. Yet as I fled down the alleys and back streets of the city, I found myself enjoying this chase. Dodging around corners, fleeing up blackened alleys, hearing the hiss of crossbow bolts sizzling past my ears I found to be invigorating. Grinning foolishly as I ran headlong into another darkened alley, I soon found my grin turning to a scowling mask of fury when the alley abruptly ended in a stone wall that completely blocked off any further escape. I was trapped! Whirling, I lifted my sword up and quickly extinguished my torch, the noise of my pursuers growing louder with each passing moment. I found the alley was enclosed on three sides with blank, cold stone walls that held neither window nor door. Cursing myself for being a fool, I silently hurried up to the opening of the alley and laid my back up against one cold stone wall and glimpsed out into the street. To my chagrin I viewed between forty and fifty warriors and Pictii priests milling about in the middle of the street exactly in front of the alley I believed was soon to be my tomb. They appeared confused, their torches filling the night air with harsh yellow light, reflecting coldly off the steel of their weapons. Cursing silently to myself again, I started to turn and slink deeper into the alley but something out of the corner of my eye made me halt and look up. The shadow of a man, in heavy robes, leaping across the gap from one building to another, came to me in the light of the moon. Amazed, I blinked a couple of times and rubbed a hand across my eyes in wonder. Was I seeing phantoms? Were the low flying, fast moving clouds creating strange shadows with the moonlight and making me think a robed figure leaped from building to building with the grace and ease of an acrobat? Shaking my head, I looked up again to see. For a full minute a cloud slid across the sky and blocked the moonlight from my eyes, throwing everything into a darkness in which nothing could be seen. But then moonlight suddenly flooded the night again and I saw the dark-robed figure leap high into the air and span a gap between two buildings no mere mortal could possibly have leaped successfully. Holding back a grunt of amazement, I saw the strangely robed creature leap one last building and disappear behind a wall. Amazed, I wondered who this mysterious figure was but had no time to think about it, for several Pictii priests and warriors in the uniform of the House of Kandar turned, with torches in their hands, and started to approach my position.

Grimly I prepared myself for the last fight of my life. Slinking back deeper into the alley I took a good grip on my sword and stepped out into the middle of the dark alley. And then to my ears came the sound of something scraping lightly across the wall behind me! Whirling, I saw through the dimness the long strand of a light rope dangling from the rooftop into the alley. Looking up, I saw the robed shadow of the mysterious leaper standing practically above me, his feet spread apart to brace himself as if to lift a heavy weight. And through the darkness I heard the voice whispering to me.

"Warrior! Warrior! Hurry! Grab the rope and scale the wall! Hurry! For they are almost upon you!"

"Aye, that they are!" I growled, sheathing my blade and taking hold of the rope quickly.

Halfway up the moist stone wall someone below me yelled as he discovered my escape route, and then suddenly the wall around me was a racket of crossbow bolts clattering off the stone. Then the mail given to me by old Fadah came to my rescue! The old armorer said that the sturdy chain mail given to me and to the Lord was impervious to almost anything, and that night I went a long way in proving that statement. As I reached up with a hand and took a firm hold of the outstretched hand of the mysterious figure, a crossbow bolt hit me squarely between the shoulders with a stunning, numbing blow. A blow that, by all rights, should have killed me. Any other chain mail and the bolt would have passed through it and my entire body, for crossbows are extremely powerful. But the mail of Fadah the Armorer, made of steel using the secret formula of the Ancient Kings, cast the bolt aside and I yet lived. The blow had been so intense that I gasped for breath, my arms numbed and my body racked with pain. But the grip of the robed figure was strong and powerful, and he quickly pulled me over the lip of the building and laid me gently down on the rooftop.

"You are wounded?"

"No, the mail made the blow glance off."

"But it squarely hit! I saw that with my own eyes!"

"Aye, but I need only to catch my breath and we'll be off again," I said, slowly moving my arms about to regain some feeling in them. As I looked into the darkness, I saw the moonlight fill the face of the mysterious Charolarl Priest with bright white light. "Aye. I should have known it would be you, priest. And glad that you came to my rescue I am too! But next time, try to save me with a little more time to spare, eh? These narrow escapes are harrowing experiences for old men of my age."

"Chatter some other time, warrior. We must hurry and find your master. I have grave news for him and we cannot tarry about."

"Aye, you are right there, priest." I growled, coming to my feet and gritting my teeth from pain. "Lead on, priest! Lead on!"

We quickly fled, leaving behind us a howling pack of infuriated pursuers. After about a half hour of leaping from one rooftop to another, we stopped to catch our breath. Looking at the face of the hook-nosed, brown-haired priest, I wiped sweat from my brow, and watched the robed figure pull from the depths of his toga a small bottle made of hard stone.

"Drink, my friend. Cheap wine it is, but something to give you an ounce of strength perhaps."

I nodded, took the stone flask and lifted it to my lips. It was only wine purchased with a few copper coins, but as it slid down my throat, it tasted like the nectar of the gods. Handing the flask back to the priest, I nodded my thanks and watched him place it back into his robe.

"We must hurry. The whole city has been aroused by the House of Kandar, and your master is to be arrested tonight. And any who claim to be followers of the Sa'yen and resist the troops sent to arrest your master are to be put to the sword without fail! The House of Kandar has even ordered two of their most powerful skyships to capture the *Black Falcon* as well. So you see, haste bids us move as fast as possible."

"Aye, that we will do shortly, priest. But tell me where is old Fadah to be found at this hour? The granddaughter informed us that he had left with you hurriedly at the stroke of midnight and she appeared worried. Where is he?"

The priest glanced down at the roof of the tall building we stood on, sadly sighed, and then looked into my face before answering. "He's dead, warrior."

"Dead? By whose hands?" I growled, suddenly enraged, for the old armorer had been but a simple and gentle man.

"By the hands of the Pictii. We came upon the shop of the old armorer right after you rescued his granddaughter from the hands of Thordak and his men. Bodies still cluttered the street in front of the old man's shop, including the body of Thordak himself. Unfortunately a group of Pictii priests entered the street as well and saw us. One of them lifted a crossbow and shot. The bolt passed cleanly through the old man."

"And you fled, leaving him dying, perhaps alive, on the street to be delivered into the hands of the Pictii?" I snarled, stepping closer to the priest in my rage, my hands curling into hard fists as I glared at the robed figure.

"He was close to death, warrior, when I left him. It was his wish that I do so. I laid him gently on the stones of the street and heard him whisper to me his last words. He wanted me to hurry and join the following of the Sa'yen. He wanted me to make sure his granddaughter fell into the arms of her betrothed. I promised him that she would just before I left him. I followed you through the streets of the city. I never could catch up with you because of the warriors who followed you. Not until you led them off into a fruitless chase was I able to help in any way."

I said nothing for some time, my rage too intense for me to speak. The death of the old man seemed senseless, pointless to me, and I had no understanding as to why the old man had to die. But then, I had not heard from the lips of the priest what had been so important in talking to the old armorer that far into the night. Looking at the robed figure, I started to ask him but my tongue was

stilled when off in the night we heard the thundering roar
of cannon fire. In the moonlight we could see off in the
distance the tower the *Black Falcon* was moored to. And
reflecting from the billowing white sails, the moonlight revealed to us the sight of two massive ships tacking into the
wind, their yardarms filled with every inch of canvas they
could carry on the upper and keel masts, their cannons
bellowing broadside after staggering broadside out toward
the *Black Falcon*. The two ships were the largest the
House of Kandar commanded, and they were coming in
just a bit higher than the *Black Falcon*. In the night, with
the wind still blowing fiercely and the clouds still racing
across the face of the moon, we saw canvas appear as if
by magic on the upper and keel masts of the *Black Falcon*. The black-hulled ship, once an Aggarian pirate's
vessel, heeled away from the landing tower it had been
moored to and shot away furiously. And it fled not away
from the attacking warships, but directly at them! Stunned,
I yelled furiously at the top of my voice for Fidor or Tallsus to take the helm and heave the black-hulled vessel
around to escape! But suddenly the hull of the *Black Falcon* disappeared into a wall of fire-spitting smoke and fury
as it delivered its first broadside to one of the approaching
warships. Holding my breath, I waited for the wind to
blow the smoke away into the night, disregarding the quiet
urgings of escape the priest was whispering to me. I had to
see if the *Black Falcon* yet survived. And I cheered like a
madman at the sight I saw. The *Black Falcon* yet lived!
And not only lived, but had wreaked havoc upon the
closest warship of the House of Kandar. Tallsus's gunnery
had completely carried away the keel masts and the upper
mizzenmast of the attacking warship, leaving the crippled
ship to flounder in the wind above the city uselessly.
Seeing the damage done to her sister ship so easily by a
much smaller ship, the second vessel of the House of Kandar heeled hard over and gave way to the oncoming *Black
Falcon*. I cheered loudly at the short but sweet fight and
then frowned. The *Black Falcon* was making no attempt to
flee the city and escape into the night. She was instead
coming directly toward us proudly, all sails set and filled
with wind, and looking to me like the proud, hungry bird

she was. Yet it made no sense that the Sa'yen did not try to escape while He had a chance. Already from the roofs of a hundred landing towers I could hear the long trumpets of the various houses of nobility blaring into the night, their calls warning all that an enemy warship was above the city, making crews of a hundred ships come alive to meet the attack. At first it did not make sense to me—this sudden foolish show of fierce pride. And although my heart filled with a glowing surge of pride and excitement at this show of daring, yet I wished for the Lord to take the *Black Falcon* on a new course that promised a chance of escape. And then it hit me suddenly as to what the Lord had in mind. He wanted to rescue us! Disregarding the hundreds of warships floating above the city and those setting sail to meet Him in combat, the Lord was determined to rescue us if at all possible. I shook the thin, robed priest joyfully, laughing like a fool.

"Come! We must make a fire! Quickly let us set fire to this building!"

"What? What do you babble, warrior? We must escape! Not create a funeral pyre for ourselves! Come, let us flee!"

"Flee? Flee? Can you not see the Lord is coming to rescue us? Look!"

And I pointed to the *Black Falcon*, all sails set, spewing out expertly timed broadsides at ships that had rashly come too close to her! For a moment or two the Charolarl Priest looked at the sight of the black-hulled ship approaching us in silent amazement. I grinned, let him go, and started to look around the rooftop for anything that might be used to make a fire. Finding many empty crates of wood, I made a large stack, and then started cursing loudly and obscenely. I had no flint or striker to make flames. Cursing like a deranged madman, I leaped to the edge of the tall building we stood on and threw my cape from my shoulders. With both hands I began waving, hoping that in the moonlight one of the *Black Falcon's* crew might see us. Yet I held no real hopes. From every quarter of the sky, ships were closing in on the *Black Falcon*, and the thunder of cannon fire was filling the night. Waving the cape back and forth over my head, I watched the gunnery of Tallsus demast another foolish ship that had tried to subdue the *Black Falcon* in a roaring broadside of fire and smoke. Standing on the rooftop I could hear all through the city the blaring trumpets of warning carried faintly in the wind, and the drumming cadence of hundreds of ship's fifers signaling their crews to their stations. And then behind me there was the sudden intake and whoosh of an explosion, and the pile of wooden crates went up in a column of white fire too intense to look upon. Leaping to my side, the Charolarl Priest nodded his head and smiled faintly.

"You have your fire, warrior. Let us hope they understand what it means."

"The Lord will know, priest. Believe me."

And He did! Almost at once we saw a large portion of the crew swarming down into the rigging of the keel masts, several holding large coils of ropes in their arms. And then faintly in the distance we heard the booming voice of the Lord Himself yelling into the night at us.

"Ahoy, Magdar! Are you capable of hauling in grappling hooks?"

Ah, such a sweet, powerful voice to my ears! I was cheering, tears running down my cheeks, gleefully pounding on the frail, thin back of the Charolarl Priest at the same time. Throwing the cloak over my shoulders again, I cupped hands around my mouth and yelled out we were more than eager to take in grappling hooks.

"And the Charolarl Priest is with me too, Master!"

"Good! Stand by to catch grappling hooks!" the Lord boomed, the *Black Falcon* now a massive black object almost over our heads and moving at an incredible speed.

Behind us a cannon ball smashed into the rooftop, showering the priest and myself with splinters and almost knocking us from the lip of the building itself. The fire behind us was rapidly consuming the roof and the heat was beginning to singe the edges of my cape. On either side of the *Black Falcon* large warships had descended from superior heights to give battle, while hundreds of other sails filled the night air and were bearing down on her. Broadside after broadside was being pumped into the night air by the *Black Falcon*, and was returned by the larger ships on either side of her. But amazingly little damage was being done to her by the fire of the two ships flanking her sides, whereas the gunnery of Tallsus was devastating. With each broadside, the *Black Falcon* shot away huge chunks of the attacking ships, the pieces of wood ripped away from their hulls and fluttering down to crash into the city streets below us. The road of cannon fire from hundreds of ships was numbing to my ears, and at each passing moment increasing in intensity. Yet I cared little of the sound but watched men in the rigging of the keel masts heave through the night air the grappling hooks attached to heavy ropes.

Each of us caught a hook with our hands, and as the ship and her keel masts sped directly over our heads, only fifty or sixty feet above us, we both took firm grips on the ropes, placed a foot into the curved shank of the large iron grappling hook, and waited for the jolting, snapping wrench that would sweep us away from the burning roof-top. And it came almost immediately. With a suddenness that almost ripped my hold from the rope, the ship flew over the burning tower and the priest and I were quickly swept up and flung madly through the towering pillar of fire. But the speed of the *Black Falcon* was enough to sweep us through the tongue of fire so quickly as not to seriously harm us. I felt intense burning pain and then sudden cold. And then strong hands started hauling in the ropes even as the battle raged on about us fiercely as more ships came in to try their luck against the Lord's master gunner.

And I was laughing! Laughing like a madman in delight as cannons belched out broadside after broadside of fire and smoke, the air filled with screaming shot and shell. I was a follower of the Sa'yen! And nothing could stop the Lord!

IX

——•◉•——

The Grief of the Gods

For days after escaping the howling mob of Pictii Priests, I had been watching the Master and the Charolarl Priest. On the night of our escape, while the building the priest and I stood on blazed brightly in the night sky, the storm which had been brewing for most of the night finally struck. And struck with such fury that for hours our only hope was to save the *Black Falcon* from running aground on the rocks cliffs above and below Triisus. But it was the storm which had permitted us to escape the raging battle above the mountain city. We had, for five straight days, been riding the strong winds of the storm's vanguard and were now far south of the mountain city I once called home.

But in those five days little had I seen of the Lord. For most of those five days the priest and the Master had been locked in His cabin, discussing what I knew not. Yet, from the look on His face when He did appear on deck, I saw ill-winds were building. The Lord had the look of a man on the run, as if pursued by demons only He could fully understand. His face was drawn and haggard, with bags under His eyes from lack of proper rest. I knew personally He had touched little food or drink. And I worried over the Lord's health.

And the priest looked even worse in his ways. He too ate little and drank hardly enough to stay alive and I wondered to myself about what the Lord and this Charolarl Priest talked so intensely. But for days there was nothing I

137

could do while the Lord and the priest stayed cloistered in the Lord's cabin.

There was for me, however, much to do. I had a ship to command. A ship that had been damaged in combat and needed repairs and I had a crew, a fresh crew barely settled in, to train and hone to a fine edge. For I was sure, on whatever the priest was informing the Master, the crew of the *Black Falcon* would be severely tested in the days and weeks to come. So I drilled the men in gunnery, in the making of sail rapidly and that of taking in sail. I screamed in fury when things were done wrong, praised those who pleased me and my demands and rewarded with good ale and a copper coin or two those who improved in their assignments. But I was rarely pleased and praised few. Sailing only a few hundred feet above valleys of virgin forests, we paused often to moor above a small clearing to hunt, gather Yab'la and Kakla wood and make repairs. And it did not take long to have the *Black Falcon* back in full readiness for the Lord's bidding.

It was on the sixth day that The Lord and the priest emerged from His cabin. finally to take in the beauty of the valley floor we hovered above motionlessly on stout mooring ropes. It was in the cool of the early evening, just after the sun had set behind high mountain walls, when it seems all things are serene and at peace with the world, that the Master joined me at the stern railing of the ship. He wore plain leather trousers, high boots and a simple cotton shirt. Strapped to His waist was a simple belt and scabbard. But in the scabbard was the blade of Fadah, the Armorer. A blade similar to mine. A blade that no other mortal maker of weapons had equaled in beauty and balance.

For some time He said nothing but stood beside me, peering out over the valley floor of dark green forest, hands behind His back and a look of infinite sadness in His eyes. I too, said nothing, fearing the Lord's thoughts were infinitely more important and not to be disturbed. Yet, as ill and unsettled as the Lord appeared, glad was I that He finally had come on deck to take in fresh air and view open spaces. And I waited for the Master to break His silence, if He so wished. Or not to, feeling pleased and honored just to have His magnificence standing beside me. What cared I of what lay ahead of us? Was I not a follower of the Sa'yen? Was I not called the Left Hand of the Lord? He had but to command me and His will would have been done. If He so ordered, I would have scaled the long walls of imperial Hakad itself barehanded, and died gladly, in the attempt. I believed then I had found my God. And I was content to be with Him.

Tallsus came up quickly behind us, bent to one knee in deep homage to the Lord and quickly rose. The Lord still frowned upon all those who thus honored Him but He had resigned Himself to accepting the practice. Those on board the *Black Falcon* were men of the Sa'yen. And we, to a man, felt our God had to be honored thusly.

I stepped from His side to hear Tallsus's question. It was of no importance and giving him instruction as to what to do, I also told the ship's master gunner to bring wine and cheese for the Lord, and also to have the crew rig tarps above the deck so as to keep the evening hawks and other brids, as well as approaching rain, off Our Master. It was my discussion of orders with Tallsus which broke the Master's reverie. He sighed, smiled sadly and looked at me for the first time in days.

"Madgar, you are a true friend."

"Aye, Lord. And even a better servant," I answered freely.

"I do not wish you to be a servant. Only a friend."

I said nothing to this but kept my eyes on His face. There are many things I, a simple Ha'valli warrior, do not understand about the Lord. But the one thing I could least understand was His sadness that sometimes filled His very soul. At times it was, this sadness, all consuming. I have never before seen such weighty concerns burden a man's shoulders, And here was my God, the Sa'yen, weighted with such heavy burdens, I wished to come to my knees, head bowed, and plead with Him to allow me to relieve some of His grief. But I was, and still am, just a simple warrior. I stood before Him, concerned and worried, but silent. I knew in time He would tell me what He wished me to know and that was enough for me.

"Magdar, old friend. Tell me, do you believe in the many legends of the Ancient Kings?"

"Believe, Lord?" I muttered, confused. "What is there not to believe? The tales of the Ancient Kings are told over and over again around campfires, over supper table, everywhere in our lives. They were once mighty and wondrous. Rulers of Hungar! I do not know what You mean when You ask such a question."

The Lord nodded, sadness again in His eyes, and He sighed heavily. For a moment or two He gazed back behind us, watching the ship's crew expertly rig up the overhead tarp, bringing tables up from the galley laden with food and finally, folding canvas chairs for Him and others to sit on in the evening twilight. He watched for a while and then returned His gaze to me.

"Magdar, have I ever said I was the Sa'yen?" he asked in a soft, quiet voice.

"No, Lord," I answered firmly. "But it is not expected of You."

"And you still think me a god?"

"Aye. The only true one! The Sa'yen!"

"And nothing will ever change your mind?"

I paused, and looked into His eyes deeply. Was this a test of my convictions? Did the Lord somehow know of the doubts which had assailed me? And finally, did I truly believe Him to be the Sa'yen? For some time I held back, not trusting myself and my answer. And then from deep within me came a sudden swell of emotion as to be undeniable in its power. I believed! Woe to those who doubted me. I believed! I was of the Sa'yen!

"Lord, you are the Sa'yen, and nothing, nothing on the face of Hungar will ever shake my faith!"

It was if I had stabbed Him in the heart. He closed His eyes in real pain, trying to hold back the tears. One slid slowly down His right cheek. But he opened His eyes again and looked at me.

"I am no god, Magdar! I am no god! I am mortal, just as you. I will die just as you. And because I am not what you think I am, I cannot live with the idea others are willing to die for me because they believe me to be their god!"

"But Lord, it is said by all our prophets even the true Sa'yen will not know His divinty."

"But your prophets could be wrong, Magdar. They could have mistaken something far in the past as godlike but not actually that of a god. Listen, I know I speak to you in riddles at times, but believe what I tell you. Do not doubt what I tell you. I am not the Sa'yen! I am just a mortal creature, fallen from another star in a fiery chariot once described by an ancient prophet long in the dim past who saw a similar happening.

"But old friend, listen to my words carefully. I am here not by accident. I came of my own free will on a mission of much importance!"

"Aye, Lord. You came to load your followers on the Wha'ta. The Sacred Pilgrimage."

"No!" The Lord let loose a scream of anguish and pain which startled and frightened those who were close enough to hear, a scream of such real pain I shall never forget. "Do you not see? Cannot you understand what I say? Gods are not real, Magdar! If they exist, and I have my doubts any exist at all, they would not come to their following in the guise of a simple warrior. Or a mere mortal. They would come in all their power and glory and show one and all what they truly wore."

I shook my head and frowned at such talk. The Lord's ramblings were far too deep for me to comprehend. Yet I could see the pain in the Master's face, and the looks of fear and worry in the faces of the ship's crew who kept a respectable distance around us. Frowning, I ordered them all to leave the deck to the Lord and myself and turned my eyes back onto the Master. I then took a great liberty upon myself by taking hold of the Master's arm gently. I had to say something to relieve the pain that was in my Lord's breast.

"My Lord . . ." I began. But He kept His face turned from me and would not listen. Glancing to see if the crew was indeed far enough away, I stepped closer to the Lord and looked at His strong profile again and spoke in a lowered, quieter voice, "Alexander, listen to me!"

Had not the Master, months ago high in the Tors

Mountains, first called Himself but just a mortal by the name of Alexander Synn? Aye, it was then when I knew this man was my god. When He said His divine name to me, a name only used by one god to another in the High Halls of Heaven, I knew then the Sa'yen was again with us on Hungar.

And the Lord looked at me sharply, hope in His eyes, a light I had ignited by using His godkin's name and I had to speak in such a way as to help Him remove some of His sadness.

"Alexander, even if You are not the True One, the Sa'yen, yet men believe you are. Men believe! All on this ship, millions on this planet have all been praying that the Sa'yen would come and lead them on the Wha'ta. I . . . I have at times wondered to myself that perhaps You are not the Lord. But even if you are not, do You not see what You bring to those who wish for the Sa'yen? You bring hope, My Lord, hope! Hope that through you, the evil which grows in this world will be exorcised. Hope that all men will grow as brothers to one and another. Hope that life, so cruel and merciless to many of us, will again be like that of the long cherished memories of our ancestors. A time when life was good and peace, everywhere, prevailed!"

"But what of the Wha'ta, Magdar? Why a sacred Pilgrimage to the south?"

"My Lord, prophets have come and gone through the ages. But all of our prophets have claimed one thing. In the south is the last stronghold of the Ancient Kings. And it is there the Sa'yen will take all of us in order to bring back the glory of the Ancient Kings and to have the Ancient Kings rule again all of Hungar!"

Suddenly He grabbed me with a grip which I thought would crush my very shoulders. And there was a look of anger, of madness in His eyes I had never before seen. I was unprepared for what he was to say next.

"What if I told you I have stood before those you call Ancient Kings, Magdar? What if I told you that I, only a mortal, on other worlds you cannot possibly know of, have actually killed creatures you call Ancient Kings? Would that not be blasphemy, Magdar? Would that not, at last, shake your belief in who you think I am? Tell me, Magdar, would it? Would it?"

I was without words! I felt as if I had been smitten with a heavy blow and left for dead. The Sa'yen, a killer of Ancient Kings? It, it was not so! Something deep within me had been badly battered and I felt weak. And He saw the deep shaken feeling in my eyes and He nodded, a smile hidden underneath His blond beard. Pleased, He suddenly let me go. Running, He leaped atop the railing which was above the ship's maindeck and lifted His arms high above His head. Men turned to look at their Lord. As I did. But I felt dazed and confused. I no longer knew what to think. My head ached fiercely and I felt lost inside. But I turned to listen to the Lord.

"Listen to me!" He shouted in a voice which would carry for miles in its richness and splendor. "I stand before you as one who denies all who claim me as their god. I am not the Sa'yen! I am a fellow mortal, a creature such as you, from a different time and place.

"But I come before you to tell you that soon, soon forces such as you have never before imagined will spring upwards and death and destruction will ravage all whom you love and cherish. I come before you to tell you they you call the Ancient Kings, those whom you have worshipped in your hearts, yet live on this planet. But live not to bring peace and harmony to one and all but destruction and famine."

I heard people gasp in surprise, growl in disbelief and mutter to themselves. Men came up from below to listen to the Lord and all faces were turned to look upon Him. He stood, feet apart, hands above His head, on the hard wooden railing of the poop deck looking down on the ship's crew and there was such a look of anger on His face as to be called incredible.

"I am not your god called the Sa'yen. But I am your friend from a far place. Your ally. And I did come to save you. Those whom you call Ancient Kings are our enemies. Those your mothers and fathers prayed would again return to their power and glory would do so only at your destruction. And it is the Pictii, and many within the following who claim to obey the teachings of the Sa'yen's prophets who lead you astray. False followers, agents of the Ancient Kings, are leading you to your destruction. They keep alive the false legends and myths about how the Ancient Kings were once good kings and fair rulers, but you all will soon die from such deception.

"Heed me! I have looked upon the faces of the Ancient Kings. I have fought those called Ancient Kings and I know what they truly are. They are evil! They are vicious! And they are ones who work their ways upon you even as I speak. Their goals are to kill you, your loved ones and all on this planet who call themselves human. They aim to murder all who believe in justice, in peace and in fairness. I know, for I have fought them since my early youth. I know what they are. And they are of the darkest forms of evil."

The ship was alive with men whispering heatedly in groups, wondering at the Lord's words. For some seconds the Sa'yen watched the men, lowering His arms slowly. And I? I could but stand behind Him motionless. I knew not what to think. But someone below on the maindeck pushed his way through the crowd and jumped atop the lower rigging of the mainmast. I recognized the lad as a younger member of the mainmast's rigging crew. A good lad with sword or musket. And even better with the handling of sail.

"Lord, I do not understand. Why would the Ancient Kings, and the Pictii, wish to destroy us? What can we do to gods? We are but human!"

"Aye, you are but human." The Lord began again, His voice strong and powerful and driven by something inside Him I cannot describe. But He held us all in rapture. It was something wonderful and exciting to stand on deck that night and listen to Him speak. "Just as human as I! Things I know about the Ancient Kings but cannot yet speak of are too hidious to describe. But what I tell you now you must believe. The Ancient Kings are not human. They do not breathe as we do! They do not live as we do. They do not die as we do.

"They are from a far past so old that even I cannot tell you how old they are. But I tell you this. Those who have told you they are, and were, benevolent, that once they ruled this world with a hand of kindness and love have all lied to you. And if you do not rise up and face your foe with a stout heart and firm hand they whom you call Ancient Kings will surely strike you down and crush you mercilessly."

The crew went into an uproar, arguing with each other; many stood to one side in silent thought, while others stood motionless and too numb to speak. For long, agonizing minutes, as I stepped closer to the Lord in anticipation, I wondered to myself what the crew as a whole would do. The Lord, in His infinite wisdom, had tried His best to shake the very core of a Hungar's beliefs. He had shaken mine severely with his words. And yet, I knew not how I actually felt. As a Ha'valli warrior, the tales of the Ancient Kings had not had for me the deep religious connotations that they had for the citizens of the northern cities. To the Ha'valli, the Sa'yen was the only god. The Sa'yen would lead; the Ha'valli would follow. For years such simple beliefs had been enough for me.

As my eyes went from one face to the next in the crowd below, my hand was on the hilt of my sword. I had called the Lord by his godkin's name. I had even confessed to Him my earlier doubts. And as confused as I felt about the Master's words, one thing I was positive of. If mutiny swept through the crew of the *Black Falcon* and danger loomed before my Lord, I would bare cold steel and fight to preserve His life. Even if it meant paying with mine.

But to my ears came a chant which began to swell through the ranks and rise in volume, a chant which brought tears both to my eyes and to the Lord's! It began with just one voice, that of old dour-face Fidor, with others adding to it with each passing second. Some reluctantly, some excitedly, and yet the excitement and thrill swept through the ranks of the crew with astonishing speed. In moments the entire ship's crew, as if one, were shouting at the tops of their lungs. And it was a simple chant, truly a simple, yet powerful chant.

"Lead us. Lead us. Lead us. LEAD US! LEAD US! LEAD US!! LEAD US!!"

And the Lord cried like a newborn babe before His children.

X

Hakadians on the Horizon

It is no easy task to practice with the rapier against the Lord. He demands much of those He practices with, and it appears I am the only one that gives Him any competition with cold steel. Others have tried, including even the gray-robed Charolarl Priest. But the Lord quickly penetrates their defenses and with a flick of His wrist disarms the unlucky opponent with a casual ease. It is, by some reason I do not understand, a different story when I face the Master. It is not that I ever win a match against Him. It is just that He takes a much longer time to reach inside my guard and touch me with the blunted point on my chain mail. And frankly, it is not unknown for me to penetrate His defense and touch Him for a point with the blunted tip of my sword. I do not understand why He allows me to do this, but I do not believe, as others have suggested, that I am as good a swordsman on occasion as He is and thus can score points. How can a mere mortal be as good as the Sa'yen? Yet it gives me a great sense of satisfaction when He drops His guard once in a great while and allows me to touch Him with the blunted sword tip. This is a great pleasure and more importantly a great honor.

We were practicing on the *Black Falcon*'s poop deck, underneath the mizzenmast behind the great spoked wheel that is the ship's helm. We were a comfortable and contented crew, with many of the men stripped to the waist and gathered about watching us. It was a warm, extremely hu-

mid day and I for one had sweat rolling off me in great
streams, stinging my eyes and making it difficult for me to
see properly. A thousand feet below, the country was a
vast, unbroken forest of Yab'lal and Kakla trees which ran
on and on, flanked in the far distance by the purple and
snow-capped ragged line of high mountains. We were far
south of Triisus, in a much warmer climate and in rugged
country I was only vaguely familiar with. The Lord
wanted us to journey to the Black Pillar Mountains, a long
voyage by any standards and filled with many lurking dangers. For to journey to the Black Pillars we would have to
travel up the mountain passes that led to the Great
Plateau. And the Great Plateau was controlled by the
ships of the Hakadians, for only four hundred miles to the
south of the pass we intended to ascend the walled towers
of Hakad itself, reputed by many to be the oldest city
still occupied on the face of Hungar. How we would ascend the mountain passes, with Hakadian ships moored
and floating above the fortress towers, I could little imagine. Those problems I allowed the Sa'yen to solve. For He
was the Lord, and I but a mere mortal. Yet I knew the
journey was destined to swirl the air with cannon fire,
spent powder smoke, and dying men. I knew the Hakadians would not willingly allow us to pass over the Great
Plateau if they perceived who we were.

But fate decided to step in and play her hand. Even the
Lord could not disregard the scheming plans Lady Fate
held in store for us. As we sailed under full canvas, with a
light breeze which barely gave us steerage, from the crow's
nest high above us on the mainmast came the call that a
foreign sail was sighted. And as we lined the starboard
railing the sailor above us yelled to us that he counted
twenty sails, all ships carrying sail cut to the Hakadian set.
I sent more eyes up with looking glasses for a better view.
But the first hail was not changed. Twenty sail, all of Hakadian set, running roughly parallel with us. Looking at the
Lord, I saw Him give me a nod that was barely percepti-
ble, and with that I ordered the helm to swing to the port
by ten degrees. I also ordered more sail to be set, for if the
Hakadians saw us I had little doubt they would try to
use every broadside they could against us to blast us out

of the sky. We still held the markings of a black-hull, an Aggarian pirate, and none of the Hakadians would hesitate in being the first to conquer and claim us as his prize. Or so I thought. For not more than fifteen minutes after setting the new course and steering away from the golden-hulls of the Hakadians, the lookouts above hailed down to the deck that another twenty sails had been sighted. But this time, all black-hulls. Aggarian pirates! Astounded, I took a looking glass from a sailor and lifted it to my eyes as the Lord quickly strode up to stand by me.

"Is it true, Magdar? Aggarians? In such numbers?"

"Aye, Lord! Look for yourself! Twenty black-hulls, and in perfect formation, like the best of any Hakadian fleet, they are too. And do You see? From every mast of each ship the pirates show banners and pennants. They come not to fight, Lord, but to bargain. And they come in strength."

The Lord held the glass up to His bearded face and peered through it for some time. The black-hulls were on an intercepting course with the Hakadians, with a great black-hull of huge dimensions leading the pirate squadron. I knew the ship well, with her highly painted mainsails depicting warriors in battle with legendary beasts, and I nodded and smiled grimly. Taking a second looking glass from Fidor, I lifted it to my eye and peered through it for a long time, examining as many of the black-hulled ships as I could.

"Lord, train Your glass on the ship leading the caravan. Do You see her size and note her sails?"

"Indeed, Magdar. I noticed that the moment I took the glass in hand," the Lord answered, His voice deep and commanding yet quite relaxed. "A very important pirate lord, I suspect. Eh?"

"The most powerful of them all, My Lord!" I exclaimed, dropping the glass down and looking into His golden-bearded face. "Yonder skyship is the *Black Emperor*, commanded by Virgantrix, King of the Aggarian Pirate Lair, himself! And worse, I note that the *Black Pearl* and the *Black Prince* and the *Black Hawk* sail immediately behind Virgantrix. Sire, each of those ships I have mentioned is captained by a leader of the Aggarian

Pirate Lair. And if Hakba Baru had the *Black Falcon* with him, it too would be in the forefront of the caravan. These pirates plan to rendezvous with the Hakadians!"

"But for what purpose, Magdar?" Fidor growled, stepping up to my shoulder and scowling as he peered out at the approaching pirate fleet.

"I have no idea, old friend," I said truthfully.

"Ah, but perhaps the reason is obvious?" the Lord muttered, a sudden twinkling in His eyes as He smiled at us and snapped the looking glass in His hand closed. "Perhaps the Aggarians come to greet the Hakadians and possibly join forces with the golden-hulls of Hakad?"

"Join forces!" the gray-robed priest exclaimed, for once losing completely the iron discipline of his emotions and registering plain surprise. "And what would the Aggarians gain by joining forces with a foe they have fought against for a thousand years?"

"Aye, a good question indeed." I nodded, just as surprised as the priest at the Lord's statement. "I cannot see what the Aggarians would gain by joining forces with the Hakadians. They are enemies, these two. Why, if they joined forces, there would be no power in Northern Hungar that could stand before them."

The Lord turned to look upon me with His deep blue eyes, and He smiled at me, pleased at my statement. He honored me by placing one of His hands on my bare arm and shaking me fondly in His grip.

"You grasp the implications of this move more swiftly than I would have thought possible, friend Magdar. And you are correct! Combined, Hakad would need not worry that any power would defeat them, in taking Triisus, for instance. And Bahir Kandar, as a puppet prince for the Emperor of Hakad, with an Hakadian and Aggarian pirate fleet at his disposal, would rule Triisus with little fear of revolt, eh? Perhaps, for the House of Kandar, the turmoil of electing a new King of Triisus goes badly for them. A sudden coup, a show of force and an overthrow of the elected government by overwhelming power, would be better suited to the House of Kandar. Aye, there are advantages for the Aggarian pirates to join forces with their ancestrial enemies, Magdar. And I fear that is what is to happen soon."

"But My Lord!" I cried, paling at the thought of Triisus under the iron hand of Bahir Kandar, the Hakadians and the Aggarians all at once. "We must do something to save Triisus!"

"Yes," the Lord sighed heavily, looking out across the valley floor at the tiny specks that were the Aggarian ships. "I am afraid we will have to take time out from our quest and do something to save Triisus. Magdar, I am going below to plan what our next move shall be. Steer a course that keeps us within sight of the approaching fleets, but with an avenue for a fast escape if we are sighted. And then adjourn to my cabin at eight bells so that I may outline to you what we shall do next."

"Aye, Lord."

The Sa'yen was blessed that night, as He always was. Heavy, dark clouds rolled in at dusk to fill the sky with jagged shadows, and the huge red moon of Hungar lay partially hidden. Only a slight breeze stirred the night air, just enough to give us steerage using only the for'top sails and main'top sails. And we stood on the poop deck, cloaks wrapped around our bare shoulders and in armor, with swords drawn and gripped with whitened knuckles. The Lord was standing slightly in front of us, the point of His sword barely touching the ship's deck, His golden mane blowing gently with the breeze that filled our sails. And He was carefully watching how the helmsman was steering the *Black Falcon* into the midst of the enemy. We were, as if by a miracle, quietly and efficiently slipping in among the hulls of the black ships of the Aggarian pirates. And yet to be challenged by a suspicious guard of the watch! Around, above and below us were the dark and menacing black-hulls of the pirates. Only a few hundred feet below, on the floor of the forest valley, were thousands of campfires winking at us in the night. So still and silent was the night that we could clearly hear the laughing and boisterous voices of men relaxing around campfires and drinking stout ale. To our nostrils drifted the aromas of roasting meat and hot, delicious Thieves' Soup, a concoction of strong onions much favored by the pirates of the Aggarian

Mountains. As the Lord had told me earlier this evening, He believed that to penetrate the moored fleets of the pirates and Hakadians we only had to work our way slowly into the darkened mass of ships. All skyships of Hungar moored above the forested floor of some valley at night to take on cut Kakla wood for the fire pits within the ships and to allow the crew to hunt fresh game for their evening meals. This night the Hakadian and Aggarian fleets took in sail at dusk in a wide, fertile valley of virgin forest and moored there in a blanket of wooden ships floating lazily in the dying sunset.

Glancing at the Lord, I lifted my head in a silent prayer to the other gods of Hungar in thanks that I served the Sa'yen. For otherwise I would have labeled the plan we now were to embark on as being the plan of a madman. The Lord had a plan that would make a strong man's knees quake with fear, as indeed mine were. For the plan of the Lord was to slip as far into the combined fleets of the enemies of Triisus and, when assured that we were as close as possible to the unsuspecting Hakadians, rip the night asunder with flame and smoke by firing broadsides from the *Black Falcon*'s guns into both the pirate and Hakadian ships. And in the confusion guaranteed to follow, we were to slip through the fleet and make our escape into the dark night. I marveled at the daring and audacity of such a plan and was confident that whatever tender threads of cooperation had been made between the pirate and Hakadian lords would soon be cut and the old enmities again resume. With this assertion of sworn ancestral hate between Hakadian and Aggarian, there would be little chance the Hakadians could take the city of Triisus by a coup backed by the fleets of the pirates. Yet small tendrils of fear still clung to my chest, gripping me with such strength as to keep me from breathing naturally. The dangers of such a plan for the *Black Falcon* and its men! If they were to be faced by the breasts of mere mortals alone, I knew we would all be consumed in the combined fire of Hakadians and Aggarians. But the Lord was with us! He, with His golden beard and cold, gray-blue eyes, I knew would lead us safely through. And no matter how much I feared for my life, doubted His actual divinity, somehow I knew all would be well with Him guiding us.

To our ears came the sounds of ships moored for the night, not suspecting the chaos that was soon to awaken them. As we passed close to a black-hull, so close I could reach out with the tip of my sword and cut the rigging shrouds that held her main'mast in place, we saw a guard of the watch propping himself up as he slept soundly with the long pole of his halberd, the huge axe blade glistening in the light from the oil-burning torches on either side of him. Twice I heard a drunken sailor from within a hull singing off-key some ballad about whoring and fighting, which these Aggarian pirates were so fond of. And the Lord, in His excellence, stood close to the helmsman, sword in hand so that it appeared to us that the ship was a thousand miles away from imminent danger.

The huge moon of Hungar suddenly appeared from behind a large cloud, illuminating the night with a startlingly brilliant glow of white and red moonlight. I lifted my hand to shade my eyes from the sudden blinding brilliance, blinked several times to clear the tears that suddenly came to my eyes, my teeth gritted together, my hand shaking from holding the sword so tightly, my breath coming to me in shallow, quick gasps. It occurred to me I had all the symptoms of being terribly frightened but dismissed this foolish thought, reminding myself that I had been born and raised among the Ha'valli. And the Ha'valli were renowned the world over as being the fiercest, most audacious warriors ever to walk. But I felt humbled and foolish whenever I cast my eyes upon the Master. He stood so calm and assured on the deck before us, a smile on His lips, His face beaming with a soothing confidence that was beyond understanding. Even with the blinding light of the giant moon of Hungar, which the Lord has told me is almost the size of Hungar itself and has an atmosphere of its own, He seemed unperturbed by the thought we were now visible to every eye of the fleet if they so glanced in our direction. But out luck held and the moon suddenly vanished behind another cloud, throwing an inky blackness about us; many of the crew let out a sigh of relief.

The Lord lifted a hand and motioned for me to step up

to His side. I did so and He lifted a sword and pointed off to the starboard bow.

"There lies the first Hakadian ship, Magdar. We are almost in the midst of both fleets. Send a message down to Tallsus to have his guns double shotted for the first broadside. Thereafter he will alternate with solid shot and grapeshot. I want as much damage done to every ship's rigging that we pass as is possible."

"Aye, Lord, Your will be done!" I nodded, stepping back and giving His instructions to a young lad who was my runner to the gundeck.

I stepped back to the Lord's side and soon stepped away again to whisper on His orders to lessen sail but to keep the sail crews up in the spars, ready to throw all canvas to the wind the moment the first broadside was fired. I no sooner stepped back to His side from passing on this order than our luck suddenly ended with the voice of an Hakadian officer hailing us from the deck of his small, ten-gun golden hull.

The Lord grinned suddenly, leaped forward to the ship's railing and grasped part of the rigging to brace Himself with one hand and lifted His sword high into the air with the other. And as His sword came down, He yelled one word into the night.

"Fire!"

XI

In The Heat of Battle

The guns of Tallsus, so lovingly cared for and made ready for just this moment, ended the placid solitude of the night with a deafening and staggering roar. Flame shot out and curled around the ship, almost engulfing the *Black Falcon* with belching fire. And no sooner was the starboard broadside fired than the ship shuddered in the night sky, skidding to the starboard a bit as the port side ripped the night air with flame and smoke. I heard men crying out, screaming from mortal wounds, in the ships of both the Hakadians and Aggarian pirates, and I cheered. The fighting lust was boiling in my veins and I was ready to have a fiery and hard-fought battle. And so, apparently, was Tallsus! Amazingly the tall, thin-framed gunner reloaded both sides of the ship's guns and a second full broadside erupted into the night even before the first shattering cannonade and its echo had run their course booming up the forested valley. Above us, the crew assigned to the masts were busily unfurling all sails and tying them down fast. The *Black Falcon* was gathering speed rapidly even in the light breeze that blew, and the helm was coming about to give us the wind gauge. Yet we were not to flee from our sudden surprise attack without meeting some resistance. As I stepped up to where the Lord was standing at the railing of the ship, intending to pull Him back to the deck, a large Hakadian frigate suddenly loomed up into the night off our port side and let go a full broadside into us. The roar and furnacelike heat blasting into us

from her guns were overpowering. I heard the whining
sound of grapeshot cutting through canvas and rigging
above us, mixed with screams of men who had been hit.
And then the portside answered the Hakadian's challenge
with a roar of its own, making the ship skid to the starboard again as all guns fired at once. Through the eye-
watering, hot smoke of spent gunpowder I saw the
Hakadian's main'mast suddenly give and then, with astonishing rapidness, come crashing down and, in doing so, en-
tangling itself into our ship's upper rigging. Our port
erupted again in another roar of cannonfire, but by now so
many ships were firing madly into the night sky it hardly
came to my ears who had fired! The night was aflame with
ships burning, with guns firing, and with the sounds of
fierce battle around us. And the Lord's plan appeared to
be working perfectly from what glimpses I could see
through the growing cloud of smoke which was engulfing
the fleets. Hakadians and Aggarians, in their confusion,
were attacking each other, and the battle was rising ferociously by the minute. I would have cheered with glee at
this development but, with an Hakadian frigate's mainmast
entangled in our rigging and anchoring the Hakadian ship
to our side as if it were a part of us, I had no feeling but
cold dread. If we could not quickly slip away from the
grasp of the Hakadians, we were doomed. For if the Hakadian frigate's full crew was on her, overpowering numbers in manpower would soon end the fight for us.
Leaping through the smoke and fury of battle and screaming at the top of my lungs, I lined up two columns of
musketmen and hurried them to the port side with hopes
of being in time to save the ship.

Around me the battle increased by the second. The
boom of cannonfire was now rolling on and on like one
continuous roar, never slackening but growing in intensity.
The smoke from the gunpowder was growing so thick a
heavy fog had apparently settled in about us, blinding us
to what happened only a few feet away. And the stench
and acrid odor of spent gunpowder made my eyes fill with
tears and my nostrils burn. I hurried the musketmen to the
port side, and we had to leap from under falling block and
tackle that had been cut from our rigging by gunfire.

Bodies littered the slippery deck that had now grown to a deep ruby red in color from flowing blood.

A breeze blew a hole in the smoke, revealing to us the Lord standing in front of a boarding plank that had been thrown onto our deck by the Hakadians, battling desperately with sword in hand to push back the mass of warriors that were trying to board us. I saw the Lord cut down three men in the time it takes one to blink his eyes, and then surge forward into the mass of Hakadian warriors themselves. Desperate to save the Lord's life, for even the Sa'yen while He is in the body of a mere mortal will eventually die, I ordered my musketmen to kneel and fire at will. And then leaving them, I leaped across the body-littered deck, jumping the gap that separated the Hakadian ship from the *Black Falcon* easily and landed feet first on the deck of the Hakadian frigate. Behind, my musketmen fired a volley, their musket balls singing past my ears a merry tune of death as I hurried to come to the aid of the Lord. Hakadians fell from the volley, momentarily thrown into confusion, giving me time to reach the side of the Lord.

"There you are, Magdar!" the Lord yelled, running his sword through an Hakadian and grinning at me at the same time. "I wondered where you might have gone. I thought you had been wounded."

"Aye, we shall be, Lord!" I yelled, parrying a thrust from a poor Hakadian swordsman and making him pay dearly for his foolishness with the tip of my blade. "We shall be sorely wounded if we do not return to the deck of the *Black Falcon* at once."

"We are not on the *Black Falcon*, Magdar?" the Lord shouted back, cutting down another Hakadian with his sword as others rushed in to cut us down.

"Nay, Lord! In Your foolish lust for battle, Lord, You leaped from the *Black Falcon* and boarded this Hakadian scow. We both shall soon be surrounded by Hakadian dogs if we do not now make the attempt to return to our ship."

And to my surprise the Lord lifted His head and laughed at His foolishness. Laughed openly and as easily as a boy would laugh at the sight of a foolish clown. I

marveled at His boldness and confidence in Himself even
as more Hakadians came to join the fray. My sword
leaped to defend us from the many blades of the ven-
geance-crazed Hakadians. I dropped two warriors before
me and the Lord dropped another. I thought we were
about to meet our deaths then, for now it was too late to
retreat back to the deck of the *Black Falcon*, as we were
surrounded. But from the backs of the surrounding Hakadians we heard a cheering and then the crackling roar of
muskets going off in a single volley. My musketmen were
coming to our rescue! There was another volley of musket
fire and the ring of Hakadian warriors thinned perceptibly
from the fire. I had hopes of cutting our way out of this
deadly trap, with the aid of the muskets my men were
using expertly, when the most dreadful thing that can happen to any skyship happened. The *Black Falcon*, rigging
still entangled with the masts of the Hakadian frigate, continued to pour forth broadside after broadside from her
guns into the golden-hull. And with each broadside the
Hakadian ship staggered heavily. But then suddenly she
staggered deeply, heaved to the port in such a violent motion that all on her were thrown to the deck. Rolling, I
gripped a piece of fallen rope to brace myself and fought
my way back to my feet. The ship shuddered again from
an internal explosion and with it the entire prow went up
in flame and smoke. Again I was thrown to my back from
the force of the explosion, the hot, searing wind blowing
past me, wooden splinters from the explosion whistling
dangerously along with it. Again I came to my feet to see
the prow of the ship, in cluttered ruins, quickly being
engulfed by tongues of hungry flames. Fire! The Hakadian frigate was afire! I looked about me to see if the
Lord lay amidst the cluttered ruins of the deck unconscious, but I saw not his body. Frantic, I started to hunt
across the body-littered deck of the stricken Hakadian
frigate to find the Lord but I saw nothing. The fire consuming the frigate was leaping and crackling about me in
startling rapidity, and yet I did not wish to leave the deck
of the striken ship without the Lord at my side. Then suddenly, through the wall of flame I heard the terrified
screams of a woman. There was a crash of cannonfire so

close I felt the blast of hot air whip about me and then through the smoke I saw the *Black Falcon* had cut herself free from the burning Hakadian. I felt pleased at this stroke of fortune, but then the screams of the woman came to my ears again through the wall of flame, forcing me to stop in my search of the Sa' yen for a moment to peer about. Was I hearing things? A woman on board an Hakadian frigate? I started to dismiss this as delusion and start my search for the Lord again, but through the flames I again heard distinctly the high-pitched scream of a woman in the grip of sheer terror. And then I saw the Lord! I saw Him high atop the burning for'top'mast of the Hakadian frigate, scampering up the rigging as rapidly as he could with the burden He carried in one arm. And that burden was a woman! A woman with long, dark brown hair who clung to Him as if terror gripped her heart. Flames, searing hot fire, had completely engulfed the ship and were rapidly following the Lord up the mast! Spellbound, for I thought the Lord was to die that night, I watched below even as the fire hurried closer to me.

High up on the for'top'gallant spar I saw the Lord use His sword and cut rigging with it before returning it to its sheath. And then, gripping the long-haired, bare-breasted woman firmly with one arm, the Lord took hold of the rope, curled it around His forearm, and leaped into the dark night just as the flames made the for'mast stagger and come crashing down into the funeral pyre that was now the frigate. Through the night sky the Lord swung from the mast with the woman in His arm. And His path brought Him directly over me, passing through a wall of flame. Then, amazed at even His luck, I saw the Lord come to the highest point of His swing and He let go of the rope to sail through the night sky and land on the deck of the *Black Falcon* on His feet. Truly amazed at this feat, even disregarding the flames that were licking about me like savage beasts eager to consume their next meal, I lifted a cheer into the night at the Lord's skill and daring. From the deck of the *Black Falcon* I saw men come to the railing with the Lord and point down at me. I saw the Lord cup His hands in an attempt to yell something at me but I heard it not. For the flames were now only inches

from my body, the heat so intense I had to escape somehow. But there was no escape! I would either burn with
the ship, perhaps my personal funeral pyre, or I could take
the final plunge and leap from the burning deck of the
ship into the night sky. I wasted no time in deciding the
matter. Preferring the clean death of plunging to the forest
below to being burned alive in a doomed ship, I waved a
farewell to my Lord cheerfully, and leaped over the burning railing of the Hakadian frigate.

And I plunged into the smoke and fire of battle while it
was still being fought about me between Hakadians and
Aggarians. I fell. And fell and fell. For what distance I
knew not. And then something smashed against my chest,
bursting the wind from my body, and I suddenly was
plunged into total darkness.

The first thing I was aware of was being cold. Very
cold. I opened my eyes, but it took some time to focus
them. And to breathe I had to grit my teeth and force air
through the pain in my chest. There were two things I
noted quickly. First, I was manacled with heavy iron at
feet and hands to chains that were bolted to massive stone
blocks. And secondly, I was in a tiny, cramped cell that
was filled with such stench as to make me instantly gag.
The cell was made of massive stone, coated with a green
slime that was distasteful to the touch. I lay on a roughly
hewn bunk made of Kakla wood filled with damp straw
for a mattress. There was a plain wooden bucket filled with
what looked like water, with a cup made of stone hanging
on a small hook in the bucket. The bucket was just inside
a heavy-looking cell door of wood studded with huge iron
bolts. There was the merest opening, not even large
enough to stick a hand through, in the door to see and between the heavy iron bars of this small hole came the dim
glimmer of a poorly burning torch. And yet all this did
not displease me. In fact, I marveled at the luxury of it
all! I was alive! Alive after a seemingly assured death
plunge from the burning deck of the Hakadian frigate!
Alive and now apparently a prisoner kept in some deepest
corner of a nobleman's dungeon. As I fought down the
pain in my chest, I wondered who my captors were and

where I might be as I struggled into a sitting position. I had not long to wait, for soon a man's voice boomed out from the other side of the door calling for the captain of the guards.

A half hour slipped by, with only the sounds of my breath whistling through my teeth as I gritted them from the pain in my chest plus the slow, hypnotic drone of water dripping in large droplets from the stone wall in one corner of my cell. I would move my arms now and then, and the rattle of chains would break the droning silence, snapping my growing desire to plunge back into a deep sleep again. And then, from the door came the rattling sound of a massive lockbolt sliding back and the screeching, protesting creak of ancient door hinges opening. Torches, several that were freshly trimmed and burning brightly, filled the cramped cell and boots stepping firmly on hard stone came to my ears. Throwing a manacled hand up to protect my eyes from the intense light of the torches, I blinked several times yet was unable to focus on the forms that filled my cell and looked down upon me with blurred faces.

"So this is the famous Magdar, called the Left Hand of the Lord by the fools who follow this imposter who thinks he is the Sa'yen. This is the swordsman that killed my trusted Captain Thordak? This scrawny, dirty dog of a boy is the murderer of Thordak? Impossible!"

I should have felt fear and dread for I now knew who stood in front of my bunk dressed in fine gowns of satin and fur, bejeweled and appearing every bit as powerful as he indeed was. Bahir Kandar himself! I should have fallen to my knees and begged for mercy, knowing full well that this was what the ruthless, merciless Prince of the House of Kandar expected. But I only lifted my head and looked up into the face of Bahir Kandar and smiled.

"I am indeed the one that killed Thordak, your personal assassin, Prince Kandar. But I take no honor in it. I expected the killer, reputed to be a fine swordsman, to put up a fight. I hardly expected to kill him with such ease."

For my answer I received a bone-jarring slap from one of the torch-bearing guards that flanked either side of Bahir Kandar. Tasting blood in my mouth, I smiled again through the pain and looked at the young, dwarfish, hawk-faced Bahir Kandar with a sneer. Dressed in the colors gray and red, the colors of his family house, the prince looked down upon me with the glittering light in his eyes and a mocking smile on his colorless lips. He had the reputation in the city of being the cruelest of masters and the most treacherous to deal with. And there was no doubt to anyone that Bahir Kandar was ruthless and sought power. One had only to look at him once, to see the greed and lust for power in his eyes, to become convinced of that. Yet none had dared to suggest that Bahir Kandar might possibly be mad. I said nothing but kept my eyes on the face of the prince and thought over the likelihood that the man was insane.

"You and your master have been great thorns that have plagued me in my plans, fool. But merely that. Only thorns. My plans have come about and surprisingly the attack you and your master made the other night upon the combined fleets of the Hakadian and Aggarian ships furthered them along more than was anticipated. For that I should thank you, you filthy peasant. My thanks will be a swift death for you and your master instead of the slow, painful exercise I had at first planned for both of you. But I am magnanimous. I am merciful. As soon as your master falls into my waiting hands in his attempt to rescue you, peasant, it will be the end of the last resistance that keeps me from ruling Triisus without a standing army on hand."

"You, Prince Kandar, as evil as you are, have not near the cunning or daring that would be needed to capture the Lord."

A torch-bearing guard stepped forward, grinning mercilessly through a dirty beard ready to strike me again, but the prince motioned the man to step back and then lifted his head and laughed softly, effeminately at my words.

"The Lord? You address your master in the tense of a deity still? Where is your God now, fool? Eh? While you rot, chained to the walls of my dungeon, where is your lord to save you? What powers will he conjure up to save you from dying of thirst and starvation? Ah, Magdar, my

sources of information have told me you were always the
bravest of the brave, as one would expect a person raised
in the ways of the Ha'valli to be. But not very bright, eh,
Magdar? Not very intelligent. How will he save you? How
can a mere being, like you or me Magdar, be a God? Eh?
I'll tell you. He's not a God! And he'll never save you! He
will try, for all fools try the impossible. But he will fall
into my grasp and I will crush you both. And when I
crush you and him together, I will crush the smoldering
rebellion that threatens to break out in my reign as Emperor of Triisus."

"Emperor of Triisus? What madness do you blabber,
Kandar?"

This time the delicate, soft white hand, laden with
heavy, jeweled rings, struck me with all the strength the
small, dwarf-sized man could muster. It stung but little
else, and I acted as if nothing had happened at all. Yet
there was fury and rage in the man's mad eyes and the
small man, dressed in his rich robes, shook violently, restraining the rage that gripped him. And then quite suddenly, like a breeze suddenly dying on a hot afternoon, the
rage left his eyes and he stood up relaxed and smiling. Ad-
mittedly, I was somewhat taken back by the suddenness of
the man's change. And I came to the conclusion that
Bahir Kandar was indeed mad. Dangerously mad. But I
said nothing and watched the small, hawk-faced prince
smile at me as he stepped to one side and lifted a hand at
the same time.

"I *am* Emperor of Triisus, you foolish peasant. And with
your help, I might add. A coup, my foolish boy, yesterday
afternoon. And I must thank you for the unplanned but
timely participation of you and your master. But let me
introduce you to the one who planned the final blow that
made me at long last the ruler of Triisus. Meet Hasdrubal,
Admiral of the Hakadian Grand Fleet, Personal Advisor
to the Emperor Hassan of the Hakadian Empire."

One of the torch-bearing guards had to step out of my
tiny cell to make room for the bearded, robed admiral of
the Grand Hakadian Fleet to enter. He was a tall man,
darkly bearded with curled hair that fell to his shoulders.
He was dressed in the blue and white livery of an Haka-

dian flag officer, and running diagonally across his chest
was the silver and red sash that marked him as one of
Hakadian's most highly decorated officers. He was heavily
scented, as all Hakadian courtiers were, and the aroma
that he wore was heavy and thick. One look at him, a man
I already knew by reputation and had once encountered
while in the presence of the Lord months before high up
in the Tors Mountains, was all I needed to know that a
deadly enemy stood before me. Looking down upon my
manacled hands and feet, the perfumed, finely dressed
courtier smiled with evil pleasure. Bowing elegantly to me,
he began playing with his curls as he spoke to me with a
voice of soft, viper deadliness.

"My Lord Kandar speaks truly that your unplanned
help furthered our plans immeasurably, fool. And I would
go so far as to say that without the intervention you and
your master imposed upon us the other day we possibly
would have failed in our ultimate goal of capturing Triisus
and placing it safely into the hands of Lord Kandar."

"Hey? What do you blabber, Hakadian? Help in capturing Triisus? We did nothing of the sort. We attacked the
Hakadian and Aggarian fleets in the hopes of disbanding
any attempts to convert the Aggarian pirates into your al-
lics. And I daresay we succeeded, too!"

"Ah, yes! You succeeded admirably, peasant! Admirably!" Bahir Kandar nodded, beaming with pleasure as he
looked at the scented figure of Hasdrubal. "And for that,
we should reward him, eh, admiral?"

"Indeed. Oh, yes indeed!" The curled, perfumed admiral
nodded, smiling in his pleasure as well. "A roommate perhaps? An old friend to while away the hours in this cell
planning impossible escapes? A comfort that will help him
along while we await the coming of his dear lord and sav-
ior?"

"Yes, yes! How deliciously cruel it will be, admiral!
Bring in the other prisoner and chain him to the walls as
well!"

Bahir Kandar and Hasdrubal, Grand Admiral of the
Hakadian fleets, stepped out of the cell to make room for
two powerfully built guards, dressed in plain breast armor
covered with the livery of the House of Kandar, to drag in

a filthy, unshaven, yet still defiantly struggling form. In the dimness of the light of the torches I had a hard time seeing who this prisoner was. But even though the small man struggled with his guards, it was apparent that much of his strength had been beaten and whipped out of him, for his robes were the tattered remains that come about only when the cat-o'-nine-tails has been used. Much of the man's body was caked in dried blood from the abuse heaped upon him and yet the man struggled valiantly. I felt admiration and gladness well up in me for the show of resistance this man exhibited. And I vowed that I would yet be free and reap the final honors from this humiliation thrown upon both of us. The two burly, hairy guards easily restrained the weak man's struggle and chained him to the walls beside the only bunk in the cell, then withdrew quickly. Bahir Kandar and Hasdrubal, Admiral of the Hakadian Grand Fleet, entered into the cell, with the Admiral now holding a torch over their heads.

"Now you have company to muse away the long hours, you dog. Ha! What a matched pair, Admiral Hasdrubal, eh? The peasant fool who thinks his god is back in mortal form to rescue his devoted followers from the clutches of evil and the pirate fool, a daring pirate chieftain himself who allowed his own ship to be captured as the spoils of victory by the very charlatan that claims to be a god."

And turning swiftly to look again at the figure chained to the wall beside me, I for the first time recognized the battered, blood-caked face of the pirate prince, Hakba Baru. Hakba Baru, once the captain of the *Black Falcon*, the very pirate chieftain the Lord captured on the hulk of the *Black Falcon* when we first found it. Captured again, but this time, like me, in the clutches of Bahir Kandar and the Hakadians. Stunned and puzzled, I tore my eyes away from the face of the pirate and looked up into the smiling, cruel faces of my captors.

"Fool! Dog! Silly peasant simpleton!" Hasdrubal sneered, striking me for no apparent reason with a gloved hand and laughing. "Do you think we Hakadians would actually lower ourselves by making allies of our ancestral enemies, the Aggarian pirates? We made every attempt to make it appear as if we were in the process of making allies with the Aggarians. We even sent Virgantrix, the Aggarian Chieftain these pirates follow, a treasure ship heavy with gold and silver to show our sincerity. We made arrangements to have a fleet meet theirs at a point below Triisus to cement what appeared to be honest attempts on our part to make them our allies. And it worked, peasant. As you well know. But our real intentions were to bring the Grand Fleet, under my command, up in the middle of the celebrations that followed soon after the pact was agreed upon between the first Hakadian fleet admiral and Virgantrix. Between two Hakadian battle fleets we would at last destroy the power of the Aggarian pirates. And it would have worked without your assistance if the admiral in command of the first Hakadian fleet had been more diligent in keeping his crews sober and manning their ships. Instead he allowed them to celebrate as well and they became as drunk as the pirates. If not for your timely intervention the fleet assigned to begin the attack before I was to come would not have been capable to do its part at all. But you forced the fight upon everybody, you and your lord. And because of that I came up in the thick of the ensuing confusion and wreaked havoc upon the pirates. We succeeded, peasant! And with your efforts on our behalf! What do you say to that?"

"And the Aggarians have been destroyed?"

"Almost to the man. Only a few, Virgantrix among them, escaped, as did your lord as well," Bahir Kandar replied, his smile gone and a severe frown upon his effeminate hawk-face as he glared at me. "I had hopes that the *Black Falcon* and Virgantrix both would be destroyed but luck rode with them. However, that shall soon be corrected, eh, admiral?"

"Immediately, my lord," the admiral nodded, playing with a dark lock of hair as he smiled upon the face of Bahir Kandar confidently. "The remnants of the first Hakadian fleet plus all of the Grand Fleet ride above the towers of Triisus now. And my staff is finalizing the plans that will track down and destroy this charlatan and Virgantrix as well. It should be only a few weeks before our victory will be total, my lord."

"Excellent!" nodded Bahir Kandar, rubbing his thin,

delicate hands together in a pleased fashion. "And when the charlatan who calls himself a god and the pirate Virgantrix are both captured or destroyed, we will deal with these rogues. But for now we must keep them alive as bait. Alive but not pampered, eh, admiral?"

"Correct, my lord," Hasdrubal, the Hakadian admiral replied.

The Prince of the House of Kandar took a final look at me and Hakba Baru and laughed in pleasure at his handiwork. Nodding to Hasdrubal, he whirled in his robes regally and left the tiny cell. The Hakadian watched the prince depart and waited for some moments before turning, torch in hand, to look down upon me. And when he did, there was a look of evil pleasure, which chilled me more than the seeming madness exhibited by the prince Bahir Kandar. The evil pleasure in his face was that of a sane man who reveled in the acts of cruel evilness which Hasdrubal was noted for. The evil in Bahir Kandar was that from an unbalanced mind, and of the two I knew not which I feared the most. But I did not show my fear as I looked up into the face of the Hakadian admiral. We said nothing for some time. Then stepping closer, the perfumed flag officer of the Hakadian court spoke to me in a low and soft voice which I found most distressing!

"I heard the prince promise you a swift death, you dog! And while I am forced by my own Emperor to be subordinate to the Prince of this city, I will yet have my revenge upon you, peasant! It was you and your lord who made me lose my own flagship when you were escaping in that windblown passage up in the Tors Mountains. I lost the best ship in the Hakadian fleet because of you and your lord, and for that I should slowly draw and quarter you over a burning fire! I almost lost my own life in your escape and for that I will kill you slowly. But you deserve to die the Death of a Thousand Stings because of another atrocity, peasant! The burning Hakadian frigate you leaped from the other night carried the entourage of the Princess Saphid. She died in those flames, dog! She, the favorite of the Emperor Hassan. And for that I guarantee the Death of a Thousand Stings will be your timely reward. And nothing, absolutely nothing will stand in my way to see you die the death I have promised you!"

And with those words he turned, threw the burning torch to one of the many Hakadian officers who were part of his immediate staff, and left the cell. The heavy cell door was pushed shut, and I listened to the massive lock-bolt slide into place. Silence, unbelievable silence suddenly hung in the tomb of the tiny cell. The chained, unconscious form of Hakba Baru hung slumped to the wall in his ragged robes beside my bunk, and off in the corner the dripping of water again came to my ears. The sudden silence draped me with a sense of immediate doom, and I lay motionless on the bunk, chained to the wall. I knew the Hakadian admiral had told no lies when he had made his promise to me. The Death of a Thousand Stings was an ancient Hakadian death reserved only for the most dangerous of enemies. It meant to die slowly, covering hours of pain-racked days, from being stung individually by the Hakadian night bees, a bee of large proportions found only on the Hakad Plateau. Each sting injects a poison into the victim's system that attacks the nerves and creates unbelievable pain. No one could possibly live through such torture. And Hasdrubal had promised me such a death.

I had no doubts that he intended to carry through his promise no matter what consequences he might eventually reap.

XII

———•◦•◦•———

Can We Ever Escape?

Through the stygian darkness, illuminated faintly by a single foul-smelling torch burning in the dungeon's hall directly in front of our cell, the pirate Hakba Beru and I whispered to each other. The fierce, black-bearded pirate with his famous hook nose and glowing brown eyes sat on his haunches, chained hand and foot to the slime-covered wall behind us. And manacled myself, I sat on the wooden bunk filled with straw, unable to move far enough to make room even for the pirate to sit beside me. Together, we had spent the better part of a month in the cell, broken only by the two hours a day we were allowed to exercise by walking up and down a twisting dungeon corridor that was sealed by huge wooden doors at either end. The corridor was wide enough for only one man to pass through at a time thus severely limiting any thoughts on our part of escaping. We sat now in the darkness, talking to each other in low voices and halting our conversation whenever boots of a guard would be heard stepping down the stone floors of the dungeon. In that time, waiting for the grand trap of Bahir Kandar to spring which might capture the Lord, I learned much of the treachery of the Hakadian Emperor and the arrogance of Virgantrix, the chieftain of the once powerful Aggarian pirates.

We also heard, through a veiled, roundabout way, of the feats of the Lord. Twice a guard, dressed in the colors of the House of Kandar, stopped just on the other side of our cell door and whispered to us the news that had spread through the city about the Sa'yen's exploits. And each time this guard stopped to whisper, disguising his voice so that we might not recognize him later, he thrilled us with the news. Twice the *Black Falcon* had appeared over the towers of Triisus, her guns blazing. Once she had appeared suddenly, like a mirage, above the palace of Bahir Kandar, emerging from a huge dark cloud that smelled most foul, with all guns firing and wreaking much damage on ships of the Hakadian fleet that lay moored and unsuspecting about the landing towers of the Kandar palace. She hovered over the city for nearly an hour, putting to blaze two Hakadian frigates in spectacular explosions that even we faintly heard. All the city was thrown into an uproar of either rage or undisguised admiration for such a daring exploit! Those that called the Sa'yen their Lord were thrilled by the fact He escaped with laughable ease and harbored great hopes of rapid deliverance. To His enemies, His feat was an insult that could never be tolerated or rectified, for the Lord had escaped, leaving the city tucked away in its vast mountain cavern blazing from a hundred fires. Yet as thrilled as even Hakba Baru was at the news of the Lord's first appearance over the city, His second appearance truly left us speechless for its audacity and daring.

His second appearance was in the teeth of a blowing, fierce winter's storm. And in the dead of night. The *Black Falcon* appeared through the blowing snow above the flagship of the Hakadian Grand Admiral. And the Lord, draped in a huge billowing cloak and dressed in the armor of old Fadah, leaped with a few devout followers to the deck of the admiral's flagship and captured it even before any knew that the Lord was upon them. And captured in the raid was the Grand Admiral himself! Hasdrubal, the Admiral of the Hakadian Grand Fleet and Personal Confidant to the Emperor Hassan himself, captured by the sword tip of the Lord! To myself and Hakba Baru, the news seemed too incredible to be true. Yet, the masked voice of the Kandar guard insisted that what he related was the truth. But more incredible, the Lord, in His Golden Bearded Magnificence, allowed the Grand Admiral to go free. To go free only after the admiral's flagship, a fifty-gun behemoth, was burnt from stem to stern, the second flagship this admiral had lost from the hands of the Sa'yen. And for the allowance of the admiral's freedom, the Lord issued to the admiral and to Bahir Kandar a challenge. And the challenge stunned both of us in the cramped, wet cell into speechlessness!

The challenge was simple, as the guard related to us earlier in the evening. Allow the captives known as Magdar the Bull, called the Left Hand of the Lord, and Hakba Baru, prince of the Aggarian pirates, to go free in exchange for the release and deliverance of the Princess Saphid, daughter and most favored of the Emperor Hassan! And for proof that the Lord indeed held such an exalted captive in His presence, He left in the hands of Hasdrubal, the Hakadian Grand Admiral, an exquisite gold chain that was last seen worn by the princess herself. For the second time in less than a month, the *Black Falcon* and the Lord escaped from above the city without absorbing so much as a glancing blow from a stray cannonball. To say that Hakba Baru and myself were ecstatic with joy at the Lord's daring boldness, as well as His incredible luck in the art of escaping, would be not fully quoting our exact feelings. We were beside ourselves with joy. And even the heavy chains that kept us tightly gripped to the cold, wet, slime-covered stone walls of our cell could not restrain us from cheering and clapping our hands. The Sa'yen! God of War! Sa'yen the Vengeful! All Praise to the Lord! For some moments we shouted and praised the Lord with all our might and in the loudest of voices. But eventually the hidden voice of the secretive Kandar guard made us restrain ourselves, for the guard had not come to relate to us the daring plans of the Sa'yen but to whisper to us secretly from his hidden spot the plans that Hasdrubal, the Hakadian Grand Admiral, and Bahir Kandar were now making to capture the Sa'yen.

Both Bahir Kandar, Prince of the House of Kandar and now tyrant of Triisus, and Hasdrubal, Grand Admiral of the Hakadian Empire, believed the Princess Saphid was dead. Died in the flames of the Hakadian frigate I had leaped from only a month before. The woman the Sa'yen claimed to be the princess was in truth merely a lady-in-waiting to the princess and not the princess herself. It was, as told to us by the mysterious Kandarian guard, rumored that one of the five ladies that waited upon the Princess Saphid was one of the many illegitimate children of the Emperor Hassan, a minor noble from a small royal house yet nevertheless rumored to be one of the emperor's own daughters. And this woman was almost an exact twin to the Princess Saphid in appearance. In escaping from the flames of the burning frigate the Sa'yen had rescued this woman, still a daughter to the emperor but not the Princess Saphid. The Grand Admiral Hasdruba did not need, then, special efforts to effect the rescue of the woman back into the safety of Hakadian hands. Thus, the Grand Admiral and the Prince of the House of Kandar conspired to trap the Lord and His entourage when they again appeared in the skies above Triisus bearing with them the woman they believed to be the Princess Saphid. This news dampened our resolve and our desire to celebrate over the Lord's twice executed appearance above the walls of Triisus and threw us into a pit of deep, scowling gloom. We were chained and helpless. And yet we knew, thanks to the treachery of one guard in the pay of the House of Kandar, the full plans of Bahir Kandar himself and his cohort, the Hakadian Admiral Hasdrubal. And we lay chained to the walls of our cell, with no apparent hope of escaping or warning the Lord of His impending doom. Or was there? A sudden thought came to me as I sat on the edge of the rough wooden bunk in the cell, my wrists and ankles chained by massive locks of cold steel. Why was this Kandarian guard so interested in telling us the fortunes and misfortunes of his master? Was it, as I truly suspected, some form of trap being carried out by the diabolical mind of Bahir Kandar? Or was it perhaps that somewhere deep within this hidden guard's heart beat a secret longing to serve the Lord? Frowning, I cleared my throat and decided to probe the man's true feelings.

"It is a pity that such a man as the Sa'yen, as many call Him, will step into the trap of your master without being warned, eh, warrior?"

There was a long pause, a pause that seemed to me so drawn out that I heard my heart pounding in my chest.

But then I heard the hidden warrior breathe out a loud sigh of regret and agree it was indeed a pity. Beaming with the success so far, I glanced at a puzzled, bearded Hakba Baru and then looked at the cell door again.

"Aye, it is such a pity, warrior. Especially if one considers what the Lord might reward one who came and warned Him of your master's trap."

"Reward?" the guard repeated, his voice trembling a bit with excitement that I could easily hear. "Did you say reward?"

"Aye! And a handsome reward that would be too, warrior! And knowing the Lord personally, I daresay He would reward that person handsomely beforehand. Would you not say the same, friend pirate?"

"Huh? Oh! Aye! Aye, that he would indeed! This strange man who calls himself the Sa'yen is quite generous with the gold of another person's treasure!" Hakba Baru stammered at first, collecting his wits about him rapidly and finishing the sentence with a firmness and conviction in his voice that pleased me.

"You, pirate, you do not believe this man to be the Sa'yen returned to us again?" the guard muttered, a note of caution in his voice as he spoke to us, still hidden from view.

"Me? Believe this man to be a god? Hah! Warrior, I am an Aggarian pirate. And we believe in no gods, don't you know. But I will say this for the rogue, friend. He stole my ship from under me, the *Black Falcon*. And she only a few weeks out of the shipyards of Triisus and in my command. And to add injury to insult, along with this rogue that sits chained to the wall beside me, that being who claims to be the Sa'yen stole all the gold and silver that I called my own. A fortune, man! A fortune that no man could spend in a lifetime! Nay, not even ten men could spend in their lifetimes!"

"Aye, but He has never claimed Himself to be the Sa'yen!" I put in hastily, knowing full well that the legends of the Sa'yen had repeatedly stated that while among us mortals, the Sa'yen would never claim to be what He really was.

"He claims to be no god?" the hidden warrior repeated,

with, now, a note of curiosity. "And yet he does miraculous things?"

"Bah! What miraculous things, warrior?" Hakba Baru coughed, winking at me to indicate he was goading the hidden guard to continue on.

"What things?" the warrior repeated, incredulous that such a question could ever be asked at all. "Why, the miracle of single-handedly fighting off a squadron of Aggarian pirates in a raging storm and capturing your ship in the process. That to me is one miracle. Or the humiliation He gave Thordak, Captain of the Guards of the House of Kandar. I knew Thordak, pirate, and I knew how ruthless and skilled he was with the sword. To disarm that man so easily and without even seeming to work at it is a miracle to me. And I have heard stories of His gift of healing the sick and feeble. Are these not miracles enough?"

It was true that the Lord had at times healed a few of the many that had gathered daily at the base of the landing tower we had been moored at only a few months back. He had pointed out to me that those who were healed under His guidance would have healed in any case but would have taken longer to do so. The devoted who flocked to His banner in increasing numbers daily would see Him walk among them and actually heal them of their sicknesses and that was enough to make His simple acts of kindness seem divine miracles. From the way the hidden guard was addressing the Lord as an actual deity, I knew our chances for escaping this prison cell and perhaps making our way to freedom had taken a leap forward. Smiling to myself in the dark cell, I again brought the conversation back to the original point.

"Ah, but what sadness fills me! As you know well, warrior, the Lord can give all His devotees a few miracles, but He still walks about in a mortal's body. He yet can be killed by the hands of others. A pity that He should die before His mission to lead us, who call Him Lord, on the Wha'ta, the March to the South!"

"Aye, such a pity!" the hidden guard said firmly, his sword's sheath scraping up against the cold, hard stone of the corridor outside.

"And what is so sad is that if we could warn Him of

His peril, he who helps us escape could ask for anything from Him and it would be granted to him freely!"

"Anything?"

"Anything the Lord, in His limited powers, could reward. It could have even been you, warrior. What would you do, friend, with a jar as tall as yourself filled with gold and jewels? Why, I know many a royal house in Triisus that does not have such a fortune in its treasure vaults."

"Aye, such a fortune!" the hidden warrior answered, his voice sounding far off and unsteady. "A fabulous fortune!"

"Aye, and all he would have to do to get it would be to help us escape and he would have such a gift," Hakba Baru said, fingering his black beard eagerly as his eyes blazed on the locked cell door. "What say you, warrior?"

"Me?" the warrior stammered, as if suddenly caught doing a terrible deed. "Me? Well, uh, escape is, uh, impossible, isn't it? I mean, uh, down this hall to your left is the dungeon guard's day room. It is staffed at all times with at least twenty men, except for this coming Monday, when the prince and the Hakadian admiral plan to spring the trap on the Lord. They will have only a few, no more than three, men in the day room plus, uh, me down in the dungeons on that day to supervise the prisoners. So, if, uh, by some impossible set of circumstances yonder door is left unlocked on a certain day and, uh, if perhaps a key is dropped too close to a cell door and two certain prisoners escape, how can one foresee the future in such things?"

"And, supposing such an impossible set of deeds did actually happen, warrior, how would the Lord recognize such a faithful servant?" the bearded, hawk-faced pirate smoothly asked, smiling through his beard as his eyes lingered on the heavy Kakla wood of the cell door.

"Recognize? Hmmm, well uh, such impossible deeds rarely happen. But they do sometimes, don't they? Yes. Well, perhaps if one matched one half of the feather from a Triisusian pigeon with the other half a certain servant might bring forward, the proper rewards might be funded?"

And a portion of a feather, broken neatly in half, appeared through the crack in the cell door at the bottom.

The black-bearded pirate looked at me and nodded, and I nodded too. As boot steps quickly hurried away from our cell down the corridor, we both understood that the Monday next would be the day we could escape from our chains!

When he came, he came on wings of silence! All through the night that we believed to be Sunday—for we knew not the actual day since neither calendar nor sand clock was part of our cell—I and the bearded, black-haired pirate sat with our ears cocked and our senses keyed on hearing the approach of the traitorous guard. But when he came, we did not hear him until he roughly pushed the key under the door of our cell and made it fly across the floor and straight into Hakba Baru's hands. The bearded pirate held the bronze, heavy-looking key up with both hands and turned to face me. Standing, we both heard the boots of the mysterious guard hurry down the stone floors of the corridor outside our cell. With growing excitement, I watched the fierce pirate take the large key and, with trembling hands, unlock the massive chains from around his wrists and ankles. With a smothered shout of glee he stepped to my side and quickly freed me and together we stood unbound from our chains for the first time in weeks.

"Freedom!" the Aggarian pirate shouted, taking my shoulders and shaking me in his excitement.

"Aye, Hakba! Freedom and a chance to save the Lord! We must hurry!"

The door to our cell we found unlocked and swiftly we moved out into the corridor. There waiting for us was my sword of Fadah's old armory and one for the pirate with accompanying scabbards and belts. We quickly strapped these on. The hook-nosed, bearded pirate took from the wall the torch which was burning brightly, and with swords gripped firmly in our hands, we moved slowly down the stone corridor in single file. The torch, held high over our heads by Hakba Baru, flickered with every gust of wind that seeped through the stone of the walls, creating huge and fantastic images and shadows which danced and twirled for our benefit on the walls, ceiling and floors of the dungeon. But we paid little heed to these mirages and hurried on in silence. Turning a corner, we stopped, the bearded pirate glancing over his shoulder to have a look at me and then nodding down the corridor in front of him. Ahead of us, bracketed by two brightly burning torches, was the heavy wooden cell door that would open into the dungeon guards' day room. What had the mysterious Kandarian guard said about how many unsuspecting guards would be lounging in the room behind that door? Only two or three? Had he spoken the truth? Or was this the first test of a possible trap of such subtleness that even we could not fathom? Glancing at the bearded pirate I saw the same suspicions being reflected in his eyes. Was this a trap? And if so, why was it necessary to trap two prisoners already safely under lock and key? Would there be only two or three guards in the room when we opened the door and suddenly entered? Or would we find a large contingent of Kandar household guards and die fighting valiantly but uselessly against impossible odds? Finding my mouth bitterly dry from fear and suspicion, I called myself a fool, gripped my sword more firmly and whispered to the bearded pirate to move on. We could not linger in the narrow, confining corridor of the dungeon in indecision. We had to press on and confront whatever grand and elaborate designs Bahir Kandar and Admiral Hasdrubal had created if we were to save the Lord! I nudged the bearded pirate to hurry him on, and we approached the heavy door of Kakla wood and halted just in front of it.

From the other side of the door we heard men laughing. The laughter came from two men obviously at ease and unsuspecting of danger being so immediately upon them. We waited for a few seconds to listen and possibly hear more voices, our ears close to the heavy wooden door. But we heard only two voices and no others and it pleased us. The bearded, hook-nosed pirate quietly slid the torch he held in one hand into a torch ring in the wall and then glanced at me. I nodded, stepped up to the door and placed a hand around the sliding bolt which kept the door locked in place, being careful not to make any sounds. Glancing at each other again, each nodding to the other

and with a swiftness of desperation driving me, I slid the
bolt of the door back and threw the door open in one motion. Together, Hakba Baru and I leaped into the large
day room of the dungeon guards and fell onto the unsuspecting Kandarian guards with a deadly swiftness that left
them without any hope of defending themselves. It was
over before they realized death was upon them and as we
stepped back and wiped our blades with the cloth that had
been spread over a large table burdened with much bread
and food heaped in many bowls, we surveyed the room
quickly. I was, at the first sight of so much food straining
the legs of the table before us, attacked with a ravenous
desire to fill my stomach. But I checked myself and only
took a large loaf of black bread and tore into it. As I
chewed eagerly on this tough but tasty bread, the bearded
pirate cut a huge chunk of meat from a ham and started
tearing it to pieces with his teeth. I grinned, threw the
bearded pirate a bottle of wine from the table, took a
bottle for myself, and motioned for the pirate to follow
me.

"We must hurry, Hakba. Already it may be too late to
warn the Lord that He enters a trap if He attempts to enter the city again!"

"Aye! Your words speak true, Magdar. But where do
we go? What can we do? We yet know little of what
Prince Kandar and that ragged, bearded thief of an admiral, Hasdrubal, plan."

"Then we must hurry and leave the palace and make
our escape even more quickly, Hakba. Hurry, follow me."

We fled from the day room and entered a wider, more
brightly lit dungeon corridor. We hurried down this corridor and then down another, neither I nor the bearded pirate sure of what direction we had to take to make our
escape. Several times we almost ran into a party of household troops as they marched in double file down wide,
tiled floors under the command of a squad leader, but
each time we somehow found places to conceal ourselves
from them. The palace of Bahir Kandar was sumptuous
and grand. The higher we fled from the dungeons the
more grand and noble the palace became. Tiled floors, of
the deepest blue in color and waxed to mirror finishes, lay

under our feet as we fled farther and higher into the upper floors of the palace. Large columns of Byrlian marble, intricately inlaid with gold and silver, lined the major corridors of the palace, affording us easy avenues of concealment when we came up onto officials of the palace. Rich, colorful tapestries of the most remarkable artistry hung from the ceiling on many walls, giving the palace an overall feeling of immense wealth and power to the onlooker. I knew the wealth and power of the House of Kandar was almost unlimited and yet I was impressed and even awed by the splendors I saw in the brief time I lingered to stare in the Kandar palace.

Yet finally, knowing full well that we were lost and that time was running out on us, we again had to hurry and hide as another large section of household troops almost found us fleeing from them. But fortune smiled upon us doubly as we hurriedly stepped into a small antechamber to hide from the marching boots of the guards. With swords still gripped firmly in our hands we both stood with our backs up against the doors and held our breath as the troops marched past. On the other side of the room were two large windows half hidden from view by thick curtains which fell from the ceiling to the floor. Leaping across the room I thought we might have at last found a route to escape, but pulling back the curtains my hopes were instantly smashed as I viewed the city of Triisus from one of the upper balconies of the palace of Bahir Kandar. Below us the city stretched out for miles, with hundreds of skyships floating moored to the thousands of landing towers. Much of the city was under a gigantic overhang of the huge cliff the city sat on. The side of the mountain that the city called its own possessed a huge lip of stone, ragged and radiating with craggy peaks on which the city itself sat. From one of the high craggy peaks that rose above the city in many locales of the city, the ancestors of Bahir Kandar had erected a fantastic, almost impregnable fortress-palace. It was rumored by many that this palace had nine hundred rooms as well as hundreds of secret passages that were both known and long-since forgotten by the current rulers of the palace. I could well believe this fortress had so many rooms! For the bearded, hook-nosed pirate and myself had been fleeing for it seemed like hours seeking a way out from under its high-ceilinged corridors unseen. And to no avail. And now, several hundred feet above the nearest street leading away from the gray, dreaded stone walls of the fortress, I thought all hope had at last run out for us.

I turned and faced Hakba Baru and shook my head in utter defeat. Trapped! Two hundred feet above the streets of Triisus and My Lord the Sa'yen soon to step into the waiting claws of the Hakadians and Bahir Kandar! The bearded, fierce-eyed pirate took hold of my arm to encourage me and started to speak. But on the other side of the room the large doors we had just ourselves entered opened and in came three officers of the palace guards. The pirate and I just had time to conceal ourselves in the large drapes that hid the windows from immediate view before the oldest looking and highest ranked officer began speaking to his subordinates.

"You know your instructions, Bazar? Kuuzi?"

"Aye, lord. We do! It will be like taking warm dew cakes from a child's cup when these impostors enter the palace!"

"Aye, it sounds so easy, Bazar! But I for one cannot believe this so-called god, this madman who calls himself the Sa'yen, would agree to actually enter the grand reception hall of the prince to exchange the Princess Saphid for his prince. It is absurd! Surely he must suspect some form of trap to be tried?"

"Be not so worried, Kuuzi! This fool, who I will reluctantly admit possesses unbelievable courage and daring, now deludes himself to believe a whole city awaits to rise in rebellion for him and is a victim of his own mania. He believes he is the Sa'yen! And a god cannot be harmed, hey? He thinks he is a god and thus cannot be harmed by mere mortals! He is insane, this man. When the Prince's plan begins to unfold, then we will show all the city who wish to follow this madman's lust exactly what genius is! Eh?"

"Precisely!"

"Undoubtedly!"

"Exactly. Now, you, Bazar, you and your chosen men

will take the upper loft positions and await the Prince's command. You have selected your men well?"

"The best crossbowmen in our pay, lord."

"Good! Assemble your men in this room, Bazar, and then take the south turret stairs to the lofts above the grand hall. Quickly now, this madman and his ship already approach the landing towers of the palace to dock! Come, Kuuzi, we have much to do!"

Through the thick folds of the drapes I saw the older officer, followed by the officer known as Kuuzi, leave. From my vantage point, hidden from view, I saw the guard known as Bazar walk across the room and open a second door that I had not noticed. He lifted his voice in a sharp command and quickly the room filled with forty men, all armed with large belt quivers of stout-looking crossbow bolts and in their hands were heavy, powerful-looking crossbows. It took only a few seconds for the section leaders to get the men sharply dressed down and in perfect formation. The small, dark-eyed officer known as Bazar waited until his subordinates had finished their work and nodded in satisfaction when the section leaders took their proper positions. With hands behind his back, he slowly walked up and down the lines in silence, inspecting each man closely. And after satisfying himself that each and every man was fully prepared, he strolled to the front of the formation of crossbowmen and looked at them fiercely before speaking.

"Each of you knows what we must do today. When the Prince rises from his throne to receive the woman whom this fool believes to be the Princess Saphid, and after the woman is clear from the charlatan rabble, we will then fire upon the rabble and kill them to a man. The Prince expects each of you to do his job without fail! Are there any questions?"

Not a voice stirred. Not one word to utter a protest over the fact the Lord would enter this palace under a flag of truce with the woman He believed to be the Princess Saphid to exchange her for myself and Hakba Baru. A flag of truce and Bahir Kandar was going to shoot the Lord down like a wild dog the moment He entered the Grand Hall. Rage filled every pore in my body and yet no

sound stirred from my lips. Hidden behind the large,
heavy drapes I made no sound, but the urge to leap into
the room, with sword in hand, and kill all that filled it and
who were enemies of the Lord consumed me and I had to
strain to keep myself from doing something so foolish. Yet
in a few short seconds this officer known as Bazar had his
section officers march the men through the large door we
had entered only moments earlier, leaving the room suddenly silent and empty. Stepping out from behind the curtains, a black rage filled my heart as the bearded pirate
prince stepped up beside me.

"It appears that your lord is doomed the moment he
steps into this foul palace, Magdar. And there is nothing
we can do!"

"We must try, Hakba! We must try!" I yelled, losing
control of my rage momentarily. "Come, Hakba. Let us
follow these assassins to the hiding places and perhaps we
may yet foil their plans."

The bearded pirate nodded, but I saw little hope of
success glowing in his eyes. Yet there was nothing else for
us to do. The Lord, on the *Black Falcon*, was at any moment to moor at the royal landing towers of the palace of
Bahir Kandar and time was rapidly running out for us and
the Sa'yen! We did not hesitate. Opening the door the
troops had so recently marched out of, we saw the corridor momentarily empty and we slipped out of the room.
Down the long, wide corridor we heard the marching
sounds of many boots and we quickly followed. Both I
and the pirate gripped our swords and felt the impossibil-
ity of the deed we were about to do weigh upon us. My
mouth was as dry as desert sands and my hands were
moist and clammy to the touch. But as silently as we
could move, we scurried along the walls of the corridor,
right behind the marching troops, staying just out of sight.
Twice we had to step up behind a huge, carved column of
rare Byrlian marble. Such marble, as I have stated before,
is rare.—black and cold to the touch, streaked in intricate
patterns of spidery webs of silver. To possess such
amounts of marble alone was enough to make the House
of Kandar exceedingly wealthy. And the palace had huge
columns of such rare stone in abundant supply. Huge

columns, fat at the bottom and tapering at the ceiling. And they made such excellent places to step behind and hide from the passing view of hurrying palace functionaries. But each time we had to hide ourselves from passing officers of the palace, we found it more difficult to hurry and catch up with the marching troops. And the second time we secreted ourselves, a band of servants, talking heatedly to themselves, took their time in passing down the corridor. Because of this, when leaving our hiding places and hurrying down the corridor to find the troops again, what we found was the corridor connecting with three other large corridors.

"Which way? Which way? I cannot hear their marching boots!" the bearded, hook-nosed pirate hissed, his face a grimace as he shook his fist in the air.

"I cannot hear their boots either, pirate. Yet, perhaps they did not take another corridor?"

"Eh? What madness do you mumble now, Magdar?" Hakba Baru growled, stepping closer to me to listen, yet not taking his eyes away from searching each connecting hall in hopes of finding some clue.

"Did you not hear their orders, Hakba? They were to take the stairs to the loft. The stairs in the southern turret. Each of these corridors leads to another part of the palace but none leads south!"

"Aye, perhaps you speak truthfully, Magdar. But where else could they have gone?"

My answer was to leap to one side of the large, wide hall and open one of the heavy, carved wooden doors. Many doors lined the halls that connected into the corridor we stood in and it took us some time of intense searching before we found the right door. Down deep into one hall off to our left was a heavy, plain-looking door with a hasp pulled to one side and a huge, ancient-looking lock of bronze hanging from the hasp, which gave us the clue we needed! Opening the door swiftly, we heard the sounds of boots marching up winding, twisting stairs of hard stone. From the stone beside the door we took from its holder a coarse-looking torch that barely danced with a flame but did so with much smoke. With torch in hand and sword in the other, I quickly started up the winding, dust covered stairs with the bearded pirate following close behind me. Above us we could hear the monotonous drone of heavy boots pounding up the stairs, and in this drone we hid the noise of our swiftness to catch up with them. But swiftly we closed the gap and slowed down, staying just one curve of the stairs behind the ascending troops. Ahead of us the noise of steel scraping against hard stone, and the shuffling sound of boots, mingled in with the smells of dark, moist layers of dust that had settled on the stairs over the years of no use, could be heard. We quickly extinguished our torch the moment we came within such close confines of the ascending troops, and the foul, strong odor of the extinguished torch was so strong our eyes watered. Yet we did not pause as we ascended further and further up the winding, spiraling stairs. And so close were we that when the troops did stop both I and the bearded Hakba almost stumbled into their midst! But luck held for us and we paused barely six feet behind the backs of the two crossbowmen that brought up the rear of the troops.

And above, we heard the sounds of a massive lock being broken and the protesting of a hasp, long forgotten and unoiled for years, being pulled open by stout hands.

XIII

The Prince Plots a Trap

Above us we heard the voice of Bazar, the officer in charge of these men, bark a sharp command and quickly the men hurried up the stairs, leaving us behind. Hakba wanted to quickly follow the rushing troops, but I stopped him by placing a hand on his shoulder and shaking my head no.

"We have come to the lofts. And this Bazar is deploying his men above the Grand Hall. If we enter now, we will be seen and cut down by his crossbowmen in seconds. Let us wait until he has positioned all his men and then perhaps we can foil the plans of Hasdrubal and Bahir Kandar."

The pirate nodded, though reluctantly, and we waited for what seemed like hours. Dimly from above we could hear the voices of a large crowd drift faintly to our ears. The grand hall of the palace of Bahir Kandar was quickly filling with the loyal followers of the prince and the Hakadian Admiral Hasdrubal. As we stood just around the winding curve of the spiral stairs which opened to the door that would lead into the lofts of the palace, I could not help but wonder if the Lord had entered the palace yet. Nor could I help but wonder if the Sa'yen was entering the palace not believing that some form of trap was waiting for Him. How could He not assume that Prince Kandar would refrain from planning a trap? Knowing the Lord, I could only believe that the Sa'yen had a plan of His own to counter the evil plans of His enemies.

"Come, Magdar, surely they are in place now! Let us hurry or your lord shall soon meet face to face with Lady Death!"

I nodded at the bearded pirate's words, and, gripping my sword with a determination to succeed in the impossible, I moved up the spiral stairs slowly. With Hakba Baru behind me, we found the wide, plain and rough-hewn door of the lofts swung open and left without a guard. I smiled at this lapse of elementary precaution by the officer in charge. He no doubt felt that in the palace of his own prince there would be little need to take such a precaution. As it was, the door to the loft was open and unguarded. We entered the cramped, dark loft high above the grand hall of the palace unchallenged. We found a dark, cramped place of huge wooden beams holding the palace roof up and large, thick ropes weaving back and forth across the space directly above the grand hall, each rope holding up massive chandeliers and other paraphernalia of the royal house of Kandar. Below, the din of a thousand voices echoed, the noise so intense it seemed to have life all its own. Smells of age and centuries of dust, mingled with the odors of all the small rodents that typically inhabit the dark corners of any large palace, assaulted our nostrils. But we silently moved deep into the wooden balcony that was known as the palace loft, high above the grand hall. Leaning up against an age-blackened beam of stout Kakla wood, I peered over the railing of the balcony and gazed downward at the sight below. And what I saw confirmed my fears, for the large marbled hall of the prince was packed with a throng of richly dressed royalty that claimed the House of Kandar as the liege lord. And there were hundreds upon hundreds of armed warriors, each dressed in their finest and most luxurious robes, milling about. Yet I felt certain that underneath all the fine silk and thick fur each wore mail and corselet of steel. For Bahir Kandar would not solely rely upon the marksmanship of his crossbowmen for the foul deed he planned. He would also have many others waiting to finish off those of the Lord's entourage that might somehow miraculously escape the first onslaught. I shook my fist silently in fury at the figure of Bahir Kandar as he sat on his raised throne amidst the splendor of his wealth.

"Careful, foolish warrior!" Hakba Baru hissed urgently in my ear, gripping me firmly by my arm and shaking me. "Yonder is the first of the crossbowman! What shall we do now?"

He nodded in the direction and I swiftly looked and found the unwary assassin with his back to us, leaning up against another massive crossbeam of aged wood. In his hands he held the plain, though extremely deadly, crossbow tenderly, as if it was a fond pet or delicate woman. At his feet were three others exactly like the one he held, cocked and waiting only for a feathered bolt to be placed up against the drawn string to make it deadly. Smiling, I glanced at the bearded pirate and nodded in satisfaction as I quickly unsheathed my sword.

"We must silence as many as we can, Hakba. But we must not utter a sound in doing so. Sheathe your sword and use your hands! I shall take this fool while you seek out the next and silence him."

The fierce, brown-eyed pirate nodded and quickly sheathed his bare blade in stark silence, and then blended into the darkness of the high loft as if he were a mirage. I smiled to myself in satisfaction. The assassins waiting to cut down the Sa'yen mercilessly with their crossbows would not suspect that two even more deadly assassins lurked among them, killing them one by one in the din of noise from below which would hide their movements. The warrior I first downed with the edge of my bare hand across the base of his neck knew nothing of the death that approached him. A swift, powerful blow and the man collasped lifelessly into my arms. Quickly stripping him of his uniform and weapons, I hurriedly donned the uniform and gear in the hopes that I might more easily approach the others of his unit without being looked upon with suspicion. And it worked much as I hoped. In a few short moments I downed five strong yet unknowing crossbowmen with my bare hands. None even uttered a groan when he fell from the blow. As the throng below continued to grow in excitement over the arrival of the Lord and the Princess Saphid, I continued on my task of circling around the high, smoked-filled lofts, silently downing those that would have killed the Lord without mercy.

I lost count when I reached fifteen. I was positive all that I had downed were not dead but none would be able to rise and fight this day. I was pleased with my efforts but was in much haste to complete my mission. I knew the Lord would soon enter the grand hall below, into the midst of his enemies' camp actually, and I had no idea how many men the bearded pirate had downed. So with frantic haste I began taking reckless chances.

One crossbowman heard my approach and turned halfway to see who came to his position. The edge of my hand caught him in his throat, spinning him around and downward in pain, where the edge of my hand again hit him, but this time on the base of his neck and cracking it in two with a sharp crack. He fell to the wooden floor of the loft before I had time to catch him, but I was already moving swiftly to another unsuspecting warrior. Coming up behind the next warrior I lifted my hand to strike swiftly when from nowhere the sharp twang of a crossbow string sang in the dark air of the loft and a bolt from a crossbow buried itself deep into a heavy beam of Kakla wood only an inch from my head! Jumping in fury, I caught the still unsuspecting warrior with the right blow just as two more crossbow bolts tore past me in a blur, missing me only by a hair's breadth. I saw Bazar, the officer of the crossbowmen, point at me from across the far side of the lofts, and crossbowmen standing beside him aimed their weapons at me. I ducked under the railing just as ten feathered bolts smashed into the heavy wooden beam above my head only inches away. Picking up the dead warrior's crossbow I stood up suddenly and fired without aiming. A man yelled on the far side of the lofts, staggered back and sank to the wooden floor. I dived for protection and suddenly the air was filled with the twang of many crossbows going off at the same time.

But the sound of all the fighting above the hall was smothered completely by the blaring of a hundred trumpets and the crash of drums and cymbals. The Lord was entering the grand hall of Bahir Kandar as if He was, even to Bahir Kandar and the Hakadian Hasdrubal, of royalty more regal than that of the host. As was the tradition of the city's royalty, the blaring of trumpets and the crash of drums and cymbals marked the entrance of such high nobility into the house of a lower nobleman. Yet, unbeknownst to Bahir Kandar and Hasdrubal, as the trumpets blew and the drums and cymbals crashed, above them a swift and deadly battle was fought with their own men's crossbows, the noise covered by the honor the prince of this house bestowed casually upon the Lord. And when the fanfare of drums and trumpets and cymbals ceased, not a sound stirred above. For in the savage melee in the lofts, the forty picked men of Bazar, not knowing who was friend and who was foe, had turned upon each other with their own weapons and wreaked deadly havoc. And as they fought among themselves, the bearded pirate and myself quietly hid in the darkness that abounded and killed those who survived swiftly and silently.

A silence complete and strangely malevolent fell upon the throng below the moment the fanfare ceased. Above, the bearded pirate joined me, our mission supposedly complete, and we had by far the best view of the whole procession below us. I saw the Lord, His yellow hair combed and pulled back over His wide shoulders, His beard a golden marvel to view, for upon this land it is rare to see the color of gold in a man's beard and hair as was the Lord's. He was dressed in the mail the old armorer Fadah had given him, the fabulous sword made from the secret steel of the Ancient Kings strapped to His side. Over the mail He had on the plain brown sarat, a thin cloth smock that covered chest and hips but left arms and legs below the knees bare, that He was so fond of. Head bare, His golden hair falling down past His shoulders and standing tall and straight as always, He was the Lord! The Sa'yen! And my heart filled with worshipping awe and thankfulness that I was one of His followers. Around Him stood the hard, stout hearts of old Fidor and tall, thin Tallsus. And in the midst of them stood a woman with long, lustrous brown hair. But not just a woman. A woman of such beauty that even I, one who usually has little appreciation for a woman's beauty, caught my breath! She was without a doubt the most beautiful woman I or any other mortal had ever looked upon. She stood dressed in flowing robes that befitted her royal personage, but such was her beauty that a simple peasant's dress would have been enough to mark her as a queen. She stood tall and straight, her head held high, her delicately upturned nose in the air. She barely came to My Lord's shoulders but she held herself in such a way that none, not one soul in the entire throng of the grand palace of Bahir Kandar, doubted who she was. She was Princess Saphid, daughter of Hassan, Emperor of the Hakad Empire!

I saw Hasdrubal, the Hakadian admiral, step up to the raised dais of Bahir Kandar and bend down to whisper something urgent into the prince's ear. I was sure the admiral was informing the prince that the Lord, contrary to what they had supposed happened, had indeed rescued the real Princess Saphid from the burning flames of the frigate I had leaped from over a month back! I saw surprise and consternation come across the face of Bahir Kandar plainly. But the evil prince was a master and quickly regained his composure and even smiled down upon the Lord from his throne. The packed throng made no sound but watched the Lord standing before the dais of the throne of Bahir Kandar. The Lord, in His magnificence, stood with His arms folded across His chest, apparently in no hurry to remove Himself from out of the hands of His enemies. And, from above, I wondered if the stalemate of silence that now gripped all below would continue indefinitely. The bearded pirate seemed as confused as I and shrugged his narrow shoulders. Looking downward again, we both saw the princess make the first effort and end the silence that had gripped everyone's hearts.

"Admiral, what means this rudeness? Attend to me."

Her words were those of a royal princess long used to commanding the most powerful of her father's commanders. And Hasdrubal, the curled, perfumed courtier of the princess's father, reluctantly came down the raised dais of Bahir Kandar and knelt to one knee in front of the princess, lowering his curled locked in submission. From the throng rose a muffled exclamation of surprise and wonder at seeing the admiral of the powerful Hakadian fleet, that now dotted the landing towers above the city, so readily acknowledge the power the Princess Saphid held over him. But neither the princess nor the admiral paid any attention to the muffled exclamations and whispers that had erupted like a whispering wind throughout the throng. The princess, in her regal haughtiness, offered her hand and the admiral took it and kissed it gently. She motioned the admiral to rise, and the perfumed, darkly bearded Hakadian rose and stepped to one side.

"My princess, I rejoice that you indeed are alive and well. A miracle has happened. A true miracle."

"Indeed a miracle! With little effort from my faithful servants or from even my betrothed to rescue me from the clutches of this vagabond, I must be insulted by being brought to the court of my future husband like a slave, to be bartered like cattle no less for more vagabonds. It is an insult, Hasdrubal! An insult! And I will not stand for it. Neither will my father when he hears of it."

I saw the curled-haired, perfumed admiral stagger a bit from her veiled threats, and surprised was I that she felt such hostility toward the person who saved her life from the flaming wreck of the burning frigate. But the Lord, even more strangely, had a mysterious smile on His thin lips and I found myself growing more confused. It appeared to me that much had happened between the princess and the Lord while He held her hostage. Yet I knew nothing and burned with an eagerness to find out. Grinning, I continued watching and saw the Lord take a step forward to speak.

"Prince, I come to your palace with the Princess Saphid, as was the conditions laid down by me, for the release of my friends, Magdar the Bull and the pirate prince Hakba Baru. I have fulfilled my promise. The Princess Saphid, as you see, is alive and very much herself. I now demand that my friends be released to me under the flag of truce we still stand under so that we may withdraw in peace."

From the crowd came a heavy mumble and a few shouts of anger. The throng was rapidly turning against the Lord, and fears new and strong gripped me. But the mumbling fury of the crowd was silenced in an instant by the shattering, high shrieking anger of the prince himself

as he leaped from his throne and dashed madly, his robes
whirling about him, down the raised dais to confront the
Lord.

"Demand? Demand? You demand from me the fools I
hold in my dungeon? Ha! You are a larger fool than I
even thought at first. You demand from me? How can a
charlatan, a leader of rabble, demand from a Prince of the
House of Kandar? I shall show you what power is, you
dog! Your flag of truce means nothing to me in my own
house. Today you die! And so dies your rabble within the
city!"

And with these words Bahir Kandar leaped back up to
his throne and lifted his hand and dropped it rapidly, grinning in evil delight in what he thought would be the sudden fury of crossbow shafts filling the air in front of him
and cutting down the Lord with a swiftness that would
have startled all in the unsuspecting throng. But no
crossbow shafts came! Surprise lit the prince's face, as well
as that of the Hakadian admiral, and both lifted their
faces upward to see what had happened to their elaborate
trap. I saw Tallsus and Fidor leap in front of the Lord,
their swords drawn to protect Him. I saw the Lord draw
His sword and push His faithful servants aside and leap
for Bahir Kandar. And then from behind me came a
blood-curdling scream of rage and pain, and then a bloodied form was clawing for my throat. I fell to the wooden
floor of the loft and fought with the demon that gripped
me with steel fingers. From below, the throng exploded
into a sustained scream of fear and terror and mass hysteria gripped one and all. As I fought and rolled with
whatever it was that clawed at me like some mad animal,
I heard from below the ringing crash of steel flying against
steel and the roar of furniture and chandeliers being
destroyed in one huge melee. Yet even as I fought I had
more concern for the Lord's safety than for my own. Desperately I tried to free myself from whatever gripped me,
but it fought with a desperation that bordered upon insanity. Hakba Baru, caught surprised and startled by the onslaught of the form that now struggled to kill me with
steel fingers, regained his senses and jumped to my rescue.
But the thing slapped the pirate to one side viciously, mak-

ing the pirate slam his head up against a wooden beam, knocking him unconscious. Yet the pirate's efforts to render assistance saved me. For, in knocking the attacking pirate to one side senselessly, the thing had to let go of his death grip around my throat. With a heave, I used an old Ha'valli wrestling hold my father had taught me as a youth and threw the man-thing off of me. With a piercing, inhuman scream of defeated rage, Bazar sailed over the balcony railing of the high loft and went screaming to his death below. Struggling to my feet, I quickly found the unconscious Hakba Baru and threw him over my shoulder. And then with one swift sweep of my sword I severed one of the many ropes that held chandeliers above the grand hall below. Leaping to the railing of the loft balcony, I gripped the rope firmly, wrapping much of it tightly around one leg. And then holding on tightly to the still unconscious Hakba Baru I shot out into the air high above the grand hall itself and went sailing downward with a swiftness that startled me.

Luck was with me that day. I swung downward in a sweeping arc and happened to land on a large, heavy table made from Kakla wood, sitting immediately behind the throne of Bahir Kandar. Jumping from the table, I dashed through the hysterical crowd, trying desperately to reach the side of My Lord. Around me people pushed and fought to flee the grand hall of Bahir Kandar. Fear, such as I have rarely seen in the eyes of mortals, filled everyone's hearts around me, but from what I had no idea. It did not occur to me that the unholy scream of a dying Bazar as he leaped from the darkness behind me in an effort to kill me was the source for the hysteria that had suddenly gripped the throng. And finally when the body of Bazar, still screaming in a piercing, high-pitched screech that was inhuman to listen to, came falling from above from out of nowhere the panic was complete. The wish of every member of the throng within the grand hall of the palace was to flee as rapidly as possible. Clawing and screaming in terror, the crowd fought with itself to escape, all sanity and reason now gone from all. And through this crowd, with the heavy, unconscious form of the slumbering pirate over my shoulder, I fought to come to the side of the Sa'yen.

"Magdar! Here!" the Lord shouted over the din of the terror-struck crowd, waving to me with one hand as He fought with five or six of the prince's personal bodyguards.

I kicked two fleeing figures from me and stepped up to the Sa'yen. Beside Him fought Tallsus and dour-faced Fidor. But both of them grinned in pleasure as I stepped up close to the Lord, lowering the bearded pirate, slowly regaining consciousness, to the floor of the palace.

"He is badly wounded?"

"No, Lord. Just dazed from a blow he received in the lofts above."

"Then it was you who threw the screaming warrior to his death from above?"

"Aye, Lord. Bahir Kandar and the Hakadian had forty men with crossbows above to shoot you down when the prince waved his hand. But the pirate and I took care of the crossbowmen and the screaming man was their officer."

"Ah, Magdar the Bull again does the impossible!" the Lord nodded, parrying a solid thrust from a Kandar bodyguard and sending the fool to his just rewards with six inches of His own cold steel.

"My Lord, will the Charolarl Priest be in time?" Fidor growled, slapping a sword thrust aside and smashing a bare fist into the face of an unwary foe.

"He will come, Fidor. Have faith in him," the Lord grinned, sending another Kandar warrior to his rewards and leaping to one side to protect the still groggy Hakba Baru from being run through the back by a charging warrior.

"I have faith in you, Lord. And maybe Magdar, but none for anyone else," Fidor growled, his sword sweeping back and forth to keep a hundred blades from finding the back of the Lord.

"What is this about the Charolarl Priest, Lord?" I asked, drawing my sword and stepping up behind the Lord's back to defend his rear.

"The Charolarl Priest and I made plans to thwart the possible trap the prince might have devised if he planned to capture us, Magdar. We did not take into the account the possibility of you and our pirate friend escaping. I find myself constantly underestimating you, friend Magdar. Glad am I that we are friends and not enemies!"

I smiled at the Lord's words, happy to hear that He thought so highly of me. But little else could be said as the fighting became intense in the small cluster of the Sa'yen's followers in the middle of the fleeing crowd. More of Bahir Kandar's personal bodyguard poured out from a side exit, swords drawn, charging straight for us. I wished to ask the Lord what kind of plan He and the Charolarl Priest had devised but no sooner had I thought to ask than I was able to see first-hand.

There was a large explosion and a giant cloud of white smoke floated upward from the floor. And out of the cloud stepped the Charolarl Priest in his gray robes, arms stretched outward and above his head. There were screams of terror from all that saw the priest appear and mad confusion reigned instantly. Even I gasped in fright at what I saw. For not only had the priest appeared suddenly from a cloud of rising smoke, but he was in flames. The back of his hands and the top of his shaven skull was burning brightly in large, yellow dancing flames. From the flames came an oily black smoke that had a terrible stench to it, so terrible it made me want to retch the moment I smelled it. And indeed many of the enemy did begin retching the moment the priest approached them. Never before had I believed in the tales of the Charolarl and their knowledge of black magic, but this frightful exhibition of burning, foul-smelling fury was enough to make even the most hardened skeptic believe. If panic and terror had set in when the body of Bazar, the crossbow officer, came screaming down from the lofts above, the panic that gripped all within the hall of the palace now was too much to possibly describe. Even the personal bodyguards of Bahir Kandar fled from us, screaming and throwing their weapons aside shamelessly in their efforts to save themselves from the mad Charolarl Priest! It was, to me, an unbelievable miracle the way the crowd fled from us. Aye, I mention that word many a time when I talk about the Lord, but miracle it was that day. None apparently

wished to stand before us when the Charolarl Priest burst
from the rising cloud, head and hands in flame. So intent
were our enemies on fleeing from us that we could have
sheathed our weapons and walked calmly from the grand
hall without so much as a finger being lifted against us.

Ah, but such a cruel day! Aye, cruel! Our enemies fled
before us, so terrified that they threw their weapons aside
in their haste to flee. The Lord, His golden mane yet un-
ruffled from the fighting He had so recently been fiercely
engaged in, led the way for us as we departed the grand
hall of Bahir Kandar. We walked as if strolling casually
through one of the many parks of the city on a bright
Sunday afternoon. Yet, the Charolarl Priest, still engulfed
in foul-smelling flames, followed up on our rear waving
his burning hands about and groaning pitifully. Fidor and
Tallsus were actually grinning, as was the Lord, because of
the groans of pain from the burning priest. But I, not
knowing how such a thing could be, was extremely
frightened and very much concerned for the health of the
burning priest. And one look into the ashen face of the
bearded pirate told me he was as eager to flee from the
burning priest as the crowd had been. Huge, white round
eyes of fear came darting madly back behind us to look at
the burning priest and sweat was pouring freely from his
brow, but the pirate stayed with our party and made no
attempt to escape. The Lord, I noticed, kept glancing at
me and at the pirate, a smile playing on His lips all the
while as we strolled down the halls of the palace. But He
said nothing for some time to us concerning the trick of
the Charolarl Priest. Then finally, rounding a corner and
into another corridor that was empty of all onlookers except for us, the Lord stopped us and spoke to me and
Hakba Baru.

"Be not alarmed at the antics of the priest, my friends.
It is only a trick, a trick that you or I can do once we
learn how. This is not magic, you see, friends. Only the
trick of an accomplished actor and nothing more. Be
calm, for yet we are in danger of attack!"

And how true His words were. How cruel His own
words were that day! And yet from the fate that befell
Him that day He arose again even stronger and more

unconquerable than ever! And I, Magdar the Bull, was there with Him that day to witness it all! Ala, Sa'yen! All praises to Him! I bear witness this day, and every day, that what was about to happen actually did háppen and I was there to see it.

We fled quickly through the palace, hurrying up sweeping spiral stairs of exquisite marble that were lit lavishly by large chandeliers of finely blown glass. Tapestries of magnificent richness in color and weave covered the walls as we fled up the sweeping spiral stairs, the main route to the royal landing towers of the palace. Thick carpets of deep Arluian purple covered the stairs and so thick were they we made hardly a sound as we raced upward. And as we hurried, none dared to step in front of us and challenge our escape. From outside the walls of the palace we heard the panic that had gripped those of the grand hall spread like fire and begin to take hold of the entire city. As the minutes fled by, the panic of the city increased, sending mobs numbering in the thousands, both for and against the Sa'yen clashing against each other. We heard cannon fire off in the distance, the ships of the Hakadian fleet suddenly coming into action one by one as the fierce followers of the Sa'yen manned ships to attack the hated enemy. The rebellion had started! The city was in the throes of a popular revolt! Stunned and amazed, I could do nothing but follow the Lord upward with the rest of His small party. The revolt had started as if He had suddenly willed it! The city was in the fight to throw off the bondage of the Hakadian fleet, hated enemies from ancestral times, without planning or apparent warning. I could not grasp the suddenness of the turmoil that had so astoundingly gripped everyone the Lord came into contact with and this, I believe, was what made me react much too slowly to the danger that suddenly emerged.

From behind us a door suddenly banged open and we heard many footsteps rush towards us! I whirled, my blade barely turning back a stoutly thrown lance that had been aimed at the Lord's back. In the blinking of an eye, ten warriors in the pay of Bahir Kandar were upon us, their blades hacking away at us and attacking in a fury I felt bordered upon the suicidal. And then I saw the reason for

their mad attack! Behind them, the robed figures of Bahir
Kandar, the Admiral Hasdrubal, and the Princess Saphid
emerged from the door and faced us, smiling at the
thought that ten of their warriors would kill us at last, as
we only numbered five armed men plus the burning
Charolarl Priest. But their eagerness to see us chopped to
pieces quickly disappeared, to be replaced by fear, for the
swords of the Lord's faithful were more than a match for
any ten set upon us that day. In the time of two heartbeats
seven of the fiercely attacking warriors fell to the palace
floor, spilling their blood on richly dyed purple carpets. I
heard Bahir Kandar give out a scream of rage and saw
him draw from his robes a small dagger, and he appeared
as if to rush us with it. But the perfumed figure of the
Hakadian admiral took the smaller, more effeminately built
man by one arm, and the Princess Saphid, that stunningly
beautiful woman, took the prince by the other and together they pulled the enraged prince back to safety. I
grinned, content in letting them flee, and the Lord made
no attempt to capture them. He too turned His back to
continue our trek upward to the landing towers of the
palace. But a sudden sound of swirling robes caught my
attention and turning I saw the Princess Saphid in the act
of throwing the curved, flat blade of a Hakad throwing
knife. I shouted a warning and leaped upward into the air
to block the whirling blade with my body, but too late!
The blade whipped past my ear, not touching me as it
sped by, and grazed the neck of the Lord before clanging
off the marbled wall of the palace. Turning, I saw the
Lord raise a hand to touch His neck. The edge of the
knife had barely touched Him; barely a drop of His blood
seeped from the wound. Relieved at such a light wound, I
turned to race after the treacherous woman and make her
a captive for the Lord. But she and the admiral and the
prince were racing down the hall; then before disappearing, she stopped and turned to peer at us for one last time.
And there was such an evil, wicked smile on her lovely
lips that I was instantly filled with dread! No sooner had
she smiled at us than from behind me the Lord suddenly
collapsed to the stairs with a crash of weapons against the
hard, cold stone.

"Quickly, Tallsus, Fidor! Pick Him up and let us get to the ship! That treacherous woman threw a poisoned blade! We must hurry to the ship so the priest can brew the antidote!"

Tallsus and Fidor nodded and quickly had the Lord in their arms. We hurried upward, gained the upper ramps of the royal landing towers and found the *Black Falcon* anchored firmly to the tower but under full sail. Half of her crew were in her masts, ready to cut the anchors away so that we might dart away from the landing towers under full sail! In the sky about the city, ships of the Hakad Navy were fighting desperately to form a line of battle to repulse the hundreds of Triisusian ships that attacked each one. Cannonfire rolled on and on above the city, and the city itself was aflame in many parts. But none of us cared for any of that! Our concerns lay with the stricken Lord as He was hurriedly taken to His cabin and placed gently on the bed. The Charolarl Priest, now with flames extinguished, was at His side, acknowledged by all aboard as the one with the best chance of saving the Lord. Any Charolarl Priest was known to have the knowledge of accomplished physicians. And they knew the antidotes of many poisons. But in this case, even he did not have the cure. Hours later, and many miles away from the burning city of Triisus, the gray-robed priest emerged on deck and with head cast downward in defeat, he gave us the bad news.

"Juli poisoning."

"The blade dipped in Juli poisoning? I have never heard of such a poison," Fidor growled, stepping up to hear the priest.

"I have." I nodded, all hope draining from me suddenly, leaving me incredibly weak. "It is a poison favored by the Caste of Assassins, Fidor. There is no antidote. The victim of Juli poisoning dies eventually by drowning in his own saliva. He never awakes after being struck down. Am I correct, priest?"

The priest would only nod his head. I saw tears flood into his eyes, and suddenly tears were in mine as well.

"He is gone from us then," I said, not even recognizing my own voice. "Just as the legends promised."

"You mean, you mean there is no hope?" Fidor growled savagely, taking the priest by both arms and shaking him wildly.

"Fidor!" I yelled, pulling him from the robes of the priest and pushing him to one side. "Begone! The Lord is stricken with Juli poisoning. There is nothing any mortal can do for Him now! As the legends have promised over and over again, He came to us for a short visit among His children and now He departs from us! Someday He will come again to lead us. But not today! Not today!"

And then grief overwhelmed me and I turned and fled to the railing to weep openly and shamelessly.

XIV

———◦◉◦———

Will The Sa'yen Prove Mortal?

Two weeks after the Sa'yen was struck down by the poisoned blade of the Priness Saphid, I stood the Thieves' Watch on the poop deck. Low, dark clouds blew about us as we were under little sail and with the wind. I had no desire to go anywhere or do anything. The Sa'yen, still alive and breathing, lay in his bed in a deep coma. He had not moved a muscle since the Charolarl Priest had pulled the heavy blankets over His body, back in Triisus. And yet the Lord was alive. Alive two weeks after being struck down, and a week longer than the usual victim of Juli poisoning usually lived. As I stood my watch, with only a young boy as the helmsman for company, I was still numb from the blow as I was the moment He was struck down.

Aye, the entire crew was still lifeless and devoid of any desire. We were mere shells of what we were, all too consumed in our mourning over losing our god to care for anything else. The Sa'yen was dying. As foretold by the legends of our forefathers. The Sa'yen, as was muttered often times to me over the fires of my father's camps, would come many times to lead His children. And many times, in the body of a mere mortal, He would be struck down before He could lead us on the Wha'ta. The Wha'ta—the Sacred Pilgrimage to the Lands of the Southern Hemisphere. Whenever the Sa'yen came to lead His childrn, He came in the guise of a mortal, with all the mortal faults. He would come forsaking all His divine

201

powers except one; and none, not even He, would know what that one divine power would be until time to use it. He would come falling out of the sky in a fiery chariot, the legends said. He could come forever forsaking the idea He was the Sa'yen. He would be like a babe among men in His knowledge of how His children lived and died on Hungar.

Below me, I knew now without a doubt that the Sa'yen had come to give us a brief visit. He had come for such a visit to renew our sagging belief in Him, to generate a new fervor in His eventual coming for the Wha'ta. And He would come again! Of this I was positive! And yet, I felt no strength in me. The Sa'yen was below dying. And I, the foolish doubter, had not fully believed in Him! It was a heavy, unbearable heart that I held that night as I stood facing the helmsman, looking out into the moonlit sky of early morning.

I would grow old now, die and not see the Sa'yen again on Hungar. The next time we met it would probably be on the Fields of Pryssian Rivers, the heaven promised to all who truly followed Him. And I was immensely sad. I wished the Lord was with us still, to lead us southwards, to be among us for years instead of only a few months. Even if He never led us on the Sacred Wha'ta, but just spent His time in Northern Hungar, I would have been content! And now, He was dead and I would never see Him again. He was gone and I would forever carry the guilt of being the doubter while He was among us. At that moment I felt such a pain was unbearable and wondered how I could live with such guilt within me. And so intense were my thoughts that I did not hear the helmsman collapse behind me nor even know about it until his outflung hand reached out and slapped me against the back of my leg. Turning, I was startled to see the young lad on the deck at my feet, all color drained from his face. Alarmed, I knelt down, fearing he had been taken by sudden illness and had collapsed from that.

And then the moon, the huge Hungar moon of blinding white and red light, came out from behind a large cloud and He stood before me. The Sa'yen! Alive and before me, one of the heavy blankets hanging from His wide

shoulders and His long blond mane dishevled and blowing
in the breeze of the night. Leaping to my feet, I reached
out and touched Him, not yet daring to believe that it was
actually the Lord standing before me. But it was! I felt a
bare shoulder, blazing hot to the touch, and I saw a fever-
filled face and fever-filled blue eyes looking at me. But it
was the Lord! The Sa'yen! He was alive and before me!
Naked except for a blanket around His shoulders and
looking terribly weak from the effects of the poison! But
alive! Alive!

And I screamed! Screamed into the night not in fright
or terror but in joy. I leaped about Him, yelling and crying at the same time, blabbering like an idiot and suddenly
pulling Him into my arms to hold Him close to me.
I was beside myself with happiness. A flooding of such
happiness engulfed me. I was like a madman that night!
I shouted to the moon, I shouted to the forest below. I
shouted to the stars above my head my joy, my happiness. And most of all my devotion to the Lord. Such incredible joy! I leaped to the stern of the ship, picked up
the slow-burning match we always kept lit to fire the stern
chase guns, and put the match to the firing hole. The small
cannon shot off into the night with a thundering racket
that was impossible to describe. And that brought the entire crew out. First appeared the Charolarl Priest, who had
for two weeks, day and night, been beside the bed of the
Lord, hoping for a miracle. He dashed to the deck after
seeing the Lord was no longer in his bed. And when he
saw the Lord standing beside me, he stopped in his tracks,
his eyes bulging from their sockets, unable to believe what
he saw! Fidor and Bidgar came next, followed by
Hagbash and Tallsus and the rest of the crew. And when
all the others saw the Lord standing before them, a roar
filled the night sky of joy and gladness which was and still
is to this day impossible to describe. Men fell to their
knees, arms outstretched to worship Him. Voices were
lifted up in common prayers to Him, and the looks of
pure joy on the faces of all was a sight I shall never forget. And I! I was just as joyful as they! I was too much
filled with energy to stop dancing. I was crying, I was

screaming, I was holding the Lord in my arms, I was beside myself with happiness. So filled with joy was I that it took the Charolarl Priest, after he had regained his composure, to approach the Lord and speak to Him first.

"My Lord, you live!"

"Yes, it certainly seems that way. Why is everyone behaving as if they have all gone crazy?" He replied, weakly reaching out with one of His hands to take a grip on the shoulder of the priest.

"You do not know, Lord?" the priest asked, taking the burning hot hand of the Lord and stepping up closer to support Him better. "Magdar! You fool! Take the Lord's other arm and let us take Him back to His cabin! He yet burns with a dangerous fever!"

"I am certainly very weak, my friends." The Lord nodded, speaking barely above a whisper. "What happened?"

"You do not remember, Lord?" the priest asked again.

"No, what?"

"You were struck down by a knife blade dipped in Juli poisoning."

"Eh, poison?" the Lord repeated in a whisper, His face filled with the burning fever as we put Him gently back into His bed. "Well, I must say your cure worked very well, priest. What was it?"

"I had no cure, Lord," the priest answered, pulling blankets back up over the Lord's chest and tucking them in under His body. "There was no cure to be had. Juli poisoning has no cure, Lord. You should be dead. Not alive."

But the Lord had drifted off into a deep, healing sleep. Stepping back from His bed, I looked at the priest, finally somewhat in control of my senses. He was looking at me, his face a mask of sheer confusion.

"He lives, Magdar. Fever still grips Him, but it is the fever of a person fighting off a bad sickness and on the road to recovery. This cannot be happening. Juli poisoning is incurable and all who are stricken by it die."

"But not if the stricken one is a god, priest. He is the Sa'yen! Ala Sa'yen!" I shouted, the praise repeated immediately by the others that had filled the cabin behind us.

"But the legends say, if you believe the legends, that the Sa'yen will return in the body of a mere mortal, subject to the fallacies and whims of all mortals," the priest went on, shaking a fist at me in anger. "And if that is so, why did the Juli poison not kill Him?"

"I am not a priest, I cannot answer such a question," I shouted back in happiness. "But do the legends not also say that the Lord always returns with one of His divine powers at His command when the time is necessary?"

"Aye, that is so," a hundred voices shouted behind me. Even the priest nodded in agreement.

"Well then, perhaps there lies our answer," I shouted, again in tears. "The Lord retained His most important divine power, priest!"

"And that being?"

"His immortality! The Sa'yen is among us as He actually is! An Immortal!"

"The Sa'yen is immortal!" The others in the cabin took up the shout and it spread through the ship like fire in dry hay.

"The Sa'yen is immortal! The Sa'yen is immortal!" The entire ship's crew began shouting together.

Immortal! What did this mean? Was this the time the Sa'yen would lead us on the Wha'ta? The Sacred Pilgrimage? But what else would He come among us for with this power if not to lead us on the Holy Pilgrimage? That spread among the crew equally as fast as the knowledge of His immortality, sending the joy of the crew into another spasm of celebration. The Wha'ta! The Lord was here to lead His devoted on the Wha'ta! The Sacred Pilgrimage! Ala Sa'yen! All praises to the Lord!

In a fury over our celebration while He still struggled with a high fever, the gray-robed priest bodily threw me out of the Lord's cabin along with the rest of the crew. But I went willingly, wishing the Lord would quickly recover so He could again lead us as He willed. And while we waited, we celebrated! Celebrated for ten entire days of song and dance and feasting.

And the Lord recovered. Recovered to lead us into battle again and again. He recovered to lead His children southward, that we were all sure of. And we were content.

It mattered little to us how long it would take before the Lord was ready to begin the Wha'ta. We could wait. For He was among us now. Among us!

Among His children! And immortal!

EPILOGUE

So you have read. And you still cannot believe. How could He, claiming to be only a mortal fallen from the stars, not die? Aye, Lady Death tried her most beguiling charms upon Him and He cast her aside. I was there! I saw! And I say to you that He could, for He was the Lord God. The Sa'yen!

And more questions still trouble your mind. What of Triisus? What of Hasdrubal, the Hakadian Grand Admiral? What of the Princess Saphid and her vicious lover, the Prince Bahir Kandar? And most importantly, what of the ancient yet still luring Fortress of the Ancient Kings that the Sa'yen was so eager to find before the bungling hands of the Pictii unleashed the havoc only the Lord could imagine?

Aye, all these questions yet must be answered. And answered they shall be. Yet now I grow tired. The cool desert evening air begins to sing her songs to me in the growing twilight, and I shall stop now and rest. Only to take up the tale on the morrow.

Presenting JOHN NORMAN in DAW editions . . .